Praise for Reba White Williams's first Coleman and Dinah Greene mystery, *Restrike*:

"There's a major new presence on the crime scene...Reba White Williams. Restrike will strike a big hit with sophisticated readers who love culture, uncommon criminals and terrific writing. You won't be able to put this book down!"
– Alexandra Penney, *New York Times* bestselling author

"Savvy, saucy, and scary – a worthy debut from a writer who bears watching."
– Jacquelyn Mitchard, *New York Times* bestselling author

"A tight, tricky plot that takes you on a breathless romp through the world of fine art prints. Captivating characters and a highly energetic plot – art smart and highly literate – I loved it!"
– Laura Childs, *New York Times* bestselling author

"A fast-paced tale of nefarious dealings in New York's art world."
– Thomas H. Cook, Edgar Award-winning author

"A captivating debut, Restrike puts on display the international world of fine art. Reba White Williams has crafted an ambitious, fascinating and textured puzzler, rife with suspects and red herrings. A polished gem of a read. Bring on the next Coleman and Dinah Greene mystery!"
– Julia Spencer-Fleming, *New York Times* bestselling author

"Starts out with a bang and keeps you riveted! A first rate debut!"
– Steve Berry, *New York Times* bestselling author

Fatal Impressions

FATAL IMPRESSIONS

Coleman and Dinah Greene Mystery No. 2

Reba White Williams

The Story Plant

Stamford, Connecticut

The Story Plant
Studio Digital CT, LLC
PO Box 4331
Stamford, CT 06907

Copyright © 2013 by Reba White Williams

Jacket design by Barbara Aronica-Buck

Print ISBN-13: 978-1-61188-131-8
E-book ISBN-13: 978-1-61188-132-5

Visit our website at www.TheStoryPlant.com
Visit the author's website at www.RebaWhiteWilliams.com

First Story Plant printing: April 2014

Printed in the United States of America

0 9 8 7 6 5 4 3 2 1

Impression:

1. *noun*, an idea, feeling, or opinion about someone or something
2. *noun*, an effect produced on someone
3. *noun*, a reprint from a book or other publication
4. *noun*, the application of pressure or force

One

March

This Monday in March, an ordinary day for most people, was the happiest day of Coleman Greene's life.

Everyone she liked best had gathered to celebrate with her. Long before she bought *ArtSmart*, her first magazine, she'd dreamed of owning a family of publications—perhaps ten, or even more. Today, with the acquisition of *First Home*, she—Coleman Greene, thirty-three years old, with financial help from her brother—was a step closer to making that dream come true. In the five years she'd owned *ArtSmart*, she'd changed it from a dowdy flop into the most successful art magazine in New York. She'd do even better with *First Home*. And then onto the next one.

Coleman looked around at the glittering crowd. So New York: artists, actors, antique dealers, landscape gardeners, architects. People Coleman had written about in *ArtSmart*. People she hoped to persuade to write for *First Home*. Her cousin, Dinah, ravishing in a lavender-blue silk suit Coleman had designed and made, with her husband, Jonathan Hathaway. Debbi Diamondstein, not only a friend but Coleman's publicist, who had arranged the lunch at the hot new restaurant on Central Park South. The immense windows allowed guests to see almost to the north end of the park—a spectacular view. A pianist played music from *South Pacific*, *Phantom*, *Les Misérables*, and other Broadway hits in a corner of the room. A buffet enticed the guests with delicious odors: smoked salmon, miniature crab cakes, tiny toasted cheese sandwiches, garlicky lamb on skewers. Huge vases of forsythia and pussy willow and smaller bowls of yellow tulips and daffodils decorated every surface, their delicate scent heralding the approach of spring. The perfect party.

Uh, oh. Not quite perfect: a man she knew and detested, greasy black hair hanging to his shoulders and in his face, black T-shirt and torn jeans, was mingling in the crowd. Trying to act invited. As if.

Debbi appeared at her side. "What's the matter, Sunshine? You were glowing, and now you look like a thundercloud. Cheer up, Madame Media Mogul, this is your big day! And you look great. That satin suit is exactly the shade of the daffodils, and your hair—clever choice."

"Two magazines don't a mogul make, but just wait, someday I will be one. Meanwhile, I just spotted that no-talent photorealist who calls himself Crawdaddy. He never stops badgering me to write an article about him. He calls me all the time and turns up in places where he knows he'll see me. He's close to being a stalker. How in heaven's name did *he* get in?"

Debbi shrugged. "A few crashers always make it through the cracks no matter how tight the security. I can have him thrown out, but he'll make a scene."

"No, I'll ignore him. I won't let him get anywhere near me."

But a few minutes later, when she and Dinah were standing by the piano listening to "Some Enchanted Evening," Crawdaddy shoved his way between them, threw his long simian arms over their shoulders, and shouted, "Photo op!" A flashbulb went off in their faces.

Within seconds, Jonathan had appeared, froze Crawdaddy with what Debbi called the Hathaway Sneer—developed during several centuries of being rich and in the top tier of Boston's social elite—and rescued Dinah. Coleman, holding her breath against the stench of Crawdaddy's body odor, struggled to remove the heavy arm wrapped around her. She was thinking of kicking the creep when Rob Mondelli appeared. Rob had been a New York City policeman, played college football, and looked it, though many years had passed since he'd scored a touchdown, or arrested a mugger. His business today, specializing in art-related crime, rarely brought him into contact with violence, but lots of gym time kept him trim and fit.

"Come have some lunch," he said. He removed Crawdaddy's arm as if it were weightless and whisked her away from the interloper.

Good old Rob—protective, warm, kind. Always there when she needed him and a lot of the time when she didn't. He was nagging her to marry him, and she couldn't convince him that would never happen. She sighed. She must do something about Rob. But not today. She wanted today to be perfect, unmarred by an unpleasant conversation.

Rob remained at her side until the last guest left and walked her and Dolly, the tiny Maltese who accompanied Coleman everywhere, to her office. In the building lobby, he kissed her lightly and said, "I wish you'd come with me to Europe. I'm seeing a number of clients about security issues, but I won't be working all the time—and wouldn't you like to meet some of the museum people? Collectors? We could have a lot of fun."

"Goodness, Rob, I couldn't go anywhere now even if I wanted to. And I can't think of anything more fun than my new magazine. But you have a good time." She looked at her watch. "You better go, or you'll miss your plane." She tried to hide her impatience, but he looked like a spanked puppy, and she knew she'd failed. Well, too bad. She was glad he was leaving town. She didn't have time for him right now, and the fact that he didn't understand the importance of *First Home* and her joy in it showed how little he understood her.

❦

It was after four when she arrived at her *ArtSmart* office. She groaned when she saw the stack of messages. She flipped through them. Mostly congratulations and calls from reporters responding to the morning press release announcing the acquisition. Hmm, here was something different: a hand-delivered letter from Oliver & Kaufman, investment bankers. She ripped it open.

Dear Ms. Greene:

On behalf of my client, a major publicly held media company, I am pleased to present this offer to acquire CG Holdings, LLC.

My client, who prefers to remain anonymous at this time, is prepared to pay twice your current rate of annual revenues, subject, of course, to normal due diligence procedures. Furthermore, my client wishes you to remain as chief executive officer of CG Holdings, LLC, and editor in chief of *ArtSmart* and *First Home* for a period of no less than two years, during which time your annual compensation will be $250,000 per year, or 25 percent of the annual pretax, preincentive compensation income of CG Holdings, LLC, whichever is greater.

Very truly yours,
Richard C. Oliver

She frowned. News of the acquisition of *First Home* couldn't have reached the writer much before noon. The letter had arrived less than six hours later. Fast work, and presumptuous. Why did these people think she'd want to sell? *ArtSmart* was her beloved creation. *First Home* was her exciting new baby. Not a very attractive *enfant* at the moment, but with potential. What was going on?

When she called Jonathan, who was her business manager as well as Dinah's husband, he explained that maybe they didn't necessarily think she wanted to sell. "Could be their client hoped to buy *First Home*, and you got there first. Or maybe they wanted *ArtSmart* and you, even before you acquired *First Home*. I know Rick Oliver. Do you want me to talk to him?"

"Would you? Tell him I won't sell at any price."

Jonathan laughed. "I can tell him, but he won't believe it. He'll say everything is available at a price."

She twisted a curl around her forefinger. "Well, can you tell him I don't need money?"

"No, I'll tell him you appreciate his offer but aren't interested—that the magazines are your true love as well as your livelihood. But the buyer might keep trying."

Coleman swallowed, trying to make the dryness in her mouth go away. "They can't make me sell, can they?" she asked.

"They won't want to. I'm sure they want *you*. A forced sale wouldn't make you a happy employee."

When she'd thanked him and hung up, she selected a message slip and punched in the number of *Pub-*

lishing News. She tried to forget about the letter, but the thought of it prickled like a tiny splinter, invisible, but a constant source of discomfort. She wished the letter hadn't come today of all days. The golden glow of the happiest day of her life hadn't vanished, but it had dimmed.

She'd return calls until six, when nearly everyone would have left for the day. Then she and Dolly would go home and enjoy a quiet evening. She'd soak in a hot tub to relax the muscles that had tensed when she read the letter and showed no sign of getting better. After her bath, she'd go in her sewing room and stay there until she finished her latest creation, a black silk cocktail dress. Designing and making clothes was her favorite form of relaxation and almost always distracted her. By bedtime, maybe the letter and her problems with Rob wouldn't loom so big.

∽

Coleman didn't drink alcohol and never had, but on Tuesday morning, she awoke an hour earlier than usual with what she imagined a hangover felt like—headache, dry mouth, sticky eyes. She'd slept fitfully, menaced in her nightmares by faceless monsters.

A hot shower and a lavish slather of her favorite almond-scented body lotion helped. After she'd fed Dolly and walked the little dog in the cool damp air, she felt even better.

She settled down on the sitting room sofa with coffee and the papers to see what kind of coverage her acquisition and lunch had received. Oh, rats, the *Soho Sun* featured a huge picture of Crawdaddy standing between her and Dinah, his arms over their shoulders as if they were best friends. Dinah looked beautiful, if startled, but Coleman's grin looked forced, and he'd rumpled her hair. Damn it. The phone rang.

"Yes, Debbi?" she said.

"How'd you know it was me?" Debbi said.

"I knew you'd call to apologize because that slug crashed my party," Coleman said.

"Oh, Crawdaddy. Yeah, he is repellent. But the other articles are good, and everyone spelled your name and the names of the magazines right. People will forget that stupid picture."

"I hope you're right. I'd be mortified to have anyone think he's a friend of mine or Dinah's—or even worse, that I like his art. I wish he'd find someone else to hound."

Two

Dinah looked at her watch: 11:25. She'd been in this uncomfortable reception room for two hours. If she sat in this torturous chair much longer, she wouldn't be able to stand. She needed to move around, and she should let Bethany know she'd be late getting back to the gallery. She'd call from the elevator corridor, where she wouldn't be overheard and the receptionist could see her.

"Greene Gallery."

"Hi, it's me," Dinah said.

"Thank goodness you called—I've been goin' crazy. Did we get the contract?" Bethany asked.

"Would you believe I haven't seen the wretched man? I arrived at nine thirty to make sure I was on time for my ten o'clock appointment, and he still hasn't turned up. We must have lost out. Why would he make me wait for good news?"

"Oh, don't say that," Bethany protested. "His tardiness probably doesn't have anything to do with us.

His train from Greenwich, or wherever he lives, may have been late."

"Maybe you're right, but if we weren't desperate, I'd leave this minute. And it's my fault we have to put up with being jerked around like this," Dinah said.

"Hush that talk. No matter what, the move uptown was the right thing to do. We were barely surviving on Cornelia Street. We'd have been out of business by summer if we hadn't moved," Bethany said.

Dinah sighed. "We may be out of business by summer anyway. I better go. I'll call you when I know something."

Back in the reception room, Dinah considered shifting to another chair, but they were all designed to cripple—icy steel bent in every way except to fit the human form, scratchy upholstery the same shade of gray as the carpet. The austere reception room declared the hand of one of Manhattan's best-known designers, but it looked and felt frigid. It was also empty of people, and this was an ordinary Tuesday, a workday. Where were the workers? The clients? She sighed and tried again to find a comfortable position.

She wished she could think of anything but the probable failure of the Greene Gallery. When she'd leased the Fifty-Seventh Street gallery in January, she'd counted on the better location to attract new artists, more customers, bigger sales. But March was halfway over, business was terrible, and the midtown Manhattan rent was murderous. In Greenwich Village she'd run her pocket-sized gallery with one assistant in a building her husband owned. The new space was much larger, and she'd been forced to hire another full-time person and two part-timers. They were graduate students, less costly than experienced gallery staff, but expenses were up, and the bottom line was red.

Today she'd learn whether she'd won the contract to select, buy, and hang art in the New York office of the management consultants Davidson, Douglas, Danbury & Weeks—DDD&W to nearly everyone. She'd been introduced to Theodore Douglas by Coleman, who'd known him from way back. He was not only one of the D's in DDD&W, he also chaired the firm's art committee. He could make or break her. Well, not break her exactly, but he could save the Greene Gallery. The fee for the job would support the gallery for a year. If Theodore Douglas ever deigned to see her.

"Ms. Greene, I'm so sorry you've had to wait so long! How about another cup of coffee?"

Oh, mercy, the pudgy receptionist with the coffee pot was standing in front of her, reeking of the scorched stench of the pot. Every time the woman, sporting a practiced smile, apologized for Dinah's long wait, she refilled Dinah's Styrofoam cup. Dinah had been too polite to reject it, but all that coffee had made her desperate to get to the ladies' room. She was sure she'd be summoned to her meeting the minute she left the area, but the receptionist promised she would come for Dinah if Mr. Douglas called. Thank goodness the restroom was nearby.

She was applying fresh lipstick in the cul-de-sac at the far end of the L-shaped room when two women came in. Dinah couldn't see them, but she could hear them. They squawked like parrots.

"You keep your hands off him, you pie-faced slut. He's mine, and don't forget it!"

The voice was cigarette husky, country South, maybe Georgia or Alabama. Dinah knew that voice, and she recognized the scent: Jungle Gardenia. Patti Sue Victor must bathe in the stuff, which Dinah knew all too well; her hated third-grade teacher had worn it. Dinah had read that it had been the favorite scent of Elizabeth Taylor, Barbara Stanwyck, and Joan Crawford. Patti Sue, like the teacher, probably thought it would transform her into a glamour girl.

Dinah met Patti Sue when she made her presentation to the art committee. The woman, whose title was inexplicably "art curator"—there *was* no art, that's why DDD&W needed someone to acquire it—was hostile. Part of it was turf defense. She seemed to be sure she could do the job better than any outsider. But Dinah thought there was more to it than that. She'd seen Patti Sue talking to others waiting to make proposals, and with them she'd been, if not friendly, at least civil.

She and Dinah had quarreled even before they met. Patti Sue had telephoned several times during the weeks Dinah was working on her presentation. Each time she reminded Dinah of the date and time of her appointment at DDD&W and tried to ferret out the details of Dinah's proposal: Why was Dinah proposing several kinds of prints? Why not use all the same type? What was the difference between a lithograph and an etching? What was a screenprint?

What was Dinah charging? If she was given the contract, when would she begin installing the art?

When Dinah balked and explained that both her fee and the time involved for the installation would be revealed at her presentation, Patti Sue had shouted, cursed her, and hung up. Dinah was sorry for the rift but felt she'd done the best she could in the circumstances.

The second voice, shrill and piercing, was unfamiliar, but it could shatter windows in Queens. "That's what you think! He's not in love with you, you redneck cracker. He knows what it's like to be married to an idiot. Why would he want another one?"

Slap! Dinah winced. She wasn't surprised at Patti Sue's role in the brawl, but her opponent seemed to be the same type. Two women who sounded as if they might be more at home mud wrestling than working at a prestigious consulting firm? Odd. A scream, thumps, groans. Should she intervene? No, she'd probably come out of it with a black eye and two enemies instead of one. She'd like to sneak out, but she couldn't leave without being seen. She'd have to lie low and pray that Theodore Douglas didn't ask for her while she was trapped.

She heard the hiss of the corridor door, the click of heels on the tile floor, a new voice.

"Ladies! Stop that noise at once. We cannot have this. Isn't it bad enough that you two pursue the same married partner, and now you use fisticuffs in the ladies' room? Get back to your desks, or I shall see that you are both dismissed. Tidy yourselves first—you look as if you've been through a tornado."

Water gushed, the whish of the door again as it opened and closed. Blessed silence. Maybe she could make her escape? Oh, no, the door opened again.

"Ms. Greene? Mr. Douglas is ready to see you." At last. Mr. Douglas's assistant had come for her.

Dinah hurried toward the door, where the woman waited, tapping her foot and fondling her chignon. She caressed that clump of hair with an air of sexual pleasure. "Hurry up," she urged. "We're very late." As if it were Dinah's fault.

Dinah struggled to keep up with her. How did she move so fast in that tight skirt and those three-inch heels? Her white sweater and black skirt covered her gaunt body like a second skin. Dinah could count the woman's ribs, perish the thought. Friends who worked at McKinsey—the best-known and most respected management consulting firm in the world—claimed that its leaders were fussy about appearance. Not DDD&W. At least not about the attire of the female support staff. Dinah hadn't seen any of the women on the professional staff, but the dress code for the men appeared to be strict: dark suits, dress shirts, and subdued ties. Strange, this sartorial divide. Jonathan had told her DDD&W demanded impeccable dress and faultless behavior from its employees. Wrong. He should have seen—or heard—the spat in the ladies' room. So far this place didn't live up to its dignified and elegant image.

But Theodore Douglas did. When he rose to greet her, she thought, as she had when she'd met him at her presentation to the art committee, how perfectly he looked his background—Princeton, Harvard Business School, Eastern Establishment. Patrician: that was the word for C. Theodore Douglas IV. Tall and slim with blondish hair, gray at the temples. Exquisite tailoring. She'd admired his manners, too, until today.

"I'm sorry you had to wait. I was in a client meeting and couldn't get away. Please sit down. Would you like coffee?"

Dinah repressed a shudder. She wouldn't drink coffee again for weeks, if ever. "No, thank you, I'm fine."

"I'll come straight to the point. We reviewed all twenty-one of the contenders for our art project and your proposal was far and away the best. The assignment is yours." His teeth gleamed in a Tom Cruise smile.

She wanted to jump up and down and shout for joy like a six year old. Get a grip, she told herself; remember you're a grown-up and act dignified. "Thank you. I'm grateful for the opportunity. I'm looking forward to a great relationship with DDD&W," she said.

"Here's the contract—I've signed it. If you'll sign here—thanks. Here's your ID for building security. Call my assistant if you need anything. Or Patti Sue Victor. You and Ms. Victor will work together, of course."

He spoke as if he were giving her a treat. Not. DDD&W's so-called art curator—"the redneck cracker" of the powder room—was the wasp in the peach ice cream. Patti Sue thought she knew every-thing about art, but she knew nothing and never missed an opportunity to display her ignorance. She certainly wasn't an art curator. Why did she pretend to be? And why did Douglas go along with it? There were signs that art had once hung on the walls here, but that made Patti Sue's role all the more puzzling. If they'd owned decent art, surely they'd have hired someone competent to care for it. And above all, what became of it?

"You'll want to see Ms. Victor and get settled," he continued. "But first, Hunt Frederick, our managing director, wants to meet you."

Dinah followed Douglas up a short flight of stairs to a part of the thirty-third floor she hadn't seen on her initial tour of the space. The thirty-second floor, where she'd waited, and the thirty-third floor had identical dark gray carpeting and light gray walls, but the offices in this area were larger, and to enter each of them you had to pass through a small secretarial room.

Douglas paused at the desk of a matronly woman in the entry area of a corner suite. "Good morning, Mrs. Thornton, this is Dinah Greene, who'll oversee the new art program. Hunt asked me to bring her around to meet him. Is he available?"

"Mr. Frederick stepped away for a few minutes, Mr. Douglas. He asked that you wait in his office. Good morning, Ms. Greene, it's nice to meet you," Mrs. Thornton said.

Aha, the voice of reason in the ladies' room. In a gray suit that matched her hair, a gray silk blouse and pearls, she looked as if she'd dressed to blend in with the carpet. Quite a contrast with the other women she'd seen. She looked like the sort of person who'd say "fisticuffs." Her role as the managing director's assistant explained her willingness to call off the cat-fight and threaten the cats.

When the Gray Lady ushered them into Frederick's office, Dinah nearly gasped out loud. A red and blue Oriental rug covered the gray carpet. The wall-to-wall window behind the desk framed a magnificent view of the East River. Carved shelves in black oak lined the other walls, floor to ceiling. The desk, chairs, a coffee table, and a sofa matched the bookshelves. The crimson upholstery on the sofa and chairs echoed the red in the rug, and the books that filled the shelves were bound in red leather. Dark red curtains hung on either side of the windows.

"My goodness, I've never seen anything like this," she said. Except maybe in a film. It looked like Hollywood's conception of the setting for a nineteenth-century executive. What a clash with the sleek modernity of the rest of the place.

"It's something else, isn't it?" Douglas said, looking around.

Good grief, he sounded as if he admired this hideous fake Victorian room. His tone was almost proprietary. "It's—uh—stunning. I'm at a loss for words," Dinah said.

A shorter, stockier man strode in. "My sentiments exactly," he said.

"Good morning, Hunt," Douglas said. "Dinah Greene, Hunt Austin Frederick, our managing director."

"Ms. Greene, I'm mighty glad to meet you."

She'd read in *Business Week* that Hunt Frederick was in his mid-forties, but he looked younger. He was about five nine, Dinah's height in heels, despite his alligator cowboy boots, which, like her Bruno Maglis, added a good two inches. His navy blue suit, white shirt, and maroon tie were conventional, but his brown hair was cut too short—it looked almost military—and his heavy gold cufflinks were too big. His looks were clean-cut and American, with strong features, and keen hazel eyes. He moved like an athlete, as if he had grapefruit under his arms, and with slightly bowed legs.

His legs, his boots, and a slight twang hinted at his Texas background. She'd read that he'd come east to study at Deerfield, Yale, and Harvard Business School and had returned to Texas to work in the family oil business for a few years before he joined the Dallas office of DDD&W. Coleman had met him at a party in the Dallas Museum and hadn't liked him—a puffed-up jerk, she'd said. Two months ago, when he'd been elected managing director, he moved to New York. Coleman said that the eyes of the business world were on him, keen to see what kind of job he'd do.

"How do you do?" Dinah said.

"Fine, thanks, but it's a challenge living up to this baronial office. The furniture and the paneling have been in every managing director's office since the firm was established in 1952. James Davidson brought it over from a castle in Scotland, and whenever DDD&W moves to new quarters, everything in here moves into an office designed to accommodate it. It's mighty fancy for a country boy like me—I'd prefer something plainer, less grand."

She believed him about the office, but he sounded a little too "aw, shucks." Country boy? Dinah bet he played that card often. She smiled to show him she knew he wasn't serious.

"Don't worry, you don't have to hang art in here," he added.

"I'm glad to hear it," Dinah said. "Nothing suitable comes to mind. Most art would be overpowered."

He raised his eyebrows. "Maybe rhino heads? I was impressed with your proposal—the price, the art, and especially how fast you plan to get it on the walls."

Dinah nodded. "We can underbid the competition because we deal exclusively in fine prints, less expensive than paintings or drawings. We'll be finished six weeks from today at the latest. I expect to start hanging tomorrow, if the young men who hang for me are available."

The quicker she could get out of here, the better. DDD&W made her uneasy, and it wasn't just Patti Sue's animosity, or the spat in the restroom. The offices were like the *Marie Celeste*, as if they had been designed for a big staff that had disappeared—too silent, too empty, too cold. Art on the walls would make it less bare but wouldn't overcome the pervasive chill. Beneath the odor of burnt coffee, the office smelled stale, like the air in an unused refrigerator.

"I'm going to take Ms. Greene down to Patti Sue's office, Hunt," Douglas said.

"Good. I look forward to seeing the result of your work, Ms. Greene. Ted, are we still on for dinner?"

"Absolutely. The Harvard Club at eight thirty. See you later."

Three

Douglas escorted Dinah back down to thirty-two and directed her toward the corridor leading to Patti Sue's office. The office was empty, but at a nearby workstation a tiny girl with wispy brown hair pounded a keyboard. She looked up. "May I help you?" Her pink nose and big eyes behind round steel-rimmed glasses reminded Dinah of a storybook rabbit.

"Hi, I'm Dinah Greene, from the Greene Gallery. Patti Sue expects me," Dinah said.

"Ms. Victor is in a meeting, but I'll, like, show you your office. I'm Ellie McPhee, Ms. Victor's assistant. You're across the hall, and I'm to, like, help you with anything you need."

The "office," probably designed to store supplies and only slightly larger than a closet, was windowless and crammed with a small metal desk, two chairs, a file cabinet, and a bookcase, all painted jailhouse gray. Thank goodness she wouldn't have to spend much time in this hideous room. She'd hang some prints to make it less grim and bring in a scented candle to get rid of that ghastly air-conditioning smell. She couldn't abide the "office" as it was, even for a little while.

"Thanks. Could you make sure I have supplies—pads, pens, folders, all that?"

"All done. And a DDD&W telephone directory with, like, office locations." Ellie looked every day of twelve and apparently couldn't raise her voice above a whisper, but she seemed efficient.

"Office services was supposed to install a lock on the door of the room where we'll store the prints until they're hung. Do you know if they did? I'll need a lock for this office, too," Dinah said.

Ellie blinked, and her nose quivered, making her look even more like one of Peter Rabbit's sisters. Flopsy? "Uh, I don't think so, Ms. Greene. No locks, I mean. I mean, Ms. Victor didn't tell me to, like, arrange that. She doesn't have a lock."

Ellie spoke as if a lock on the door were a status symbol. Maybe it was. Theodore Douglas's office had a lock, and Hunt Frederick's had two: one on the door to the anteroom, and another on the door to his inner sanctum. Dinah didn't care. She had to have those locks. Her insurance company demanded them.

"I need locks because I'll have art here on approval," she explained. "When art is stolen from a corporate site, it usually happens before it goes on the walls."

"Uh...I mean, like, you'll have to ask Ms. Victor," Ellie said.

"Ask me what?" Patti Sue pushed past Ellie into the room.

"Hi, Patti Sue. I asked Ellie about the locks for this door, and the art storage room."

"Not possible," Patti Sue said.

"I'm sure it is—it's standard when you have art waiting to be hung, and it's in my contract. I have to have a secure place to keep the prints," Dinah said, trying not to sound like a kindergarten teacher.

Patti Sue tightened her lips, smearing her purple lipstick. "Then I gotta have a set of keys."

"I'm afraid not. Until the prints are on the walls, I'm responsible for them, and I'll keep the keys."

"We'll see about that. I'll take it up with Ted Douglas." She flounced out, Ellie scurrying behind her.

Dinah closed the door behind them. Patti Sue's leathery skin, straw-like mane, and long bony face reminded Dinah of a bad-tempered pony she'd encountered as a child. She looked to be in her fifties, but her hairdo and clothes were designed for a teenager, or a hooker: Lurex, gaudy colors, miniskirts, and platform shoes. Dinah sighed. The woman's appearance was none of her business, but Patti Sue's attitude was a problem. Argue, argue, argue. Insisting on involvement and getting in the way. This lock issue was typical—all about power and control. Oh, well, with luck she wouldn't encounter Patti Sue again after the job was finished, and that couldn't be too soon. When the prints were installed,

Dinah would be out of here, check in hand, as fast as she could walk, never to return.

She called Douglas's assistant, who promised to have the locks installed right away. Half an hour later they were in place, and the keys were stowed in Dinah's handbag. She checked out the storage room, making sure the key would work, and returned to her cubbyhole. Now the fun part: telling Bethany. She made the call, and when Bethany answered, announced, "We got the contract!"

"Hallelujah! When do we start?"

"Today. Would you call the warehouse and arrange delivery of the prints early tomorrow? We'll start hanging Wednesday night, if the guys are available. And would you messenger over that set of William Seltzer Rice prints—the southern flower series in the black frames—and my tool kit? They'll dress up this hole of an office."

Her next call was to Jonathan, but he was in a client meeting, and Coleman was out to lunch. She left her cousin a jubilant voice mail, and was on the phone with one of the men she employed to hang art, when Patti Sue barged in and slammed the door against the wall.

"It's against policy to keep your door closed," she announced.

"Thanks. I'll see you Wednesday," Dinah said, and hung up. She'd never heard of a closed-door policy. Could it be possible? This place was a zoo. So far she'd been reminded of parrots, cats, a rabbit, and a pony in her short time at DDD&W. Their standards were so bizarre, perhaps they did forbid closed doors and give locks only to top management. "Nonsense. I'll be discussing money and prices. I need privacy, and a quiet place to make my calls," she said.

Patti Sue, ignoring her, rattled on. "And I gotta have a key to your office, and one to the storeroom. Frannie Johnson, head of human resources, says so." She spoke as if that settled the matter.

Dinah took a deep breath. "Human resources didn't hire me, and I am not a DDD&W employee. I'm an independent consultant, and according to the terms of my agreement with the company, if I'm not available, if anyone needs access to my office or the storeroom, one of my employees will take care of it." She stood up and stared at Patti Sue. Maybe she would go away.

The woman's face was scarlet. "I am well and truly sorry you got the job here, Miss Stuck-Up! I saw your picture in the paper showin' off and actin' like a big deal. You make me sick. Everybody wanted Great Art Management to come back. When they helped me with the collection, they didn't put on airs, or have locks, and secrets. I'm gonna get you thrown outta here, see if I don't!" She stormed out.

Dinah wrinkled her nose. Jungle Gardenia had replaced eau de refrigerator. She wasn't worried about Patti Sue's threat—Jonathan's lawyer had drawn up her airtight contract—but she wished the ugly scene hadn't occurred. What was "the collection" and what happened to it? Marks on the walls in the corridors, the reception room, and the managing director's office, where pictures had once hung, revealed a ghostly presence no one mentioned. And who was Great Art Management? She looked at her watch. Noon: time for a break. While she nibbled the chicken salad sandwich she'd brought for lunch, she looked them up on her laptop. Headquarters in Miami; branch offices in Boston, Chicago, Los Angeles. Big. But not in New York, and not well known, or she'd have recognized the name. How had they "helped" Patti Sue? Never mind. Whatever they did, that was then; this was now, and the Greene Gallery had the contract.

When the Rice prints and her tools arrived, Dinah hung the exquisite aquatints of magnolias, roses, camellias, and lilies in simple black frames. She backed away to admire them and stepped on a large brown envelope. Someone must have slipped it under the door while she hammered. Inside were colored photocopies of two paintings she recognized as the work of George Stubbs, an eighteenth-century English artist famous for his images of horses. The paintings were portraits of a woman in elegant riding clothes on a beautiful bay, and a similarly attired man on a larger black horse.

Why would anyone give her these pictures? Everyone knew her gallery dealt exclusively in American prints. Could they have been sent to her by mistake? No, the envelope had her name on it, hand printed in tiny letters. The note inside, in the same writing, was also addressed to her: *Dinah Greene: you should know about these.* She tossed the envelope and its contents in the wastebasket and stowed her tool box in a drawer in the file cabinet. A few minutes later, she had second thoughts and retrieved the Stubbs photocopies. Maybe they were important, although she couldn't imagine why. She stuffed the envelope in her pouch with her laptop and her other papers. There was nothing else she could do at DDD&W today. She might as well go home. On her way out, she'd stroll through thirty-one and thirty and take the elevator to the lobby from there. She wanted to see those floors. It seemed odd that she'd been asked to install art on thirty-two and thirty-three but ignore the lower floors.

Whoever decorated the thirty-first floor must have been color-blind. The walls were painted mustard and the carpet was cow pie brown, which still couldn't disguise coffee and other stains. Dusty fake plants in filthy plastic pots were scattered around the corridors. Wads of crumpled paper lay on the floor near wastebaskets and fax machines; empty cardboard coffee cups and soft drink cans cluttered desks. A big table draped with a stained paper tablecloth stood in an open area. It was littered with crumbs, dirty paper plates, and plastic spoons and forks. A mouse scurried across the table and, twitching its whiskers, paused to nibble crumbs. Ugh. She smelled pineapple and brown sugar. Pineapple upside-down cake, maybe? Yep, someone had ground a maraschino cherry into the carpet.

A throng of people was moving down the corridor, talking and laughing, headed toward the sound of shouting. Dinah followed the crowd, expecting any minute that someone would ask who she was and why she was there. But no one even glanced at her.

All eyes were on a man jumping up and down on a table surrounded by bystanders. The table, like the one where she'd seen the mouse, stood in an open area, but it was covered with piles of paperwork instead of a tablecloth. The tall Ichabod Crane–type on the table gibbered and shuffled the papers with his oxford-clad feet. His audience cheered, and Dinah stared in disbelief while the man unzipped his fly and peed a great flood all over the papers and the table. His audience clapped and yelled encouragement. She nearly gagged. The stench of urine mixed with pineapple upside-down cake and the odor of the sweaty crowd was nauseating. Who could the lunatic be? And why did people act as if he were a rock star? She turned to a nerdy young man standing near her. "Uh—who is the man on the table?"

He stared at her. "You must be new. That's Oscar Danbury. You know, as in Davidson, Douglas, Danbury & Weeks. That's how he lets people know he doesn't like their work." He snickered, as if this sort of thing happened often. Maybe it did.

"Oh, yes, of course," she said, and ran for the elevator.

Four

In the subway car on her way downtown, Dinah was unable to concentrate on *The Girl with the Dragon Tattoo*. She couldn't erase the revolting image of Danbury from her mind. How could that man have done what he did? And the crowd cheered him on. She'd looked forward to telling Jonathan about her contract, and how weird DDD&W was. She'd thought he might be able to explain the emptiness of the office and why the people were such an odd assortment. It was hard to imagine how the likes of C. Theodore Douglas IV and Patti Sue Victor ended up in the same company, let alone working together.

But Oscar Danbury was in a class by himself. His behavior was beyond strange. The word *madness* came to mind. If Jonathan heard about his exposing himself, and his public urination, not to mention the degradation of the wretched employee he was "punishing," he'd never let her go near DDD&W again.

Well, she wouldn't tell him. She was determined to complete the job and get the gallery on firm ground.

She had changed out of her cranberry wool suit into jeans and a sweater and checked the pot roast she'd left in the slow cooker all day, but she was still thinking about Oscar Danbury when she heard Jonathan at the door.

He was bursting with news. He had to be in Los Angeles on Friday, and he'd reserved a suite at the Hotel Bel-Air. He and Dinah would fly to California tomorrow night and return to New York Monday. They'd have a long romantic weekend in one of their favorite places. He beamed, certain she'd be as pleased as he was.

When Dinah explained she couldn't go to Los Angeles because she had to hang prints Wednesday and Thursday, Jonathan blew up: "Why must you work at night? When we agreed you'd expand the gallery and move uptown, night work wasn't part of the deal."

She told him she'd already hired people to hang the prints Wednesday night. That they'd have lots of opportunities to go to California, but she must complete the DDD&W project right away. He knew how much the contract meant to her business. They'd discussed it often enough.

His anger tonight was part of a familiar theme: Jonathan wanted all of her time and attention. Until their marriage ten months earlier, she'd been the curator in a Connecticut museum. He'd expected her to retire as soon as they were married, but she wanted to work a few more years, and after a lot of arguing, they'd compromised. They'd bought the house in the West Village, where they lived in the apartment upstairs, and she ran the gallery in the street-level space, almost like working out of her home. A cottage industry, and about as profitable.

Coleman had warned her that an art gallery in the West Village wouldn't succeed; she'd said a gallery needed to be near other galleries to get drop-in business. Jonathan had disagreed. The Village was convenient for his commute to Wall Street, and he insisted the gallery would be fine. Anyway, she didn't need to earn money; the gallery was just something to pass the time until she had children. The location would be ideal when she had a baby. She'd be able to take the baby with her to work.

She'd gritted her teeth and once again explained that she wanted to run a *real* gallery and make it succeed—that she was years away from having a child. He'd sulked, and when it became obvious the gallery would fail unless it was relocated, he'd balked at her request to move. Chelsea was her first choice, but Jonathan didn't want any part of that area—too bohemian, he said. After weeks of arguments he'd finally agreed to her renting Midtown space for a two-year trial period. If the gallery failed, she'd retire. If it succeeded, they'd renegotiate.

But now the battle had resumed about her plan to move ahead with fulfilling her contract with DDD&W. He was cold and distant during dinner, and afterward, instead of helping her clear the table and load the dishwasher as he usually did, he disappeared to pack for his trip to LA. While she tidied the kitchen, she forced herself to close cupboard doors gently instead of slamming them shut, and to avoid clashing pots and pans. Technically Jonathan was right: they hadn't discussed her working at night, but he worked nights, and weekends, too. Investment banking was not a nine-to-five job. But neither was an art gallery, and for the next two days, DDD&W had priority.

When she went into the bedroom, she met Jonathan coming out.

"I'm taking Baker for a walk," Jonathan said.

Dinah nodded. "I'm exhausted; I need an early night." When he returned fifteen minutes later, she pretended to be asleep.

∽

Ted Douglas and Hunt Frederick had finished their steaks and had covered a series of client-related issues. They were at the coffee stage, and Hunt was looking at his watch, ready to head for home, when Douglas asked, "What did you think of Dinah Greene?"

"She's a beautiful young woman," Hunt Frederick said. "Those blue eyes with that dark hair are extraordinary."

Douglas shook his finger. "Now, now, naughty, naughty. None of that."

Hunt frowned. "Don't be ridiculous. There's no law against admiration. Now, one more time: are you positive she's right for the job?"

"Absolutely. She's excellent at what she does. Her gallery has a good reputation, and she should make real money with the move to Midtown, but she has temporary financial problems. She needs this job. She'll complete our project on schedule, she'll do as she's told, she won't ruffle feathers, and she won't poke her nose in where she shouldn't. Jonathan Hathaway is a successful investment banker from a prominent family, and one of the biggest stuffed shirts that ever came out of Boston. Trust me, he wouldn't tolerate anything but a docile yes-girl as a wife. She's thirtyish, but she comes across as naïve, almost childlike, except about her business. You heard her—she's a Southern belle, born and bred in North Carolina. Nothin' could be finah than our gal Dinah. Sweet as pecan pie," Douglas drawled, in a misguided attempt to mimic Dinah's accent.

"Okay. But if you're wrong, we're all in trouble. And I don't like it that her cousin is a journalist. Make sure Dinah doesn't learn anything her cousin can use," Hunt said.

"I'll vouch for Coleman," Douglas said. "I've known her a long time. She won't cause any trouble—she'll want Dinah to succeed."

"I hope you're right," Hunt said. "She could kill us with a negative article about us."

Five

Dinah woke up Wednesday morning still worrying about her failure to tell Jonathan what she'd seen on the thirty-first floor. She didn't believe in keeping secrets from him—she intended to tell him everything—but not until she'd finished hanging the prints. Meanwhile, she'd never set foot below the thirty-second floor again.

When Jonathan left without breakfast or a goodbye kiss, she was annoyed, but she mentally shelved their quarrel and thoughts of Oscar Danbury. She had work to do. She rushed through her morning chores and was in the gallery by eight o'clock, working through her checklist to make sure everything was on track for the print installation that night. Gambling that she'd win the job, she'd bought hundreds of prints she hoped to hang at DDD&W. She'd acquired all the works she needed to complete the decoration of the reception areas and the dining room. If DDD&W hadn't hired her, she could have sold the prints elsewhere, but it would have taken time she didn't have, given the gallery's financial situation. Thank goodness her bet had paid off.

At eight thirty, she packed her bag with the papers she needed and had started out the gallery door, when she remembered the Stubbs photocopies. She turned back to give them to the senior graduate student and asked her to find out everything she could about their ownership, location, and history. Then she hurried down to the street to grab a cab to DDD&W to meet the movers.

But when she reached the freight elevators near the storage room on thirty-two, Patti Sue awaited her, clipboard in hand. Dinah raised her eyebrows. "Good morning. How may I help you?"

"I'm here to check on the art when it's delivered," Patti Sue said, her voice and manner declaring that she was in charge and intended to stay that way.

"That's kind of you, but I already have an assistant—she's videotaping the unpacking. It's standard procedure—my insurance requires it," Dinah explained.

As if on cue, Bethany, carrying a video camera, appeared. "Good mornin'," she said.

"Why? I never heard of such a thing," Patti Sue said, ignoring Bethany.

"Let me introduce you to Bethany Byrd, who works at the gallery with me," Dinah said. "Bethany, this is Patti Sue Victor."

Bethany smiled. "How do you do? I've heard a lot about you."

Patti Sue continued to ignore Bethany and glared at Dinah. "Why are you filming the prints?"

"As I said, it's standard procedure. We check to see that everything we stored arrived, that nothing went missing in the warehouse or in transit. We'll photograph the installations, too."

Patti Sue shook her head. "We don't do that here," she said. "Gimme the list of prints you're gonna hang. I'll check 'em off."

"Sorry—no checking by anyone except my staff," Dinah said. "It's in my contract."

"I'm sick and damn tired of hearin' about your contract!" Patti Sue shouted. "I don't believe a word of what you say about it, or about your insurance. I got a right to do this: I'm art curator—this is DDD&W's art!"

Dinah put her hands over her ears. "Keep your voice down," she said. "People are coming out of their offices to see why you're yelling."

"I don't give a damn who hears me! This is *my* job!"

"Patti Sue, this nonsense must stop. I can't get my work done with you having tantrums all the time. Why don't you ask Mr. Douglas for a copy of my contract? If you read it, you'll understand and stop arguing with me."

Without warning, Patti Sue threw the clipboard at Dinah. Bethany reached out and caught it on the fly. She got a baleful look from Patti Sue, who trotted down the corridor at a fast clip. Before she disappeared around the corner, she looked back and shouted, "I'll have both of you outta here before the end of the week!"

Dinah and Bethany exchanged exasperated glances. The arrival of the elevator with a load of prints gave them a chance to turn their backs on the spectators who'd come out of their offices to enjoy the action. Bethany began filming, while Dinah checked off the prints on her lists. The curious returned to their offices.

～

Soon after seven Wednesday evening, Dinah and her three helpers arrived on DDD&W's thirty-third floor. They hung the architectural prints—bridges, skyscrapers, Manhattan-skyline views—in the reception area first: a great improvement. The river and harbor scenes, ferries, tugs, and ships transformed the nearby dining room, softening its starkness and complementing the magnificent water view. After the last print went up on thirty-three, they took the elevator to the thirty-second floor reception area. When the nineteenth-century landscapes and seascapes were on the walls, Dinah could scarcely recognize the depressing room where she'd waited so long. The area was welcoming and gracious, despite the uncomfortable chairs and the unpleasant odor of scorched coffee.

When everything was completed, Dinah photographed the three rooms. Tonight they'd hung nearly one hundred and fifty prints, about fifty in each room. They were off to a great start. If Jonathan hadn't gone to California, she couldn't have remained at DDD&W so late—he wouldn't have allowed it—and she would have had to devote two nights to what they'd accomplished in one. As it had worked out, she would be able to join him in Los Angeles on Thursday. She'd bought her plane ticket as soon as she realized they'd be able to finish tonight. Jonathan would be pleased, and she'd enjoy the weekend with a clear conscience.

They'd begin hanging the next six hundred prints in the corridors next week. Arranging them would be challenging, because the prints would vary in theme, image, and size. Still, she had plenty of time, and she'd already acquired about half the needed works. To avoid Patti Sue and other bystanders, she'd decided to continue hanging at night, although the silent office was eerie. She heard a faraway clock strike midnight. She shivered, glad for the company of the hangers, gladder still to leave the place. Its emptiness and all the dark offices were intimidating.

Six

By five thirty Thursday morning, Dinah had eaten a light breakfast, dressed, and packed. At 5:45, Tom, Jonathan's driver, picked her up in the Lincoln Town Car. Tom would drive her to the DDD&W office in the Fry Building, wait while she made a final check of last night's installations, then take her to the airport in time for the nine a.m. flight to Los Angeles.

They dropped Baker at his vet's for the weekend and were on their way uptown by a few minutes past six. Dinah mentally checked everything she should have done. Her suitcase and carry-on bag were in the trunk, and she was dressed in a favorite travel outfit, a navy blue pantsuit and a crisp white shirt. Her ticket was in her bag, as were her sunglasses, *The Girl with the Dragon Tattoo*, and cash in small bills to buy newspapers or magazines, and for tips. She'd remove the jacket when the plane arrived in warm LA. The New York weather was typical for March: cold, damp, and overcast. She smiled. In a few hours she'd be in sun-shine, surrounded by the beautiful Bel-Air gardens, enjoying a loving welcome from Jonathan. Making up after a quarrel could be fun.

At the Fry Building, she took the elevator to the thirty-third floor. She paused to admire the prints in the reception area, then hurried toward the dining area. But before she reached it, she noticed the door to the anteroom of the managing director's suite was open. Hunt Frederick must be in. She'd invite him to join her for a tour.

The door to his office was ajar. Dinah called his name but got no reply. Maybe he was on the tele-phone and couldn't hear her? She tapped on the door and pushed it open. The carnage jumped up at her, a vision in a nightmare, and the smell was horrif-ic—blood, urine, feces, and—oh, God—a whiff of Jungle Gardenia. The heavily carved bookshelves on the left had pulled away from the wall, and shelving and books lay all over the floor. Beneath the jumble of dark wood, red leather, and white pages splattered with blood: a body—and more blood, black against the red carpet. Blonde hair soaked in blood. A blood-stained beige platform shoe. A hand with purple painted nails.

Dinah tiptoed into the room, avoiding the blood, and touched a white wrist: no pulse, and the skin was cool. Nothing could help the poor woman.

Fighting nausea, she backed into the corridor and called 911 on her cell phone. "There's b-been a f-fatal accident," she said.

Told to wait at the scene, she leaned against the wall. What should she do? She didn't know anyone's extension at DDD&W, and the telephone operators wouldn't arrive until eight. She didn't know how to reach the security people in the lobby. There was no point in calling Jonathan—it was the middle of night in California, and he couldn't be here for hours, even if he left immediately, even if he could get a plane so early.

She'd call Coleman. Her workaholic cousin was always in her office at *ArtSmart* by six.

"Coleman," she whispered to herself, listening to the phone ring on the other end of the line, "it's Dinah. Please p-pick up, it's an e-emergency." Oh, hell, she was stammering. She'd stuttered as a child when she was upset but rarely since. Well, she had good reason: she was alone with a dead body.

When Coleman answered, Dinah explained what had happened and begged her cousin to come to the DDD&W offices as soon as possible. "I'm in a st-state, I'm not th-thinking st-straight, I m-might throw up. I don't know what to d-do. P-please, please c-come quick as you c-can."

Coleman, predictably calm and controlled, promised to hurry. Dinah felt as if she'd been on the thirty-third floor for hours, and it wasn't even seven o'clock. She wished she'd gone downstairs to call 911 from her office. At least she'd be able to sit down. If only Hunt Frederick would turn up. Or his assistant. Anybody.

She heard the sound of the elevator and looked down the corridor. Ellie McPhee hurried toward her.

"Ellie, I've n-never been so g-glad to see anyone," Dinah said.

Ellie, wide-eyed, whispered, "What is it? What's the matter?"

"Something awful's h-happened. The b-bookcases in Hunt Frederick's office c-collapsed and fell on—k-killed—s-someone."

Ellie's face paled. "Have you called for, like, uh, security?" she asked.

"I called 911, but I d-don't have n-numbers for p-people here. You don't have your cell phone with you? No? Would you g-go d-downstairs and phone s-security, and anyone else you can th-think of? I have to w-wait here."

Ellie nodded and raced off. Dinah leaned against the wall again and closed her eyes. Time passed, but Ellie didn't return.

When Dinah began to think no one would ever come, all at once people were everywhere—two building security men, medical technicians, uniformed police, and the Lord be thanked, Coleman.

At the sight of her cousin, Dinah was so relieved she nearly lost it. She forced herself to maintain control, promising herself she'd collapse later. With Coleman there, she could get through this. She wouldn't let these people see her faint or go into hysterics, and damn it, she wouldn't cry and she wouldn't stutter.

Hunt Frederick appeared with Theodore Douglas and a short bald man Dinah hadn't met. They were trailed by a chesty woman whose teased black beehive, stiff with hairspray, looked like a bowling ball.

"What are you doing here, Coleman?" Douglas asked. "And Dinah? You look awful. Are you ill?"

"I'd like some answers, too," Hunt Frederick said, glaring at Coleman.

"Good morning, Teddy," Coleman said to Douglas, before turning to Hunt Frederick. "Dinah came in early, and your door was open. The bookshelves have collapsed, and there's a dead body beneath the rubble."

Hunt Frederick rolled his eyes. "Yeah, right, and there's an elephant in the dining room. Are you covering the—uh—events for your magazine?"

Coleman stared at him. "Dinah is my cousin, and after she called 911, she called me. Excuse me, but aren't you the CEO here? I repeat: there's a corpse in your office. Shouldn't you be attending to your duties instead of interrogating me?"

Hunt Frederick flushed and addressed the security guards. "What do you know about this ridiculous story? Why are you here, anyway?"

"When the ambulance and the cops got here, we come upstairs with 'em," the senior guard said, tugging his Groucho Marx moustache. "We got a call, too, but it didn' make sense. We'd of come anyway, but these people got here first."

The medical team reappeared. "Nothing for us to do here; the woman's been dead for hours. No one should go in there until the detectives arrive," one of them said as they departed.

The policemen and the security guards exchanged glances. "The detectives should be here any minute," a cop said.

"Detectives?" Hunt Frederick asked, frowning. "What are you talking about? There really is a body in there? Who is it? What happened? An accident of some kind? A heart attack? What's going on?"

"We had a call from a dame there'd been a murder here," the senior security guard said, still tugging his moustache. "We told the cops."

Hunt Frederick glared at Dinah. "Were you the idiot who made that call?"

"I did not. I called 911, and Coleman. That was it," Dinah said. Thank goodness she'd managed to speak without stuttering. Hunt Austin Frederick had called her an idiot, and was treating her like a criminal. Well, he could go to the devil! It wasn't her fault she'd discovered the accident. She wouldn't mention Ellie. She wouldn't subject that child to Hunt Frederick's bullying. If Ellie had misunderstood and thought someone had been murdered, so what? It would be cleared up when they learned why those bookcases fell.

"They'll have tapes of those calls," Hunt Frederick warned Dinah.

Dinah sighed. "Yes, I know. I watch television, too. I was in your office for seconds. I saw the collapsed shelves, and the body. I have no idea what caused the shelves to fall. I assumed it was an accident," she said.

"Did you recognize the—uh—person?" Ted Douglas asked.

Dinah shook her head. "I can't be certain, but I thought it was Patti Sue."

Hunt Frederick, still scowling, said, "What made you think so?"

"Purple nail polish, platform shoes, bleached hair," Dinah said.

Coleman intervened. "I think Dinah should sit down, have something warm to drink."

The bald man spoke. "I quite agree. I'm Mark Leichter, the office manager. And you are?"

Douglas looked at Hunt Frederick, apparently expecting the managing director to make the introductions. When Hunt, who looked dazed, didn't speak, Douglas said, "Oh, sorry, Mark. Dinah Greene, our art consultant, and her cousin, Coleman Greene. This is Mark Leichter and his assistant, Naomi Skinner."

"I regret we weren't introduced earlier, Ms. Greene," Leichter said. "I'm so sorry you've had this terrible experience. If I can be of assistance, let me know. You'll have to excuse me now. I have a great deal to do, as I'm sure you can appreciate. This sad death will create a lot of problems." He departed, trailed by Hairspray Woman.

"Why don't we go in the dining room?" Douglas said. "There should be coffee by now. The—uh—detectives can talk to Dinah there."

"I'd like to go to the restroom first," Dinah said.

Coleman nodded. "I'll go with you."

When they were alone, Coleman said, "I phoned Jonathan and Rob. They're coming home as soon as they can. We're all going to meet at your place this evening at seven."

Dinah splashed her face with cold water and patted it dry with paper towels. "I'm glad," she said. "Thanks for calling them."

"Rob and Jonathan and I think you should have a lawyer. If this is murder, you could be a suspect, if for no other reason than that you found the body. I've read that maybe 80 percent of murders are committed by the person who 'discovers' the corpse. And if it's Patti Sue who's dead, you told me she's been threatening to get you fired ever since you arrived here, and quarreling with you even before then. I'm sure everyone here has heard about it. A lawyer will make life a lot easier for you," Coleman said.

Dinah, who had applied fresh lipstick and was brushing her hair, shook her head. "Oh, Coleman, you read too many mysteries. It isn't murder. It's bound to have been an accident."

Coleman didn't answer. She hoped Dinah was right, but she'd learned to be prepared for the worst.

"Where's Dolly?" Dinah asked.

"I left her at home. As you know, I formed an unfavorable impression of the Cowboy when we met in Texas, and I thought he'd have Dolly and me arrested if I brought her—I'm sure this office has a no-dog rule. Anyway, Dolly's a snob. She wouldn't like it here. She might even bark to let the world know what she thinks of the place."

Dinah smiled. Dolly, six pounds of adoration focused exclusively on Coleman, had been taught not to bark, partly because Coleman took her everywhere, including places she might not be welcome, and partly because her bark was so piercing it hurt the ears. In the four years Coleman had owned Dolly, as far as Dinah knew, the little dog had barked only three times, always at Coleman's command.

"Come on, let's go face the police," Dinah said.

Seven

Coleman hadn't eaten breakfast, and the dining room smelled down-home: coffee, toast, bacon. But there was nothing cozy about the two enormous men waiting for Dinah. They looked like they'd come off *The Sopranos* set, and their expressions were hostile. Had they picked up attitude from Hunt Austin Frederick? And why had *he* been so nasty? And where was he? Frederick and Douglas had both disappeared.

Coleman wasn't surprised. In her experience, corporate types were rarely brave, and their chivalry didn't run deep. She'd known Ted Douglas for years, and he'd never struck her as a hero. As for Frederick, he reminded her of a big bullfrog on a lily pad, croaking away, telling the world how important he was but disappearing under the dark water at any threat or challenge.

An overweight blonde Amazon appeared, carrying a huge tray of coffee and doughnuts thickly frosted with chocolate, vanilla, and pink icing, and plate-sized pastries oozing cherries, pineapple, and cheese. Her top-heavy figure reminded Coleman of *Mad Men*'s Joan. What a bosom! The giantess smiled at the cops and set the tray on their table. She left the room, ignoring Coleman and Dinah.

Coleman rolled her eyes at Dinah. Another rude and hostile person. DDD&W should add Disagreeable to their list of *D*'s. She collected a glass of orange juice for Dinah and coffee for herself from the buffet before approaching the detectives. Neither of them rose or invited them to sit down. Coleman pulled out a chair for Dinah at a table near theirs and sat down beside her.

"I'm Detective Ed Harrison," the bald hulk said, "and this is Detective Joe Quintero. Which one of you found the body?" Quintero had dark circles under his bloodshot eyes. A drinker? Or an insomniac? He smoothed back his sleek black hair, and Coleman caught a whiff of coconut. Hair oil? Yuck.

"I did—I'm Dinah Greene. And this is my cousin, Coleman Greene."

"Why are *you* here?" Harrison asked Coleman through a mouthful of doughnut.

The man looked as if he usually ate babies for breakfast. His bald head contrasted with his several days' growth of black whiskers. He was sporting the need-a-shave look often seen on Hollywood hotties. Too many men cultivated stubble and thought they looked cool. It was nearly always a mistake. Precious few had handsome faces like those beneath the stubble of the stars—Harrison was no George Clooney.

It would take more than a shave to make the cop look halfway decent. His eyebrows were bushy and unkempt, and the backs of his hands were furry. His hair was in all the wrong places. Maybe he was a werewolf?

"I'm standing in for Dinah's husband, Jonathan Hathaway," Coleman said. "He's on his way back from California. Do either of you know Robert Mondelli? He's a former police officer and one of Ms. Greene's lawyers. He's on his way here, too. Mr. Hathaway and Mr. Mondelli expect me to stay with Dinah and, if I think she's too tired or distressed in any way, to take her home."

Harrison raised his caterpillar eyebrows. "We need to talk to Ms. Greene alone. You'll have to excuse us—*ma'am*."

Coleman smiled. So this was going to be power play time. Bully the women, right? The man was laughable. He sounded just like *NYPD Blue*'s Andy Sipowicz on a bad day. Sarcastic politeness. Tedious.

She'd long since known that the best defense against sarcasm was to ignore it, or to pretend she thought it was sincere. "Dinah will not talk to you alone. If I leave, you'll have to wait until her lawyer arrives to speak to her. And I suggest you let your supervisor know that Dinah Greene is Jonathan Hathaway's wife and Robert Mondelli's client," she said.

Both detectives glared at her. "Wait a minute," Harrison said. "I reckanize you. You're the one made a mess of things at that crazy art party in February, right? You interfered with the police investigation, screwed up a slam dunk. Keep your meddling hands off my case, got that? Or you'll be sorry."

Coleman considered telling him that her "interference" had solved the case, but why waste time arguing and prolong their questioning? Her cousin needed to get out of there.

Quintero was looking at Dinah. "How'd you happen to discover the corpse?" he asked.

Dinah, sounding exhausted, explained again why she came in early and what she'd seen.

"Did you tell anyone it was murder?" Harrison asked.

"No, I told the 911 operator there'd been a fatal accident—they'll have the tape—and I called Coleman. I made both calls on my cell phone. And I don't think it *was* murder."

Harrison's eyebrows rose to where his hairline should be. "No? Why do you think the cases fell? Magic?"

She shrugged. "Poor installation, maybe. Or blasting in the neighborhood. Something like that."

"You identified the victim?" Quintero said.

"I couldn't see her face, but I thought it was Patti Sue Victor. She wears nail polish and shoes like those I saw, and she has long, bleached blonde hair like the dead woman's," Dinah said.

It was Harrison's turn. "You got a key to Frederick's office? Or his secretary's?" he asked.

Dinah shook her head. "I have a key to my office on thirty-two, and a key to the art storage room on the same floor. Both have conventional locks. Most of the offices here unlock with pass cards. I'll only be here a few weeks, and my ID—it's also my pass card—doesn't let me in any of the offices." She took the card out of her purse and handed it to Harrison, who glanced at it and put it in the pocket of his windbreaker.

"I'll keep this—you won't need it. Can I look through that purse?" Harrison said.

"Of course." Dinah handed him her handbag. Coleman studied her face. The dark color of her jacket emphasized Dinah's unusual pallor; she still looked as if she might faint. Small wonder. Her cousin had suffered a terrible experience, and these guys were inconsiderate buffoons.

Harrison took Dinah's diary out of her purse and skimmed through it until he must have reached today's page. He looked up. "You planned to fly to California this morning?"

"Yes, to join my husband."

"Don't count on leaving New York for a while," Harrison said, his lips pulled back in a grimace. Maybe it was his idea of a smile. His yellow teeth and the miasma around him suggested he was a two-pack-a-day man. He smelled even worse than Coconut Quintero—he must smoke both cigarettes and cigars. Coleman could hardly wait to hear what Rob Mondelli had to say about these creeps. Rob was a modern cop—law degree, polished manners, clean-cut and clean smelling. Just the opposite of these thugs. Drat, she hadn't wanted to think about Rob. She'd have to deal with him soon, but not today.

"As you see, I don't have a pass card for those doors," Dinah said.

"You coulda hid it, or flushed it down the toilet."

Coleman stifled a laugh; he pronounced it "ter-let." Harrison was a joke. If Dinah weren't involved, Coleman would enjoy this experience. She'd always wanted to meet a Harrison. She'd put him in a novel someday, or maybe she'd put him in an article sooner than someday. But he didn't amuse Dinah. Her face was even whiter than it had been earlier. "Are we about through here?" Coleman asked.

Harrison ignored her. "You've been in Frederick's office before, right? Did ya touch anything?"

"I was in his office Tuesday for a few minutes, but I didn't touch anything," Dinah said. "I wanted to run a hand over that carving, but it didn't seem appropriate, and anyway, there wasn't time. Today I was in there for seconds. I just touched the woman's wrist." She shuddered.

"Why'd ya do that?" Harrison asked, leaning closer to Dinah.

Dinah flinched and moved her chair back. Coleman wasn't surprised. His breath must be deadly. "To see if she was alive, of course. If she needed medical treatment, or if it was too late."

"And?" Quintero said.

"No pulse, and her skin was cold. She'd been dead a while."

Harrison scowled, and his eyebrows overlapped. "You've had a lotta experience with death?"

"My grandmother and my great aunt," Dinah said, tears welling up in her eyes.

Coleman reached out for her hand and squeezed it. Dinah cried easily and often, over everything from a romantic movie to a dead pigeon on the sidewalk. Coleman was amazed that these were her first tears of the day.

"Back to Frederick's office. We're going to finger-print that room. Are you sure we won't find your prints in there?" Quintero said.

"Positive," Dinah said.

"Oh, please," Coleman said. "She's already answered that. Ms. Greene is tired. We're leaving. You should go do something useful, like fingerprint that room."

"We'll say when Ms. Greene can leave," Harrison said, shoving his face into Coleman's.

She nearly gagged. His breath was even worse than she'd imagined. "No, you won't, not unless she's under arrest. If you keep on harassing her when she's about to pass out from fatigue and shock, you're going to be sorry. Don't say another word, Dinah. Listen, Detective, you get one more chance to save yourselves a lot of trouble. I'm calling a lawyer you've heard of—he's known as the Cobra, and for good reason. He'll drop everything to help Dinah, and he won't care what he has to do to anyone hurting her." Coleman, cell phone in hand, turned to Harrison. "But while I'm calling, you better talk to your boss. This is the last time I'm warning you: stop bullying Ms. Greene."

Harrison's face turned purple. "Don't threaten me. Show a little respect, big mouth, or we'll teach you how to behave. You're asking for trouble."

"What are you going to do? Hit me? Please feel free. Beat me up, big man. I'm five feet tall and I don't weigh as much as one of your hands. You'll be a real hero. I can hardly wait to see you in court," Coleman said, and punched in the number. His threats didn't bother her a bit, and Dinah might be exhausted, but she wasn't intimidated. Coleman could see that the police were puzzled because their threats weren't working. They exchanged glances, and Quintero left the room.

Coleman could hear the murmur of Quintero's voice in the corridor. Good, he'd finally called a senior officer. She knew what he'd learn, too: Rob Mondelli's detective agency specialized in art crime. He was a consultant to the NYPD on art-related cases and was highly regarded by the NYPD and city hall. These idiots would be told all about Mondelli, and that the Hathaway name had an asterisk by it that meant "handle with kid gloves." They'd be in big trouble if they kept beating up Dinah.

She cancelled her call. It was past time to get Dinah home.

Quintero came back into the dining room looking furious. "You can go," he said, nodding at Dinah.

On their way to the elevators, Coleman said, "Do you want to speak to anyone here before we leave?"

Dinah shook her head. "No, I'm so tired I can hardly move. I want to go home, pick up Baker, take a shower, eat something. I was so happy this morning, proud of the job we'd done last night, and looking forward to California, and then that horrible scene—God, I'll never forget it. What a ghastly experience. Surely it can't get worse."

Coleman hoped Dinah was right, but a police investigation into a suspicious death was bound to be unpleasant. If it turned out to be murder, it could get a whole lot worse, and Dinah was in the middle of it.

Eight

After she'd seen Dinah into the car where Tom waited to drive her to Cornelia Street, Coleman collected Dolly from her East Fifty-Fourth Street apartment and walked the little dog to *ArtSmart*'s offices on Third Avenue. They rode up in the elevator, and Dolly followed Coleman to the office they shared and curled up in her basket. Coleman settled down at her desk to read an article one of her writers had just turned in.

But she couldn't concentrate. Why had Harrison been so nasty to Dinah? Hunt Austin Frederick, whom she thought of as the Cowardly Cowboy, had been rude to her, too. Odd. Dinah was the gentlest of creatures, and unlikely to offend anyone, except, apparently, Patti Sue Victor, who, according to Dinah, had pounced on her like a chicken on a june bug. It was hard to believe that resentment of Dinah's role at DDD&W was Victor's sole motive for declaring war on Dinah, but what else could it have been?

And it seemed unlikely that Harrison and the Cowboy should be hostile to Dinah because *Victor* disliked her. What was going on?

The only way she could think of to help Dinah was to try to learn more about DDD&W. Luckily, she had a good source—Amy Rothman was an old friend, who worked as a consultant there. Coleman had hired Amy to help with the hundreds of details leading up to the acquisition of *First Home* and had been impressed. She had recently extended Amy's contract to cover the implementation of the merger. What would Amy think about this mess? She dialed her friend and reached her right away. Coleman didn't have to describe the early morning events at DDD&W; Amy knew everything.

"It's all over the office," she said. "People think it's murder, and that it has something to do with the art project, and that Dinah's a killer. Absurd, I know, but the people working here need to think a stranger did it, if anyone did anything. Do you know for sure that it *was* murder?"

"They haven't told Dinah either way. Have they identified the body?" Coleman asked.

"I thought it was Patti Sue Victor. That's why people think Dinah did it. Everyone knew Patti Sue didn't want Dinah working here and was trying to get rid of her," Amy said.

"Dinah didn't know for sure it was Victor. Dinah only saw a shoe, nail polish, and hair. She said it *could* have been Victor," Coleman said.

"Oh, God, then it might be Frannie Johnson, Patti Sue's older sister, the head of human resources.

They dress alike, wear the same makeup, have the same hairdos."

"Shouldn't someone know by now? After they uncovered the body, someone must have identified her," Coleman said.

"I'll find out and call you back," Amy said.

Ten minutes later, Amy reported that the dead woman was Frannie Johnson. Patti Sue, eyes red and face swollen from crying, was screaming to anyone who'd listen that her life was in danger, insisting that she needed protection. Everyone was ignoring her, or trying to. "Since it's Frannie, we know how she got in Hunt's office. Frannie had access to everything," Amy said.

"Why do they have different names? Are they trying to hide that they're sisters?" Coleman asked.

"Frannie's divorced, Johnson is her married name. Everyone knew they were sisters. They not only looked alike and dressed alike, they were always together, shared an apartment. Anyway, just because it's Frannie who was killed, Dinah won't be off the hook. They'll say Dinah murdered Frannie by mistake, thinking she was Patti Sue," Amy said.

Coleman let that pass. "Isn't that kind of nepotism unusual? Two sisters hired, with one in a sensitive job? Human resources has access to a lot of confidential information, and the sisters' relationship means Victor probably knows everything Johnson knew."

Amy sighed. "Yes, it's unusual, and it's worst practice. We advise our clients not to hire relatives, especially in sensitive positions, and then *we* do it.

The sisters came in with Danbury & Weeks when we merged with them. The people here should have let them go. I don't think Frannie was necessarily a bad person, and neither is Patti Sue. But they were way over their heads, trying to do jobs they weren't prepared for, in an environment they didn't understand. Frannie was ignorant and tacky, and so is Patti Sue, but I don't believe either one of them would do anything criminal. Pathetic is the word that comes to mind."

Coleman tapped her pencil on her desk. She needed to know a lot more about DDD&W if she was going to help Dinah.

"I can't make myself work. I'm too worried about Dinah," Coleman said. "She's innocent of any wrongdoing, but I'm afraid this thing will ruin her reputation. I have to do something, but I don't know what. Maybe you can advise me. Are you free for lunch?"

"Why don't you come over here for lunch? I can't promise you good food, or even good advice, but you'll learn a lot about this place," Amy said.

"I'd love to see DDD&W's offices, but most of all, I want to talk to you. Is twelve thirty okay?" Coleman asked.

"Absolutely. See you then."

Nine

Coleman arrived on DDD&W's thirty-third floor ten minutes early. She wanted to see the signs of the missing art that Dinah had mentioned. Yes, despite all the prints that had been hung, Coleman could see indentations and walls lighter in spots than the surrounding paint. Dinah, thinking it might be a touchy subject—had they been desperately in need of money and forced to sell their collection?—hadn't asked anyone at DDD&W about the missing art, but Coleman wasn't so diffident. Its disappearance could be a story for *ArtSmart*, and maybe learning about what had happened to the missing pictures could help Dinah.

Amy appeared, smart in a vivid purple suit and a becoming new haircut. But her round rosy face below the mop of black curls was troubled.

"What's the matter?" Coleman said.

Amy stared at her. "You mean other than an unexplained death in the office? This is where I work, remember? Where I get my paycheck. This death won't do our business any good."

"But DDD&W is very successful, isn't it? Surely an accident won't seriously cut into your business," Coleman said.

"A bizarre accident wouldn't be as bad as a murder, but it could still cause unwanted publicity, draw attention to what a mess we are. Anyway, we're not nearly as successful as we used to be. I'll explain at lunch," Amy said.

When Coleman saw the food on the buffet in the dining room, everything else went out of her mind. "Good Lord, Amy, who's your chef? A refugee from a fifties diner? Even looking at this food, I'll gain weight. Chicken pot pie, fried pork chops, chicken fried steaks, white rice, mashed potatoes, macaroni and cheese, two kinds of gravy, corn, butter beans. I don't know when I've seen an array of food like this. Maybe at a Sunday school picnic when I was a toddler? Did anyone in the kitchen ever hear of green, as in vegetables?"

Amy sighed. "Later," she said. "Let's try the salad bar, although it's just as bad."

They served themselves and sat down with their unappetizing greens, mixed with a few exhausted vegetables. Amy was silent while she struggled to cut an impenetrable slice of unripe tomato but finally gave up, set aside her knife and fork, and looked at Coleman. "This food is a paradigm for everything that's happened. Did you ever hear of the Davidson & Douglas food program?"

Coleman pushed a piece of limp brown lettuce to the side of her plate and nodded. "Yes, I read about it in the *New York Times*. That's why I was surprised to see all that greasy, starchy food. Davidson & Douglas used to have a sensational chef who specialized in low-fat meals, long before other business dining rooms changed their food from heavy to healthy. What happened?"

"When Davidson & Douglas acquired Danbury & Weeks, D&W took over the management of the back office. They fired the chef and hired Trixie's Treats, a caterer who specializes in so-called 'home cooking.' Trixie is a buxom blonde who eats the stuff she serves, and shows it. The food's not only unhealthy, it's tacky. I can't bring clients here, old friends like you excepted. The DDD&W people don't eat here, but the DWs love their thirtieth-floor cafeteria, which serves the same food." Amy looked at the dessert buffet. "Do you want dessert?"

"Are you kidding? Banana pudding? Coconut cream pie? Fudge cake? Whipped cream, or ice cream toppings? Trixie must be trying to kill the people here—uh, sorry, tactless of me. How's the coffee?"

"I'll get it," Amy said, and went over to the coffee station.

She returned to the table with Coleman's coffee and a glass of iced tea and continued where she'd left off. "Aren't the desserts unbelievable? The DWs—the Dreary Wearies—are sugar addicts. They eat doughnuts and frosted pastries all morning, and after a big dessert at lunch, they have what they call a 'snack' at three every afternoon—another dessert, usually some kind of cake or pie. They flock to it, brag about it, slurp it up. The new food program is one of many post-merger culture clashes, and a huge waste of money. We pay people to serve this awful food, but hardly anyone uses the dining room, the food goes in the garbage, and we run up expenses taking clients out to restaurants."

Coleman looked around the vast room with its beautiful view and, thanks to Dinah, wonderful art. Amy and she were the only people in sight. "I'm not surprised no one's eating here. The food's all wrong for this century."

"It's not just about bad food. I told you, the food is just an example of everything that's wrong. You'll encounter a lot worse if you spend much time here."

Coleman laughed. "Oh, Amy, lighten up! How bad can it be? I don't have to eat here, and I'll rarely use the restroom, and when I do, I'll try to avoid banshee battles."

Amy frowned. "What are you talking about?"

Coleman grinned and described Dinah's encounter with the catfight. "Any idea who Patti Sue's opponent was? Or the identity of the partner-lover? Or the peacemaker?"

"Not a clue. I'm not tuned in to office gossip—I've traveled so much in the last year, I hardly know where my office is. But nothing would surprise me. This place is a cesspool. We've had a series of weak managing directors who've let everything fall apart. Hunt was elected as a reform candidate, partly because of this merger, which is a disaster. We need a new broom, and he qualifies, never having worked in the New York office. He's supposed to clean house. I'm keeping my fingers crossed. Now that you know what we're like, do you want to look for a well-managed consultant?"

Coleman shook her head. "No, but I don't plan to eat here again, and I have questions. Did DDD&W have an art collection?"

Amy sighed again. "James Davidson's will."

"What do you mean?"

"James Davidson and Campbell Douglas, the founders of DDD&W, both died in the early nineties. But for more than forty years, they ran the place with iron fists in iron gloves. The art collection belonged to Davidson, but it always hung in the office. He left the collection to the firm as long as a Davidson worked here, but if a time came when the firm no longer employed a Davidson, the collection reverted to any Davidson heirs. If there are no Davidson heirs, the art goes to a museum. The Davidson male line ran out a long time ago, and the partners fought the will for years. They lost. The art collection left here last year."

Coleman frowned. "Aren't there any female Davidsons?"

Amy shrugged. "If there are female Davidsons, and if a female Davidson would have satisfied the terms of the will, the partners must not have thought they or she were suitable. Or they decided they'd rather lose the art than hire a high-status woman. DDD&W is a male-dominated firm, and they'd have to treat a Davidson better than they treat the few professional women here. Management didn't care about the art, although I'm sure they'd rather have sold it than given it away."

"What was it like?"

"Americana—prints, posters. Some good, some worthless. The good stuff was mostly Audubon and Currier & Ives prints. Davidson also left the paneling and furnishings of the chairman's office to the firm, and the income from a huge trust fund, as long as the managing director's office remains as it was designed. DDD&W sure wouldn't want to lose the money."

Coleman nodded. "Dinah told me about that office. She said there are spots where art used to hang, on either side of the door."

Before Amy could comment, four men entered the dining room. Coleman waved at Ted Douglas. He smiled and waved back before he and two of his companions paused at the buffet to serve themselves. The fourth man, Hunt Frederick, frowned and strode over to their table.

"Amy, how are you? Ms. Greene, what brings you here? I hope you aren't planning to write a story about us," he said.

"We don't publish much on corporate art. It's rarely newsworthy, even with Dinah in charge," Coleman said.

"That's a relief," Hunt said. He nodded, went to the buffet and filled his plate before joining the other men at a table at the far end of the room.

"What *is* his problem?" Coleman asked.

"He doesn't want anything in print about the art project. An article about it could be an embarrassment."

"How so? I'm sure Dinah has already improved the appearance of this place enormously. The reception room and this dining area must have been bleak before she hung these prints," Coleman said.

"Yes, but management might have to admit they lost the Davidson collection, and why. As you know, Dinah's assignment is to put art on the walls of thirty-two and thirty-three—Hunt insisted something had to be done because the place looked so grim after the Americana collection came down. The walls of thirty and thirty-one, the floors where the D&W people work—human resources, accounting, the mailroom and the cafeteria—are to be left undecorated. The Dreary Wearies don't want art. They think it's a waste of money—another culture clash. Hunt wouldn't be happy to see *that* in print. I think he hopes to try to integrate the two firms before outsiders learn how catastrophic the merger is. It's not just the inability to meld the two organizations, either. We don't make the kind of money we used to make. We didn't pick up any new clients with the merger; in fact, we lost some. Hunt is supposed to bring in a lot of new business while he cleans house," Amy said.

Coleman shook her head. "Sounds like a tall order. I hope he's up to it. As for the D&W people, they sound really strange. No art. This food. It takes all kinds, doesn't it? I met that bald man with Ted Douglas and Hunt Frederick earlier today. Mark Leichter? What does he do? And who's the fat man? I thought you said nobody used the dining room."

"Just a handful of insiders who don't care what they eat, or have to show the flag. The fat noisy guy in the red suspenders is a big deal investment banker. His name is Michael Shanahan, but everyone calls him Moose. He's a Texan, played football for Texas A&M. He and Hunt know each other from way back. DDD&W hired Moose from Bache, Gold & Glatz a few years ago for a ton of money to get us into financial services and mergers and acquisitions big-time. They're supposed to be growth areas, but so far, all we've seen is a lot of expenses without much result. Moose is one of the people who wanted this merger, and he said we had to have a lot of computer geeks and accountants—bean counters—to help attract new business. Moose is usually trailed by a bunch of baby investment bankers turned consultants. He's the chief of a tribe of adoring sycophants."

Amy sipped her iced tea and made a face. "Ugh, it's presweetened. I should have remembered. Back to our fellow lunchers. The one you met—the prissy-looking bald guy in the short-sleeved dress shirt—is Mark Leichter, our office manager and chief operating officer. He's the son-in-law of Weeks, one of D&W's founders. Weeks retired about a year ago and anointed Leichter as his successor," Amy said. "How's your coffee?" Coleman shook her head. "Dishwater. What's Ted Douglas's position here? I've lost track if I ever knew. I used to see him at parties, but not recently. Is he still married to Glenda the Ice Queen?"

"He's a member of the senior partner committee, and he's Hunt's chief link with the Old Guard. He's also probably the closest friend Hunt has here, except for Moose. Ted's a rainmaker—belongs to the best clubs and hangs out with a lot of big deals. Nobody dislikes him, but he's a lightweight, the typical son of a famous father. He wanted the managing director's job in the worst way—politicked for it for months—but it was hopeless. He's still married to Glenda, although she's failed in her most important role: she's never produced an heir," Amy said.

The DDD&W story was fascinating, but Coleman couldn't see how anything she'd heard would be helpful to Dinah. She needed to get back to the office. The papers on her desk were calling her. She arranged to meet Amy and several of her associates Monday afternoon at DDD&W, when the team would present a detailed timetable for implementing the planned changes at *First Home*. After saying goodbye, she headed toward the elevator, thinking about picking up a sandwich to eat at her desk. Lunch had been long on gossip, but short on food.

Back in her office, Coleman outlined the article she'd like to write about DDD&W, its management, and its art. Hunt Austin Frederick had annoyed Coleman—she didn't like being snubbed—and he'd be easy to caricature. But she didn't want to interfere with Dinah's project; the article would have to wait until Dinah had finished her job. And maybe she should hold off on the article until after her own association with DDD&W ended. No point in biting the hand that was helping her. She summarized all she'd learned from Amy and added her impressions of DDD&W and Hunt Austin Frederick. She would need her notes when she wrote the article, but for now, she'd fax them to Dinah, Jonathan, and Rob.

Ten

After Dinah showered, shampooed, and dried her long dark hair, she put on comfortable black slacks and an oversized matching sweater. She forced herself to make and nibble an egg salad sandwich and sipped a Diet Coke. But when she'd eaten, cleaned the kitchen, and unpacked her suitcase, the rest of the day stretched endlessly before her. Her thoughts turned again and again to the horrible scene in Hunt's office. The room's nauseating odor seemed to cling to her, despite a generous use of lemon-scented soap and shampoo. When she was able to force the death scene out of her mind, it was replaced with the repellent picture of Danbury urinating on the desk, accompanied by the disgusting odor that pervaded the thirty-first floor.

She needed distraction. Cooking usually soothed her, and she considered baking a cake or cookies but decided against it. That wouldn't work today, this Thursday that was the worst day of her life. She craved companionship. She'd go to the gallery, where she'd be among friends and where there was always work to do.

She grabbed her red suede jacket, and after locking up, hailed a taxi headed uptown on Sixth Avenue. When she entered the gallery and saw Bethany's welcoming face and the friendly smiles of the others, her spirits rose. She felt even more herself when Bethany hugged her and ushered her into the little conference room. "I want to hear all about everything," Bethany said.

Telling Bethany about Oscar Danbury was a relief. Her friend was shocked, but she chuckled. Dinah couldn't see the funny part, but something deep inside eased at the sound of Bethany's laughter. Maybe it wasn't quite as awful as she'd thought. She found it far more difficult to describe her discovery in the managing director's office, and she began to cry again. But Bethany's sympathy helped, and she was feeling almost normal when Coleman called to fill Dinah in on everything she'd learned from Amy.

Dinah only half-listened. She detested DDD&W, and anything bad that happened to the people there was probably less than they deserved. She was more interested in Coleman's reaction to the Oscar Danbury story and wasn't surprised when her cousin was properly disgusted. As always, Coleman was supportive and encouraging. Neither Coleman nor Bethany suggested Dinah try to get out of her contract; they assumed she'd resume hanging prints as soon as she could. Dinah was grateful for their understanding. Jonathan would have a different take on everything. She dreaded arguing with him about her determination to complete the work at DDD&W.

When Coleman asked for an update on the Stubbs photocopies, Bethany put the phone on speaker and briefed both Coleman and Dinah. "None of us has learned much. The paintings have perfect provenance, but I didn't find any recent articles about them. As far as the world knows, they're still hangin' at DDD&W," Bethany said.

Dinah frowned. "That's odd. I guess they could be on loan to a museum or out being cleaned or restored. But why wouldn't Hunt Frederick have told me about them? Oh well, just one more weird thing about the place." She couldn't wait to finish hanging the prints, deposit her money, and forget that DDD&W existed. Tonight she'd have to go over everything that had happened since she got the job on Tuesday, answering questions from Rob and Jonathan. Good Lord, was Tuesday only two days ago? She felt as if weeks had passed.

What should she tell them about Ellie? When she was first questioned, she'd been certain that the death was an accident, and she hadn't wanted Hunt Austin Frederick or the police screaming at Ellie, so she'd kept quiet about the girl's presence in the office Thursday morning. But hadn't the guards signed Ellie in? Or out? Had they reported her to the police? Ellie *must* have been the woman who'd told the police the death was a murder. Why had she thought that it was murder? And why hadn't she come forward since then? Was Dinah breaking the law by not telling people about Ellie's presence near the death scene?

Eleven

Coleman ate her turkey sandwich, drank a cup of coffee, and tried to settle down to work, but she couldn't concentrate. The bits and pieces she'd learned buzzed around in her head like a swarm of angry yellowjackets. Dinah's story about Danbury was repellent, and the missing paintings were mysterious, but what, if anything, did they have to do with Johnson's death? She felt as if she were trying to put together a jigsaw puzzle with half the pieces missing. If only Frances Johnson's death would turn out to be an accident, she could forget the whole mess. Maybe there was news. She telephoned Amy again. "Do they know yet whether the woman's death was an accident? Or have they decided it was murder?" she asked.

"Everyone in the office is saying it's murder. I think the police must have told someone that it's murder, and the news has been leaked all over the place. I hope Dinah has an alibi. If she does, everyone here will shut up about her being involved," Amy said.

Coleman's heart sank, then settled somewhere in her stomach. "Do they know when Ms. Johnson died?" she asked.

"I've heard early this morning, but that's all," Amy said.

"Without knowing when the woman died, it's hard to say whether Dinah has an alibi, isn't it? Anyway, why would that woman have been in Hunt Frederick's office?"

Silence. Coleman could almost hear Amy thinking.

Finally, "Maybe something to do with two paintings that usually hang in that office," Amy said.

"Two Stubbs paintings?" Coleman asked.

"How could you possibly know that?" Amy asked.

"Someone put photocopies of two Stubbs portraits under Dinah's door at DDD&W. According to the catalogue raisonné, they should be at DDD&W in the chairman's office. You were going to say something about them at lunch before Frederick turned up, weren't you?"

"I swear, Coleman, sometimes I think you're a witch," Amy said.

"Yeah, right. But I still want to know why Frances Johnson was in that office in the middle of the night."

"I have no idea. Maybe she heard the Stubbs were missing. We may never know," Amy said.

"Which part of the will covers the paintings?" Coleman asked.

"That's the multimillion dollar question, isn't it? If they're part of the art collection, they probably left the office with the other Americana and are in the museum that inherited them. But if they're part of the chairman's office fittings, and they've been lost or stolen—that will cost the firm big-time. I'm not sure DDD&W could survive. I think we need the income from the Davidson trust to stay in business."

"I can tell you one thing: those paintings are valuable. The pair should sell for at least twenty million dollars, maybe a lot more. Several Stubbs paintings have fetched big money at auction in the last couple of years, including a record sale at Christie's—thirty-six million, I think," Coleman said.

"Oh, my God, I had no idea. The paintings must be insured, right? Someone should be worried about them, unless, of course, they were part of the art collection. But surely management would have tried harder to keep the collection, if anything that valuable was part of it. They might have even gone so far as to hire a female Davidson," Amy said.

Coleman laughed. "The supreme sacrifice, huh? Don't say anything about the paintings to anyone until we know more. I'll get a list of everything that arrived at that museum. Maybe the paintings are there. What's the name of the museum?"

"Wait a minute, let me think...it's a place I'd never heard of. It's Scottish, and royal. Mary, Queen of Scots? No—the Prince Charles Stuart, that's it. And the town is Stuartville, New York."

"Thanks. I'll let you know when I learn anything."

Before she placed the call to the museum, Coleman checked her e-mail and her voice mail. Jonathan had left a message repeating his request that she join him, Dinah, and Rob at Cornelia Street that evening to discuss the DDD&W situation. She texted him that she'd be there. Rob had called and wanted her to call him. She'd ignore that one. She was too busy to argue with Rob about their relationship. She'd see him soon enough. Time to call the Prince Charles Stuart.

The director of the museum chirped and twittered like an excited canary at the prospect of an article in *ArtSmart* about their new Americana collection. She promised to fax the list of the art they'd received first thing Friday morning, explaining that "it needed a bit of organizing before she could send it, but she'd work on it this afternoon and tonight." Coleman sighed at the delay and called a paralegal at *ArtSmart*'s law firm to ask how she could obtain a copy of James Davidson's will. The young woman explained that the will was a public document, all that was needed was a trip downtown, and described the process step-by-step. But Coleman couldn't get downtown and complete her research before the Chambers Street office closed. The will would have to wait until Friday. She'd take Dolly for a long walk, and then they'd go home so Dolly could have supper and Coleman could change clothes before heading for Cornelia Street.

Twelve

Coleman's emergency summons caught Robert Mondelli at Heathrow. He was on his way to Paris to spend the weekend with friends, but since he had only a carry-on bag with him, he was able to catch the British Airways 1:40 flight to New York scheduled to arrive at JFK at 4:10. He texted his assistant in New York to cancel his Paris engagement and to arrange with Brown's Hotel to overnight the rest of his baggage to New York.

Interrupting his trip was inconvenient. He had several appointments at museums to discuss security arrangements. They'd have to be rescheduled, which meant a time-consuming return trip to Europe, when he was already overcommitted. He had two new and demanding clients, both needing his attention as soon as he returned to New York. He was swamped and significantly understaffed for all he'd promised to do, even before hearing about Dinah's problem. He needed to hire more people, but when would he find the time? Coleman wouldn't have asked him to come home unless it was urgent. Dinah? A suspect in a murder investigation? Treated like a criminal by the police? Absurd. This had to be a mistake. Maybe he could wrap it up in a few hours and turn to his other clients.

And then there was Coleman. He should be thinking about his business, but he couldn't get her out of his mind. When she'd telephoned, for a heart-stopping few minutes he thought she was calling to say she was flying over to join him in London. But while her voice reflected concern for Dinah, her manner in dealing with him was distant. Her attitude toward him had changed in March when he'd asked her to marry him. Her refusal had been curt, and when he'd explained he wanted to take care of her, prevent anyone from hurting her ever again, his explanation seemed to make her angry. She'd said she didn't need anyone to take care of her, and she'd reminded him that she had warned him the first time they went out that she had no interest in marriage.

"I told you then that I've never married, never been engaged, never lived with anyone, and that I never will. That I like men in small doses—flings. That I love living alone. And I said that if you were looking for a wife, or even a roommate, *forget about me*. I'm not interested. Didn't you hear me?" she asked, her green eyes icy.

He remembered every word, but he hadn't believed she meant it at the time, and he still didn't. All women wanted to be married, to have a family, to have a husband to support them. He and Coleman had gone out together almost every night since their first date in January. Every occasion had been wonderful. He was in love with her, and he was certain she was in love with him. He was confident that he could persuade her that they were meant to be together. It was just a matter of time.

But the more he pursued her, the more she retreated. When he talked about children and a house in Connecticut, perhaps Darien or Westport, she shook her head and looked at him as if he were a Martian. Before she'd acquired *First Home*, he'd tried to persuade her not to buy another magazine, advised her that given the country's economic problems, buying it was a bad risk. In any case, she shouldn't work so hard, keep such long hours. Since then, she'd refused his every invitation. He could rarely reach her on the telephone. He sent flowers, candy, books, notes, and cards. He received brief thank-you notes, until she'd e-mailed him, asking him to stop the "annoying" barrage.

Still, he would keep trying. He was determined to marry her. Surely she would come to her senses and see how much better off she'd be as Mrs. Robert Mondelli. Retired from the cutthroat world of publishing. Taking care of babies instead of a lap dog. A big beautiful house in the suburbs instead of her tiny apartment in dangerous New York, where she'd been mugged, and where she met such awful types, like that filthy artist who accosted her at her party.

He tried to call both Coleman and Jonathan from the limo that met him at JFK. Coleman was out of the office, but Jonathan, who hadn't yet arrived from

Los Angeles, had e-mailed asking Rob to come to Cornelia Street tonight at seven. Rob left word with Jonathan's assistant that he'd be there and that he would call Jonathan as soon as possible. He phoned Dinah at home, got her machine, and tried the Greene Gallery.

A shaky little female voice answered the telephone—probably one of Dinah's graduate students, getting a taste of the real world and not liking it. "This is Robert Mondelli. May I speak to Ms. Greene, please?"

"Welcome back. We missed you," Dinah said, picking up the line. Her chatty tone suggested that today was an ordinary day. Could something have changed since he spoke to Coleman?

"What's happening, Dinah?" he asked.

"The detectives are here waiting to interview me again. I thought they'd asked me everything early this morning, but I guess not, and Coleman said I mustn't speak to them without a lawyer—"

Bad news. The police shouldn't be after her again so soon. She must be their only suspect. She shouldn't be in the office; she should be at home, resting and inaccessible, especially since it was after five.

"Coleman's right. I'll be there as soon as I can. Don't say a word till I arrive. Can you transfer me to one of the officers?"

"Yes, of course. Thanks, Rob," she said.

The next voice he heard was deep and gruff.

"Harrison," the man said. Rob identified himself as Dinah's attorney and said he'd be with them in an hour. "Till then, I don't want you to speak to my client. Is that clear?"

"Yeah."

He sounded surly, but Rob was confident Harrison would do as he was told, at least for now. Before Rob saw Dinah or talked to the police waiting to interrogate her, he needed information about this death. When he spoke to Coleman, she hadn't been sure that it *was* murder. Maybe the problem had disappeared. If only. He telephoned a highly placed friend at One Police Plaza and inquired about the case.

"We're treating it as a suspected homicide. Someone loosened the brackets holding the bookcases to the wall, and after that, it didn't take much to pull them down. The woman was crushed—killed instantly—those bookcases and books weighed hundreds of pounds. The victim was Frances Victor Johnson, fifty-five, divorced, head of human resources at DDD&W. She was identified by her sister, Patti Sue Victor, who also works there. Because of Johnson's job, she could open any locked door, but she had no business in that office. No one knows why she was there," his friend said.

"When did Johnson die?" Rob asked.

"Between two and four Thursday morning. The brackets must have been loosened earlier, but someone had to be in the office at the critical moment to make sure the bookcases fell on the right person. Hunt Frederick—the big deal whose office it is—was with clients in Chicago on Wednesday. Came back on a charter jet in the wee small hours, landed at

Teterboro Airport at five thirty this morning, and went straight to the office. He's in the clear."

Rob made a few notes. Then, "Okay, got that. What else?"

"Frederick's secretary said the office was locked, and no one—including her—went in there all day Wednesday. She ate lunch at her desk and left for the day at five thirty. If she's telling the truth—and we think she's squeaky clean—someone got in after five thirty Wednesday night to loosen the brackets—and—"

"Wait a minute, how do you know the shelves were loosened that night? Couldn't someone have slipped past the secretary during the day?"

"We think whoever did it wouldn't have left the shelves hanging loose for long—they might have fallen accidentally, or might have been spotted. And no one could have been sure the office would be empty all day Wednesday, or if she left her desk, that she wouldn't return and catch him or her in the act. To get out of the frame, Ms. Greene needs an alibi for the hours between five thirty p.m. Wednesday and five a.m. today. The suits at DDD&W will throw her to the wolves if they can. It's CYA time," his friend said.

"How strong is the case against her?" Rob asked.

"It's pretty good. Her gallery is in financial trouble, and she needs the DDD&W job. Patti Sue Victor didn't want her at DDD&W—Victor wants to be in charge of art and wanted DDD&W to hire a consultant that sucked up to her and gave her credit for everything to do with the company's art collection. Victor told everyone that Dinah Greene was trying to

steal her job, and her sister supported her. Both Johnson and Victor were agitating to oust Ms. Greene,
and some people think they would have succeeded.
There's your motive, whether Ms. Greene intended
to kill Victor or Johnson: get rid of the sisters before
they got rid of her, and try to make it look like an accident. As you know, Ms. Greene discovered the body,
and her excuse for being in the office this morning
is weak. Why would she come in to check on work
she'd finished last night? And everyone knows Ms.
Greene hangs prints and can handle tools as well as
a carpenter. She's physically capable of doing the job.
She's the only stranger in the place, and the murder
took place right after she started to work at
DDD&W. If she doesn't have an alibi, they'll have
nearly enough to arrest her," his friend warned. "If
she was a nobody, I think they'd indict her with what
they have. But given who she is, they'll have to go
slow."

Rob wasn't surprised that the brass knew all
about the crime. A murder inside a company like
DDD&W would make headlines, and the Hathaway
name would raise warning signs all over the case.
There'd be a lot of pressure on the police to solve
this one fast, but they'd want to get it right. They
wouldn't arrest Dinah unless they were sure she was
guilty, but they wouldn't do anything to help her
either.

The limo slowed, and Rob glanced out the window. They had arrived at the building on Fifty-Seventh Street where the Greene Gallery was located.

Thirteen

When Rob saw the massive detectives looming in the spare black-and-white gallery, he wasn't intimidated—he was as big as they were—but he was annoyed. They'd obviously hoped to catch Dinah without Coleman or a lawyer at her side. They'd reckoned without the steel in that magnolia, and they hadn't known about Bethany Byrd, assistant manager of the gallery, and one of Dinah's closest friends.

Rob greeted Dinah, who whispered that Bethany had refused to allow the detectives to enter the private part of the gallery and had threatened to call the police. Told that they *were* the police, Bethany said she found that hard to believe, and they'd have to show her a search warrant before she let them in. She knew some real police, she said, and they didn't look and act like bozos. She said that if they'd been halfway polite, she'd have offered them chairs from the conference room. But they'd been so rude, they could stand there all day for all she cared. After firing her barrage, Bethany had returned to her desk and her paperwork, while Dinah studied auction catalogues in her office, pretending not to hear the disturbance in the gallery.

The detectives gnashed their teeth and snarled, but Bethany, all five feet five inches and 110 pounds of gorgeous in a golden brown knit suit that matched the color of her skin, held her Nefertiti head high and ignored them. Dinah said Bethany looked like a Siamese kitten hissing and spitting at a pair of pit bulls. The pit bulls had retreated.

Dinah seemed fine, maybe too relaxed given the situation, but in good shape to answer questions. She'd snapped back fast after her gruesome early morning discovery. Rob had seen Coleman behave the same way; he never ceased to marvel at the Greene cousins' resilience. Maybe that's what a tough childhood did for you—they'd been orphaned at an early age, grew up desperately poor, and had worked hard for everything they'd achieved.

He joined the detectives in the outer gallery. "What exactly do you want?" Rob said, after examining their identification.

"To talk to Ms. Greene," Harrison said.

"Didn't Coleman Greene tell you that Dinah Greene Hathaway wouldn't speak to you without an attorney present?"

Harrison scowled. "Little blondie with the big mouth? Who'd listen to her? She screwed up a case for friends of mine earlier this year. She better stay outta my way, or she'll find out what happens to a bimbo obstructing the NYPD."

Rob clenched his fists. "You've been misinformed. Coleman Greene solved that case when the police went in the wrong direction and looked like fools. *You* should have listened to her. Now listen to *me*: if you approach my client again without an attorney present, I will take every possible step to see you unemployed."

"That blonde is a nosy busybody, and the cops I know say different about her. What makes you think you know better than them? I won't have her messing around in my case!" Harrison shouted.

"We're just trying to do our jobs. We could take her downtown," Quintero whined.

Rob considered Quintero. The guy had huge bags under his bloodshot eyes. Was he ill? "You could, and I'd be there, and I'd tell her not to speak to you. I'd also make sure that the press turned up so we'd have plenty of evidence of your mishandling of this case. I know you've been told to walk on eggshells, so look out. I'll watch your every move. What do you want to ask Ms. Greene?"

"Where she was yesterday and last night," Quintero said.

"All right. Keep it polite, and make it brief. My client is exhausted. And Harrison, stop shouting. Nobody's deaf here."

They sat down in the little conference room, where the walls were hung with brilliant colored woodcuts of cheerful land and seascapes Rob recognized as scenes from Provincetown, Massachusetts.

This was a room people usually enjoyed. Not today. The cops didn't notice the prints. They looked like hungry hyenas regarding Dinah as prey.

Dinah laid a green file folder on the conference table. Rob picked it up, glanced through the papers inside, and nodded approval. Dinah's brain was working. When required, the steel emerged from beneath the creamy fragrant petals.

"Where were you all day Wednesday?" Harrison asked.

"I was at DDD&W early to meet the movers delivering prints, and then back here in the gallery from nine thirty to six thirty. Around six thirty yesterday evening, I left here to go back to DDD&W. I took a taxi and got there about seven."

"You say 'about seven.' Can't you be more exact?"

"No, but I'm sure the building's security people can. The guards checked our ID when we arrived, and the guys who were with me to hang the prints can help, too."

"I'll need their names," Harrison said.

Dinah handed him a typed sheet of paper. "I thought you would."

Harrison glanced at it and passed it to Quintero.

"Were you and these guys together all night?" Quintero asked.

"I went to the restroom once," Dinah said.

"While you were on thirty-three, did ya see anybody?" Harrison wanted to know.

"Early in the evening, there were people wandering around, but I didn't see anyone I knew," Dinah said.

Harrison leaned closer to Dinah, and she moved away from him, pushing her chair back from the table.

"Was the door to Frederick's office open?" Harrison asked.

"I was never in the corridor outside his office."

"C'mon," Harrison said, scowling. "Stick to the facts, lady. You were working in the dining room. It's next door to his office."

Dinah took a photocopied floor plan of the thirty-third floor from her folder and handed it to him. "We came up this way," she said, pointing out the alternative route to the dining room.

Harrison leaned closer. "Why'd ya go that way?"

"It's the nearest way from the elevator," Dinah said, scooting her chair back from the table again. Rob could see she was trying to get as far away as possible from Harrison. Not surprising. The man smelled like an ashtray after an all-night poker game.

"Why use the elevator and not the stairs? You're young and healthy," Harrison said. He leered at her breasts, subtly outlined under her loose sweater. When he noticed Rob glaring at him, he licked his lips.

Rob gritted his teeth. Harrison was looking for a fight and he'd get one, but not today. Rob needed time to marshal his forces.

Dinah's cheeks turned pink, but her voice was steady. "The men were carrying tools, hanging materials, framed prints, and two ladders. I was carrying prints and sketches of how I wanted them hung. It made sense to use the elevator."

"What time did ya leave?" Harrison asked.

"Around midnight." She handed him another piece of paper from her folder. "Tom, our driver—he's a retired policeman, this is his address and telephone number—can tell you exactly when, I'm sure, as can the building people. They signed us out."

Harrison sneered. "That's the second time you've mentioned the building guards. I bet it's pretty easy to get by those guys late at night."

Dinah looked at him, her expression thoughtful, then turned to Rob. "Rob, you should talk to the building owner. It's the Fry Building at Forty-Eighth and Park—Jonathan and Greg Fry were at Harvard together. The Frys will be interested in Detective Harrison's low opinion of their guards. If people hear that the police think the building has poor security, it could hurt the Frys financially. I'm sure they'd be unhappy about what Mr. Harrison has to say about their building."

It was Harrison's turn to flush. He stood up and loomed over Dinah, his face close to hers. "Feel free to quote me, but if that's a threat, you're wasting your time. If I was you, I'd be looking to prove you didn't leave your apartment this morning between one and five."

Dinah's smile was polite. "Thank you for the advice. Is there anything else you want to know?"

"You say you left the Fry Building around midnight Wednesday. What time did you get home?" Quintero asked.

"I rode with Tom to take the guys home, and then I walked the dog outside our house. It was around one when I locked up for the night. Again, Tom can tell you exactly—he waited to see me go in. I was in bed with the lights out by one thirty."

"Can anybody swear you stayed in from one till...what time did you say you left home this morning?" Harrison asked. He was still standing, still looking down on her. But if he was trying to intimidate her, it wasn't working. Dinah looked as cool as a snowy December morning.

"Around six. Tom picked me up; he can tell you. And the guards saw me when I arrived at the building."

The cops exchanged glances, got up, and left without another word. But seconds later Quintero reappeared. "Just one more thing, Ms. Greene...you seem like a nice lady, so I'm surprised you aren't sad about that poor dead woman. Don't ya care?"

"I'm sorry she's dead, but I didn't know her, never even met her," Dinah said.

Quintero, glowering, departed, and this time he didn't come back. But Rob was sure he *would* return, and even surer about Harrison. Harrison seemed to have a hate on for Dinah, although he'd almost certainly been told to treat her politely. Why wasn't he following orders? Something was up, and Rob would have to find out what. Unless another suspect turned up, or Dinah could prove she didn't leave the Cornelia Street building all night, the police weren't going to leave her alone.

Fourteen

Back in his office, Rob called Jonathan and reassured him about Dinah's attitude and well-being before summarizing the news from One Police Plaza and describing the police interviews. He went on to comment on Coleman's notes on DDD&W.

"I believe Coleman when she says something's wrong there, something more than the problems created by the merger. She's not usually troubled by atmosphere, and she's not fanciful. This is the first time she's ever even hinted to me that anything or any place freaked her out," Rob said.

"I agree. She's fearless. I can't see her getting nervous about anything unless it's truly terrible. I blame myself for all this. I gave Dinah the go-ahead on that wretched project. I know some of the DDD&W people, and I thought they were okay," Jonathan said.

"Maybe most of them are. But one of them must be a murderer, and murder is usually about love or money. Either or both could be an issue at DDD&W. Another thing: a murder investigation might uncover a lot that people want to keep hidden. Having guilty secrets can turn bad guys worse. People kill every day to protect their secrets. I think that office is dangerous."

"They can all kill each other far as I'm concerned. I just want Dinah out of it. Do everything you can to help her, Rob. Spend whatever it takes. Hire experts. Get every kind of test, whatever. Make a list of things you want me to do. Anything you want, you've got. I'll call on everyone I know, cash in every IOU."

"It's worrying to have Dinah mixed up in this, but remember: the police still have a long way to go before they have a case against her. They can't come up with how she got in that office, and they have no idea what was used to loosen the shelves. Of course, if Dinah has an alibi, their case is toast," Rob said.

"I know. But I want Dinah out of this mess with her reputation undamaged—that's going to take some doing. She could be all over the tabloids at any minute, and if that happens, she'll never recover. It would devastate her," Jonathan said.

"I'll do my best," Rob promised.

Fifteen

Rob looked at his watch. He had to make a phone call before the meeting at Cornelia Street. He hadn't been free to tell Jonathan that he'd encountered DDD&W during his work for another client. He needed to call the district attorney's office to find out how much information he could pass on to his friends.

The DA was investigating sales-tax evasion by art dealers and buyers. The problem was huge: a person could buy expensive art, jewelry, furs, whatever, and arrange to have the vendor send empty boxes to an address outside New York, since items purchased for use outside the state weren't subject to the nearly 9 percent sales tax. Meanwhile, the goods remained—tax free—in New York.

A lot of money could be saved that way, and people—even the very rich—kept trying to get away with it. But some of them got caught. The late Leona Helmsley testified before a grand jury that she'd avoided paying $38,662 in taxes on Van Cleef & Arpels jewelry. She admitted that store employees sent empty boxes from the retailer to her Connecticut estate, while she took the jewelry to her home.

In 2003, Samuel Waksal, founder and former CEO of ImClone, pleaded guilty to dodging $1.2 million in city and state taxes on nine paintings valued at $15 million that he purchased from a New York art dealer. He'd claimed the art was for use outside New York, when, in fact, it was delivered to Waksal's Manhattan apartment.

Ex-Tyco chief Dennis Kozlowski was indicted in 2002 for conspiracy to avoid paying sales tax on six paintings, including a Monet and a Renoir, by shipping empty crates to Tyco's headquarters in New Hampshire. In 2006, Kozlowski agreed to pay $21.2 million to resolve the tax evasion case.

There'd been no recent big arrests, but the investigators in the district attorney's office thought that those who'd been caught were the tiniest tip of a mammoth iceberg, and they were on the hunt for others up to the same tricks, perhaps with new approaches. DDD&W was on their "suspects" list, but so far, they hadn't charged the firm with anything.

Rob reached his contact, who confirmed that DDD&W remained on the DA's watch list. He insisted that Rob tell him everything he knew about the company and the nature of his friends' involvement before he gave Rob permission to tell them anything. Rob told him all he knew about the consulting firm and how Dinah came to be involved with them.

"So your client Dinah Greene is their art consultant?" the ADA asked.

"Yeah, but she only got the assignment Tuesday, and she met the DDD&W art committee for the first time a few weeks ago. She can't possibly be involved in a long-term sales tax evasion scheme," Rob said.

"I'm sure you're right, but can you fax me copies of her contract and her presentation? If her name comes up, I'll need to be able to prove she's in the clear."

Rob smiled. Tactfully put. "Sure. Anything else?"

"Has anyone at DDD&W mentioned other art consultants they've employed?"

"Yeah, wait a second...I've got the name in my notes. Here it is—their curator told Dinah they'd employed a firm called Great Art Management. Dinah doesn't know exactly what they did for DDD&W. There's a lot of weird stuff going on at that place. This is Dinah's first venture into the corporate world, and she's had one hell of a baptism," Rob said.

"What do you mean?"

"Oh, that's right, you couldn't know yet. It only happened this morning—it seems like weeks ago. There's been a death at DDD&W. The police think it's murder."

"My God! Does it have anything to do with art?"

"Maybe. The head of human resources was killed, but it could have been by mistake. She's said to have looked just like her sister, Patti Sue Victor, the 'curator' I mentioned. Dinah says Victor doesn't know anything about art, and there's no art at DDD&W for her to curate, although they used to own a collection of some kind," Rob said.

"And it was this Patti Sue Victor who mentioned Great Art Management?"

"Yes, do you know of them?"

"I certainly do. I'll fax you our report on them. They're up to their ears in sales tax evasion. But we hadn't heard DDD&W's name connected to GAM until now."

"What made you suspect DDD&W?" Rob asked.

"Confidentially? An anonymous letter."

"That's interesting. Dinah Greene had an anonymous communication, too," Rob said, and went on to describe the delivery of the Stubbs photocopies, their disappearance and the potential problems the firm faced if they were sold, lost, or stolen.

"Sounds like there's at least one bad guy and a 'Deep Throat' inside DDD&W. Does Ms. Greene have any idea who her informant is?"

"Not a clue, but if she gets any more anonymous mail, I'll send you copies. If Dinah still has the note about the Stubbs, I'll send you that. I hope Deep Throat didn't suggest Dinah was doing anything illegal?"

"No, not at all. The letter didn't mention her—just advised us to check up on DDD&W personnel who collect art. If either of you has any ideas about who might be involved in the art tax dodge, let me know right away," the ADA said.

Rob promised to stay in touch and glanced at the wall clock. He had a little time before he had to leave for Cornelia Street. Whom should he call? Law school, his years as a cop, and even more years as a private investigator specializing in art crime had brought him into contact with a lot of people employed in the pursuit of criminals. He could call on friends in police work all over the US, and in many other countries. But given DDD&W's major activity—consulting to business organizations—he decided to start with the Securities Exchange Commission. His SEC contact was available, and after a minimum of small talk, Rob asked if his friend had heard anything about DDD&W.

His friend hesitated. Then, "Why do you ask?"

Rob explained, adding, "I think plenty could be going on there, based on the little I know. Dinah has run into some very odd people. I don't have to tell you that if there's one illegal activity going on, there are probably more."

"I can't comment formally, but your instincts are good. We got interested in the company because of the merger. Davidson & Douglas was a consulting firm, but Danbury & Weeks is an accounting firm. Many of the legal problems in the headlines about accountants in trouble involve firms that are auditing clients for whom they're also consultants. Auditors have to be independent. If they get consulting fees from the clients they audit, it's a conflict of interest."

"Do you think that's going on at DDD&W?" Rob asked.

"They have the same potential conflicts as other firms we've investigated, and some of those firms are now out of business. As you say, if you find one illegal activity at a firm, there's usually more. Kozlowski's art sales-tax indictment was the first indication that he might be involved in other crimes. We're hearing from many informants and investigating every allegation. I'm sure you know we get a lot of our information from whistle-blowers."

"Are any of your tips anonymous?" Rob asked.

"Yes, why?"

"My client, Dinah Greene, had an anonymous communication from someone at DDD&W, and so did the Manhattan DA's office. Both tips had substance," Rob explained.

"That's interesting. I might be in a position to share some information with you soon. I'll call you, okay?"

"Absolutely. And if I hear anything solid, or even a good rumor, you'll be the first to know," Rob said.

The SEC investigator had been discreet, but Rob was now sure both the SEC and the DA were investigating DDD&W. Rob didn't know how what he'd learned could help Dinah, but the investigations certainly opened up some possible motives for murder. As he'd told Jonathan, people will kill to hide other crimes. DDD&W could have plenty to cover up.

Sixteen

When Coleman arrived at Cornelia Street, Dinah, in a blue silk caftan that Jonathan had given her to wear for evenings at home, was telling Jonathan and Rob that she couldn't understand why they were so worried about the police investigation into the death of Frances Johnson.

"So what if I can't prove I was home all night? They can't prove I was at DDD&W, because I wasn't. Isn't a person innocent until found guilty?" she said.

"Dinah, if we can't clear this up, you'll always be under suspicion," Rob said. "This is murder, and so far, you're the only suspect. If they don't find the guilty person, this thing will hang over you for the rest of your life. We have to prove your innocence. That means proving you didn't leave home after one a.m. when Tom took you home until he picked you up this morning a little before six, or discovering who the killer is. Or both."

"But I had no reason to hurt that woman, or even Patti Sue," Dinah insisted.

Coleman sighed. Reasoning with Dinah in a stubborn mood was like trying to teach a billy goat table manners. Luckily, she didn't have these moods often. Coleman was sure Dinah was terrified and covering her fear with her obstinate denials.

"Yes, Dinah, but you and Patti Sue argued constantly, and she complained about you all over the office. Amy says she was trying to get you fired, or force you to quit. We know you wouldn't kill anyone, but the cops can make a case that you had a reason to want her out of the way," Coleman said.

"I *didn't* want her out of the way. I don't plan to be around that place more than another week or so. Why should I care whether she's there?" Dinah said.

Coleman caught Jonathan's eye, who, seeing that it was hopeless trying to make Dinah face the situation, changed the subject.

"Do you think Patti Sue was the target?" Jonathan asked. "Or was the killer after the Johnson woman?"

"If the killer meant to kill Patti Sue, it almost has to be about art, and an art-related murder wouldn't surprise me a bit," Coleman said. "The missing Stubbs and whether the Prince Charles Stuart Museum received everything it was supposed to could be big problems. Maybe Patti Sue has been stealing art from the company and was afraid Dinah would find out?"

Rob nodded. "Yes, those areas have to be investigated. And there's an art-related sales tax issue." He summarized the suspicions at the DA's office, and the role of Great Art Management, following up with the possible investigation by the SEC.

"I don't know why you're so sure it's about art," Dinah said to Coleman. She turned to Rob. "I've heard you say murder is usually about love or money. What about the woman who fought Patti Sue in the restroom? She sounded as if she'd like to kill Patti Sue."

Rob nodded. "Good point. We need to get that story to the police. Who saw the fight besides you? I'd like to keep you out of it, if I can."

"I heard it, I didn't see it, and I didn't see the woman who intervened, but I'm pretty sure it was Hunt's secretary, Mrs. Thornton. She's the only woman I've met there who speaks in that ladylike way. But Patti Sue knew the person she was fighting with—ask her," Dinah said.

"But will Patti Sue talk? And if it *was* Hunt's secretary, will *she* talk?" Coleman said.

"They'd have to be stupid not to cooperate in a murder investigation," Rob said.

"Oh, Rob, get real. If their bosses tell them they'll be fired if they talk, they *won't* talk," Coleman snapped. "Back to motive: if the intended victim was Patti Sue, could she have been killed over something to do with the art tax evasion scheme? She might know who was involved, and could testify against people."

Rob shook his head. "I doubt if anyone would kill over that. If they're guilty, Great Art Management is in trouble, but the law enforcers rarely go after individuals for that kind of crime unless they want to make an example of them. They're after the art galleries or art consultants, the jewelers, the furriers. They rarely do more than make the buyers pay the tax they owe, plus interest, and maybe a fine. Anyway, I suspect more serious criminal activities are going on there, and that means there could be other motives for murder."

"What could be 'more serious' than the theft of the Stubbs paintings? We're talking *big* money here. Not to mention the income the firm will lose if the paintings are gone," Coleman said.

Rob shook his head again. "We don't know that any art *has* been stolen, or is even missing. Let's summarize what we *do* know: the New York County District Attorney's office is investigating whether some of the DDD&W people are avoiding sales tax on art. We think the SEC is investigating DDD&W for conflict of interest. The Stubbs paintings may be missing, and if they are, as far as we know, their disappearance hasn't been reported, which could be fraud, since there's a penalty attached to their disappearance. If the company has sold them, that's illegal. But we don't have a lot of facts about any of the art issues," Rob said.

"How can we assist the investigators?" Jonathan asked.

"I don't think we can contribute to the government investigations, but they could help us. We could try to persuade them to speed up their activities. They're moving slowly, and we need answers *now*. Meanwhile, we can investigate all the people involved to see who needs money badly enough to steal. We can check to see if anyone has a criminal record. We should learn all we can about the art. Most of all, we have to do everything we can to prove Dinah wasn't at DDD&W at the crucial time," Rob said.

Jonathan took off his glasses and polished them. He put them on again and said, "I'd guess that the DDD&W people will shove Dinah down the throats of the police, trying for a fast solution that doesn't involve anyone they employ. But won't they know we'll retaliate and expose any illegalities we can uncover at DDD&W?"

"I'm sure they know we could put a spotlight on their criminal activities, but if they can focus the attention of the police, their employees, their clients, and the press on Dinah, they might be able to buy enough time to cover up some of their nefarious doings. That's why we have to move fast. We've got to see that they're caught before they destroy evidence. Frankly, I'm surprised they haven't already tried to convict Dinah in the press. That's probably next," Rob replied.

"I think so, too. Well, I'll be damned if I'll let them destroy Dinah's reputation," Jonathan said.

"I feel the same way," Coleman said. "Let's decide who's going to do what. I'll take care of the art side—check out the Davidson will, work with the museum on what they received, try to get a list of what they were supposed to get, see if there's a big difference. See what I can find out about the Stubbs paintings. And I'll work with Debbi on PR, planning what we can do to counter any bad publicity."

"I'll help Coleman with the art questions, and acquire the prints needed to complete the project," Dinah said. "I want to be ready to go to work the minute I can get back in there."

Jonathan frowned, but Coleman noticed he didn't comment on Dinah's plans to finish the job at DDD&W. She was surprised. She'd been sure Jonathan would prevent Dinah from returning to DDD&W. Maybe he planned to discuss it with Dinah privately. Dinah was already upset, and he might want to soften the blow.

"I'll talk to our lawyers, any friends I think can help with the government investigation, and the Frys. We need the guards' records—when Dinah came and went, anyone they thought was suspicious," Jonathan said.

"I'll take care of everything else," Rob said, yawning.

Coleman considered him. He looked tired and worried. Well, she was too, but she'd never let Dinah see it, and Rob shouldn't either.

"Oh, this is making my head ache," Dinah said. "Let's eat. We're having spring specials: green pea soup with fresh mint—my own recipe—pasta primavera and strawberry shortcake." She smiled, a hostess-y, Martha Stewart-ish smile, as if this were an ordinary dinner with family and friends.

Coleman, exasperated by Dinah's refusal to admit that her situation was serious, rolled her eyes at Jonathan. They tacitly agreed to put aside the subject of Dinah's predicament for the rest of the evening. But avoiding discussion of DDD&W, the murder, and the police investigation was a strain, and they broke up early, Rob and Jonathan pleading travel fatigue.

Rob offered to share a taxi uptown with Coleman, and she accepted. She was sure he wouldn't bother her about their relationship while she was so preoccupied with Dinah's problems. He didn't speak until they were nearly at her apartment, then, "I wish Jonathan had come up with more tonight. I thought he'd have a lot of ideas about how he could help," he said.

"Don't worry about Jonathan," Coleman said. "He'll move heaven and earth to clear Dinah. I wish Dinah would wake up. She's in a dream world."

"Surely she'll come to her senses after Jonathan's had a chance to talk to her. God, I hope this doesn't get picked up by the press."

Coleman nodded, but she was only half-listening. She was still thinking about Dinah's refusal to face her dangerous situation. Coleman had read books in which a person was convicted of a crime he or she didn't commit. Surely something that terrible couldn't happen to her cousin. But she knew all too well that there was truth in the saying that bad things could happen to good people.

❧

Late Thursday night, when he finally had a few spare minutes, Rob telephoned a detective he employed for surveillance work and asked if the detective and a friend who worked with him could interview every-

one living or working on Cornelia Street. Had anyone seen Dinah come home at one a.m. Thursday? Or
seen anyone leave the Hathaway house between one
and six a.m.? When did lights in the building go off
or on? Did anyone see Dinah leave the house at five
forty-five a.m.? Tom and the Fry guards could vouch
for her, of course, but neighborhood witnesses would
be impartial and convincing. The two detectives were
available and would start Friday morning.

Seventeen

Coleman lay in bed listening to the pounding rain, waiting for the slap of Friday's papers against the floor outside her apartment door. When she heard it, she rushed barefooted in her nightgown to bring them in. Back in bed with the papers and a fresh cup of coffee, she leafed through them to see whether anyone had picked up the story of the death at DDD&W. Thank goodness, the *New York Times* had nothing, and the two tabloids that mentioned DDD&W described the death as an accident. Still, it was only a matter of time till the murder became headlines. She'd call Debbi later today. They'd need to put their own spin on everything happening at DDD&W. There'd be no point in calling now; Debbi was a late riser.

She hurried through her shower, dressed in a St. John beige knit pantsuit and her Burberry, put on her Wellingtons, and fed Dolly. Dolly hated rain, so Coleman carried her in her pouch and walked with her at a fast clip to the office. Once there, Coleman checked the fax machine. Hallelujah, the list from the Prince Charles Stuart Museum had arrived. It was much shorter than she'd expected, given the amount of wall space at DDD&W. But the note with the list reported that this was everything. She stuffed the list in her carryall for closer study later and checked her e-mail.

Groan. Rob had invited her to dinner at his apartment Saturday night. She'd try one last time to get him to back off, and if he didn't—well, that was that. She sent her reply:

"Rob: I'd like to have dinner with you. We have a lot to discuss. But if I come, you *must* lay off the marriage talk. If we can't be friends—and only friends—I can't go on seeing you. Let me know if we have a deal." Surely that was clear enough? If only he'd stop pushing her. She'd like to keep him as a friend.

Her first task of the day was to search the Internet for James Davidson's obituary and for articles about him. Good, everything she needed was there. Davidson drowned at the age of sixty-four, while swimming in a lake near his weekend estate in Connecticut. His only child, a son, had been killed in a traffic accident many years earlier. Three years before Davidson died, he'd divorced and remarried. Twin daughters from his second marriage, Margaret and Elizabeth, survived him. What had become of them? And where was their mother? She wasn't mentioned in the obituary. Was she dead? If both parents had died, someone must have been appointed their guardian until they were old enough to take care of themselves. Why hadn't they joined DDD&W when they were old enough? Could the will have specified a male heir or heirs? Would that be legal? Oh good, here was Davidson's New York address: 4 Sutton Place South. She'd need that information at Chambers Street.

She put the Davidson material aside and researched the Prince Charles Stuart Museum. Their endowment was tiny, but there wasn't much to support; the director, three junior people, and a modest building housing a small, not very valuable collection—a few obscure paintings, a little furniture, old weapons brought from Scotland. She didn't recognize the names of any of the staff, or of anyone on the board. She faxed the board list to Jonathan to see if he knew any of them.

She turned to the papers in her in-box, all of which related to *First Home* or *ArtSmart*, and started through them, making notations on some, writing instructions on others. She stacked the marked-up documents in her outbox for collection by the mailroom girl, who'd see that they reached their destination. She'd made a respectable dent in the piles when the offices downtown opened. She checked her e-mail again before heading out. Rob had replied: "Deal." She hoped he meant it.

The helpful paralegal had warned Coleman about tight security at 31 Chambers Street, so Coleman left Dolly, sad but resigned, at *ArtSmart*. Inside the building, she showed the guard her photo ID and passed through a metal detector. The building was old and grand, and the lobby was lavishly decorated with beautiful Beaux Arts details, but the people guarding the doors and the machinery were serious, hardworking, and twenty-first century in appearance and attitude.

In Room 402, she spotted a smiling woman with waist-length brown hair and recognized Elaine, whom she'd been told to seek out—"a real person, not a bureaucrat," the paralegal had said.

Coleman gave Davidson's name, address, and the year he died to Elaine, who took notes. A few minutes later, she located the will and gave Coleman a form to fill in requesting it. When the form was completed, Elaine gave Coleman a blue cardboard folder. "Here's your will. You can make a copy if you like—the copier's on the wall to your right. If you need change for it, there's a machine in the corner," she said.

Coleman thanked Elaine, opened the folder, and flipped through the pages. There they were: Stubbs, *Portrait of Lady J*, and *Portrait of Lord J*. They were listed as part of the office suite. If the paintings were missing, DDD&W would lose them—a huge loss given their value—and forfeit the income from the trust, potentially disastrous for the firm. Who got the pictures and the money in the trust if the firm had sold them or had allowed them to be stolen? The will was clear: they'd go to Davidson descendants; if none existed, then to the Prince Charles Stuart Museum. Davidson's heirs were his twin daughters, Elizabeth and Margaret. She copied the will and headed back uptown.

On the subway, Coleman studied the section of the will dealing with the Americana collection. As Amy had said, James Davidson had left the collection to DDD&W, conditional on a Davidson being employed there. The sex of the Davidson descendents wasn't specified—they *could* have hired a woman or women. Since no Davidson worked at DDD&W, the Americana collection should have gone to the twins. Only if there were no surviving Davidsons should they have gone to the museum. The inventory list of objects in the Americana collection was several pages long.

She took out the list of the objects that had been sent to the Prince Charles. The two lists should be nearly identical, although DDD&W might have acquired or lost a few items over the years. Luckily the objects in both lists were numbered: 1,049 objects in the DDD&W list, and 414 objects sent to the Prince Charles Stuart Museum. Good grief, some shortfall! Surely DDD&W couldn't have *lost* more than 600 works of art? She should compare the lists to determine what was missing, but a comparison would require hours of concentration, and she couldn't do it in a subway car. Anyway, it was the kind of pernickety job she hated. Maybe one of Dinah's assistants could do it.

Back in her office, she summarized everything she'd learned about the Davidson estate and e-mailed the summary to Jonathan, Dinah, and Rob. She also e-mailed copies of the two lists of the Americana collection to Dinah, asking her if she could arrange a comparison.

The next item on her to-do list was calling Debbi. She tried, got voice mail, and left a message: "Call me. Urgent." She wracked her brain to see if there was anything else she could do to help Dinah but couldn't think of anything. She sighed and returned to her day job.

Eighteen

Jonathan spent most of Friday morning talking to Hathaway lawyers. The lawyer who would be Dinah's major defender was Sebastian Grant, known as the Cobra by everyone who'd come up against him and most people who worked for him. Grant, who'd met Dinah at their wedding, was properly horrified at anyone suspecting her of murder and leaped into the fray, making threatening calls to Hunt Austin Frederick and various lawyers attached to DDD&W, explaining exactly what would happen to them and their associates if Dinah were defamed. Backing up the Cobra were dozens of minions, all of whom required documents of one kind or another, including descriptions of what Rob was doing and information on everyone involved, all of which Jonathan supplied.

At last, satisfied that the Cobra and company had everything they required, Jonathan turned to his friend and classmate Greg Fry to discuss what Jonathan needed from the Fry Building security office: tapes, sign-in records, names of guards on duty at the critical hours. Anything else Greg thought would be helpful in establishing when Dinah had arrived at and departed from the Fry building during the critical period.

⌒

Rob sent an e-mail assigning background checks on Patti Sue Victor and Frances Victor Johnson to Pete, a computer whiz kid who worked for Rob's agency more or less full-time, including weekends. Pete was a graduate student at City University of New York, who seemed able to handle both school and Rob's assignments. He needed the money, but he also loved the work. He would enjoy researching the Victor sisters' histories, their finances, everything he could find.

Rob had waited anxiously for Coleman's reply to his invitation to dinner Saturday night. He was thrilled when she accepted. He agreed to her terms—she wouldn't come otherwise. But deep down, he couldn't believe she meant it. "Only friends." He didn't see how that was possible.

He worked on other clients' problems until Coleman's notes about Davidson's obituary arrived. He studied the notes carefully and e-mailed everything to Ace, a friend of Pete's who helped out occasionally, with a list of follow-up questions: Where are the daughters? Was there any obvious reason why they hadn't been employed by DDD&W? What happened to their mother? Was she alive? He marked the material urgent, and returned to his other cases.

Nineteen

Dinah had been instructed by both Rob and Jonathan to stay at home, to ignore anyone who came to the door, and to let the answering machine pick up calls. She had agreed, but she didn't like it. She prepared an egg white omelet and turkey bacon for Jonathan's breakfast and nibbled a bran muffin while he ate. Worried and preoccupied, neither of them found much to say.

When Jonathan left for the office, she'd have liked to take Baker for a long walk, but the rain was beating down on the skylight. Walking in that downpour was impossible, even if she hadn't promised to stay inside.

She spent the day on the telephone, calling dealers to acquire prints for DDD&W. Every half hour she called Ellie. Ellie's office extension, which was also Patti Sue's, rang and rang, but no one answered. Soon after noon, Patti Sue answered, and Dinah hung up without speaking; Patti Sue might recognize her voice.

Maybe Ellie was at home, traumatized by what she'd seen Thursday. Maybe she was avoiding the police. Dinah tried to track her down, but neither the Internet nor AT&T information turned up a listing for Ellie or Ellen or Eleanor McPhee in the five boroughs. She tried New Jersey and Connecticut, also without success. Of course, Ellie could be short for lots of names, not necessarily beginning with an *E*, but she telephoned all the McPhees she could locate, and no one had heard of an Ellie. Danielle? Isabel? Marcella? Much as she hated contact with the place, she'd have to try Ellie again Monday at DDD&W. Drat. She was anxious to tell Jonathan everything, but she didn't feel she could expose Ellie before giving the girl one more chance to come forward. She wanted to tell Jonathan about Oscar Danbury, too, but she couldn't bear the thought of the temper tantrum she was sure that story would provoke.

When Coleman's e-mail on the will and the list of items from the museum arrived, Dinah sat down at her desk to compare the Americana collection listed in the will to the items sent to the museum. This was the kind of task she enjoyed, and for a while, she forgot her problems.

Almost immediately, she struck gold—or the absence of gold. Someone had stripped the DDD&W collection of its most valuable objects. The 414 works sent to the museum were junk: advertisements, faded and battered chromolithographs of kittens and ducklings, tattered woodcuts ripped from the pages of moldering books, incomprehensible cartoons by unknown artists from forgotten newspa-

pers, and nearly worthless reproductions of
Audubon and Currier & Ives prints issued by museums and other organizations. None of the items
would sell for as much as $1,000; most would sell, if at
all, for $100 or less. The total value of the works the
Prince Charles Stuart Museum received was less than
$25,000, maybe less than $10,000.

The DDD&W collection was nineteenth century
and not Dinah's area of expertise—the Greene
Gallery specialized in American prints of the first
half of the twentieth century—but she knew the
missing objects included all the best works in the collection and that many of them were very valuable.
Davidson had owned a complete set—all 435—of the
first edition of Audubon's *Birds of America*, printed by
Robert Havell, Jr. A similar set had sold in New York
recently for $7.9 million, and before that, in London
for about $11.5 million. An individual print from a
broken Havell set, *American Flamingo*, had sold for
nearly $200,000 at Christie's, while some of the other
prints in the same set went for up to $150,000. She
was confident that the Davidson works would sell for
as much or more than they had in the past.

DDD&W had also owned both the original "Best
50" big and "Best 50" small Currier & Ives prints.
Dinah didn't know recent auction prices for most of
those works, but she knew that *The American Nation-
al Game of Baseball* had set a record at $76,000, and
she knew that other Currier & Ives prints had sold
for between $25,000 and $45,000. The museum had
suffered a huge loss. The thief had chosen well.

She summarized her findings and faxed the report to Jonathan, Coleman, and Rob. What next? She looked up at the skylight. Rain was still pounding down, matching her mood. Not long ago she'd planned on spending this dreary Friday in California. No point in thinking about that. Back to the telephone to buy prints for a client she hated—a client who was accusing her of murder.

Twenty

D ebbi didn't return Coleman's call until after four Friday afternoon. She'd been in Philadelphia all day with a client. She was furious when she heard why Coleman was calling.

"Dinah? Murder? No way! Those people must be out of their effing skulls."

"Exactly," Coleman said. "I'm worried about the press. What do you think we should do?"

"The same as you think: preempt. Put our own spin on it. What have you got? Tell me all about it, and I'll handle it," Debbi said.

Coleman outlined everything she knew about DDD&W and the Cowardly Cowboy. Despite her fears about Dinah's situation, when Debbi chuckled, Coleman joined in.

"What jerks! Got it. Start watching for our stuff. Read the tabloids every day, and keep me posted on developments," Debbi said. "We'll fix the bastards. They think they can slaughter that innocent little lamb? Little do they know the Dragon Lady is on Dinah's team, and the war path."

Coleman was still laughing when she hung up. When they'd first met, she'd nicknamed Debbi "the Dragon Lady" because her friend was always smoking and because she had such long red fingernails. But Debbi had recently quit smoking, and Coleman had begun to think of her as Smokey the Bear—Debbi was great at putting out fires and knew that the best way to stop a dangerous fire was to counter it with another one.

Twenty-One

Soon after five Friday evening, Ted Douglas stopped by Hunt Frederick's office. Hunt, who'd spent the day discussing Frances Johnson's death with lawyers and DDD&W's public relations firm, was signing the letters his assistant had typed. He wanted to get them in the mail right away and was far from thrilled at Ted's interruption. He sighed but raised the topic he knew Ted wanted to talk about.

"What a mess this thing is. What are people saying?" Hunt asked.

"People in the office think Dinah Greene killed Frannie. Ms. Greene looks and acts like an angel, but so have other murderers," Ted said.

"Yeah, well, I'm sorry Ms. Johnson is dead, although I didn't like her. But I'm even more concerned about the timing of her death—it couldn't be worse. This is going to get us a lot of media attention before I have a chance to clean this place up. God knows what will come out."

"Don't you think we should release the story to the press? Let them know the killer is almost certainly an outsider?" Ted asked.

"No. I want to keep up the pretense that it was an accident as long as I can. If reporters start digging—well, you know what our situation is. Clients will lose confidence if they find out how bad things are. I'm taking some steps I hope will soothe both the staff and the clients."

Ted raised his eyebrows in question but Hunt had no intention of explaining and prolonging the conversation. He wanted Ted to go away so he could return to his letters.

"Do you think Dinah did it?" Ted asked.

Hunt shrugged. "Who knows? I don't know much about Ms. Greene. But I do know Frances Johnson wasn't very smart and was available to anyone who'd have her. That fool of a woman even came on to me."

Ted raised his eyebrows. "So you think it's personal? Nothing to do with the business?" he asked.

"I think it's personal, and the killer has to be somebody who works here—unless it's Dinah Greene. I can't see how anyone else could have access. I sincerely hope it *was* Ms. Greene—I hate to think one of *us* is a killer. On another topic, Teddy, is there anybody here we can put in charge of human resources? I'd like to hire a pro, but we can't afford it," Hunt said.

"How about Mark Leichter's assistant, Naomi Skinner? Leichter thinks highly of her."

Hunt sighed again. "I don't have a better idea. Make it happen, would you? And see if you can find out what the police have on Greene, whether they're anywhere near an arrest. I wish I'd never laid eyes on that young woman. Even if she isn't a killer, something she did must have precipitated—provoked—the murder. The timing can't be a coincidence: she arrives, and two days later someone dies."

"I think so, too," Ted said.

"What do you know about her cousin, Coleman? The magazine woman?" Hunt asked.

Ted looked amused. "She's cute, isn't she? She looks like a sweet, cuddly little thing—so tiny, blonde curls, dimples. But she's not a bimbo. She owns an art magazine that's the talk of the town, and she just bought another magazine. She's sharp and tough. And don't forget, she's connected by marriage to Jonathan Hathaway."

"Never mind all that. Will she write about DDD&W and this mess?" Hunt asked.

"I doubt it. She's very protective of Dinah," Ted said. "I'll watch her."

"Well, if she shows any sign of writing about us, it's your job to stop her—however you can."

Twenty-Two

B y seven Friday evening, Coleman was so tired she could hardly move. She'd worked through most of the papers on her desk, although new articles, queries, and memos seemed to arrive every hour. She packed up the papers she hadn't read, snapped Dolly's leash in place, and plodded to East Fifty-Fourth Street through a freezing downpour. Her umbrella turned inside out in a gust of icy wind, and she tossed it in a trash can. She'd be happy to see March over and April arrive; she was ready for sunshine and forsythia and daffodils. She'd be happier still to see someone other than Dinah arrested for the murder of Frances Johnson.

She and Dolly were drenched and chilled by the time they reached home. In her snug apartment at last, she lifted Dolly out of her sodden pouch, toweled her dry, and fed her. She ran a hot tub and took a mug of Swiss Miss hot chocolate—only twenty-five sinless calories a serving—into the bathroom, along with a paperback copy of Stieg Larsson's *The Girl Who Played with Fire*, the second of the author's trilogy; she'd loved the first book and looked forward to this one. After several tub refills of hot water, when the chocolate was long gone and the knots in her muscles had dissolved, she felt better but ravenous.

Dry and warm, wrapped in her favorite green cashmere robe, she put a Weight Watchers pizza in the microwave and phoned Dinah.

"How are you feeling?" she asked.

"I'm okay—just waiting for Jonathan to come home. I have a leg of lamb in the oven. I hope it doesn't dry out. I think my husband spent most of the day tilting at windmills, so he had to stay late doing his real work," Dinah said, sounding annoyed.

Coleman felt her shoulders tense. "He's trying to help you, Dinah," she said, forcing herself not to speak sharply. Dinah ought to be grateful for the help she was getting.

"The whole thing is ridiculous," Dinah said.

"I hope you're right. Have a nice dinner and sleep well," Coleman said.

She hung up, carried her pizza on a tray into the sitting room, and turned on the DVD player to watch for maybe the twentieth time *Gaudy Night* from Dorothy Sayers's Lord Peter Wimsey series. Both the video and the book it was drawn from were on her top ten list. Like Jane Austen novels and DVDs made from them, she turned to Lord Peter and Harriet Vane when she was worried or under stress. She fast-forwarded past the credits, looked at Dolly, half-asleep on the sofa beside her, and said, "I wish Dinah would get her head out of the clouds and understand that she's in real trouble. I think it will take a bomb dropping on her doorstep to get her attention."

Twenty-Three

The bomb fell in the form of a hand-delivered letter to Dinah from Hunt Austin Frederick, which arrived on Saturday morning while Jonathan and Dinah were eating breakfast. Because of the "strong feelings" at DDD&W about the death of Frances Johnson, the firm's "highly regarded" head of human resources, and her death's association in the minds of DDD&W employees with Dinah Greene, Dinah should not return to their offices until the mystery of Ms. Johnson's death had been solved. The pass allowing her access to the premises had been revoked.

Coleman's presence in the office was also unacceptable. All press visits and inquiries must be approved by Hunt Austin Frederick. He had instructed the receptionists and the security people not to admit Coleman without his written authorization. A copy of this letter had been delivered to Coleman.

Dinah took in the contents of the letter and felt her face grow hot. "Does this mean I won't be able to install the rest of the prints, and I won't get paid?" she asked.

Jonathan shook his head. "No, of course not. Our lawyers drew up your contract, and I know exactly how it reads. If DDD&W prevents you or your representatives from entering DDD&W's offices during the installation period—that is, between the day they hired you and the deadline cited in the contract—they have to pay you in full immediately. Meanwhile, they owe you for the work you've already done. Prepare an invoice, and I'll have the lawyers deal with it."

Dinah got up and selected a sheet of paper from her shoulder bag lying in a nearby chair. "I've already made out the invoice," she said, handing the paper to him. "I'd planned to give it to Ted Douglas this morning."

He skimmed it and nodded. "Okay, you've completed 20 percent of the work, and they owe you forty-five thousand dollars. I'll get the lawyers to press for immediate payment."

Dinah followed him down the hall to the library, Baker at her heels.

"Hunt Frederick must know about the contract. He has lawyers, too. So why is he doing this?" she asked.

"Hunt Frederick is trying to divert attention from the people who work there by making it obvious that management thinks you're guilty. So far he's been careful not to risk a lawsuit, and we'll make sure that continues. Meanwhile, the worst they can do to you is pay you for everything, even though the work is incomplete—which would be just fine, but they won't do it—or force you to send someone else to finish the installation. I wouldn't give them the chance to do that. I think we should tell the lawyers Bethany will complete the work in their office. You'll buy the prints, map out their locations, and run the operation from the gallery. Bethany can handle the installation, can't she?"

"Absolutely. Go ahead and tell the lawyers that's what we'll do."

She could see that Jonathan was even angrier than she was, but he'd shifted into an icy business mode to deal with DDD&W and Hunt Frederick. Dinah had her own plans for her erstwhile employers. She couldn't remember ever being so furious. She had never been accused of anything—not even driving too fast, not even littering. How could anyone think she could *kill* someone? And lock doors against her? Did they think she would kill again? She wasn't going to sit around idly and let those creatures ruin her reputation, even her life. She needed to talk to Coleman and Bethany and work out a strategy for showing the world the kind of rats that ran DDD&W.

Twenty-Four

Saturday morning Coleman checked the papers again before she left for the office. Oh, joy, the *Express* had printed an item based on information provided by Debbi:

Is it possible that DDD&W, the consulting firm once famous for its art collection, has lost its greatest treasures? Recent visitors to the DDD&W offices on the thirty-third floor of the Fry Building report that two exquisite portraits by the eighteenth-century English painter George Stubbs titled *Lady J* and *Lord J* are missing from the office of the managing director, where they are said to have hung for more than fifty years. A spokesperson for DDD&W declined to comment on the missing works of art.

Coleman laughed. Well, that should put the cat among the rats. And a good thing, too; she wanted those Dastardly Disgusting Dreadful Worms on the defensive. If they were forced to answer questions from the press about their dirty little secrets, they wouldn't have time to attack Dinah. With a sense of having trumped their opponent's ace, she and Dolly headed for the office. She always worked Saturdays, and today would be no exception. She was looking forward to reading a couple of articles submitted by a new writer. She felt better than she had for days, despite the continued cold, wet weather.

But when she arrived at *ArtSmart*, Hunt Frederick's letter drove everything else out of her mind. She read it three times and compared it to the contract Amy and two other senior members of the DDD&W consulting staff had signed and messengered to her on Friday. The contract defined the scope of the work that Amy and her associates would undertake for Coleman and her magazines. The contract had been signed by the "Co-Chairmen of the Practice Committee," who, according to Amy, had to approve all DDD&W engagements. Hunt Austin Frederick had insulted a client and had forbidden that client to enter the office where she was scheduled to meet Amy and her team Monday afternoon. Talk about right and left hands.

Could the man possibly be as foolish as he appeared? Maybe he was seriously rattled and not thinking clearly. Whatever. Hunt Austin Frederick was at best an ass. Maybe he was worse than an ass; maybe he was a criminal. Coleman had disliked him when she met him in Texas, loathed him in the DDD&W dining room, and detested him when she encountered him at the murder scene. She'd like to pillory him before the world. But revenge would have to wait. She faxed Frederick's letter to Rob, to her lawyer, to Amy, and to the two DDD&W bigwigs who'd signed the contract. Then she called Dinah, who sounded more upbeat today, despite her eviction from DDD&W.

"I'm on my cell phone talking to Bethany about Hunt's letter right now," Dinah said. "Bethany's going to finish the installation. She'll move into the office they gave me at DDD&W. The hangers will work with her, but I wish I had somebody I trusted to stay with her full-time. That place is a swamp, where snakes and alligators and all kinds of vicious crawlies are waiting to sink their teeth into her. She needs somebody to watch her back."

"What would you think about Loretta Byrd assisting her?" Loretta was Coleman's most recent hire for *ArtSmart*, and Coleman didn't know her very well, but she was related to Bethany, who had recommended her for the job.

"Bethany would love it," Dinah said. "Can you spare her?"

"Yes, she's too new to be a contributor. I'll give her leave of absence so she can work full-time with Bethany. The sooner they get started at that hellhole and get out of there, the better. To make everything legitimate, you should provide Loretta with business cards and a Greene Gallery photo ID, and pay her salary until the installation is complete. She'll be your employee, if only temporarily. I'll take care of the *ArtSmart* paperwork giving her leave," Coleman said.

"When can Loretta start?" Dinah asked.

"Monday, if your lawyer clears it with DDD&W by then, and if you have her identification done," Coleman said.

"Everything will be done," Dinah promised.

Coleman leaned back in her desk chair, wondering if she had just made a bad decision. She didn't know Loretta Byrd well, and she wasn't certain she was trustworthy or reliable. She'd joined *ArtSmart* the first of March as a junior writer. She was twenty-four, had a degree in writing from Caldwell Creek, a college near Greensboro, North Carolina, and had written articles for *Carolina Arts* in Raleigh for two years before coming to New York.

Loretta was smart as a tree full of owls, and a talented writer, but she didn't bother to hide the boredom she felt with the assignments she was given. She obviously thought she should have a bigger role at the magazine. Her impatience and aggressive ambition annoyed the other writers.

Then there was the matter of her looks and her outside interests. She was very different from her cousin, both in appearance and attitude. Loretta was shorter and curvier than Bethany, and her skin color was café au lait, not golden. Bethany spoke in a soft Carolina drawl, while Loretta had a near-Yankee accent, picked up from her father, who had lived in Massachusetts before he and his wife moved to North Carolina after Loretta was born. They had different styles, too.

"What do you think of the way Loretta looks? The way she dresses?" Bethany had said after the introductory lunch Coleman, Bethany, and Loretta had shared.

"Interesting," Coleman had said. "She carries it off well."

"She works at it," Bethany had said. "When she was fourteen, she was plain—dull-looking. You wouldn't notice her in a crowd. Then she took a high school film class that featured vintage classics, and she reinvented herself to look like the great film stars of the 1940s. She had no trouble buying retro clothes on eBay, and here in New York, she spends all her spare money at Hamlet's Vintage on Bleecker Street and Star Struck Vintage on Greenwich Avenue."

"I know the stores and have friends who shop there, but they just wear forties outfits occasionally. She's really into it," Coleman had said.

"Oh, yes, she's joined a vintage film club and located the theatres that show the things she likes, and she's considering taking a course on classic films at The New School. She's met a bunch of girls who share her interests. They call themselves the 'Retro-guards,'" Bethany had said.

"I'm glad she's found some girlfriends. I don't think she'll have any trouble attracting boyfriends. Every man who sees her does a double take."

Loretta wore her long black hair parted in the middle and pulled into a bun at the nape of her neck, which should have made her look like a dowdy old maid. Instead, she looked like a younger and more attractive Wallis Simpson, and she adopted 1940s movie star makeup—heavy mascara, dark red lip-stick—to go along with her clothes. Coleman was clothes-crazy herself, but Loretta seemed obsessive, and reckless. She hoped Loretta didn't take all those films seriously, inspiring her to do something stupid at DDD&W.

Oh well, she wouldn't get in trouble with Bethany watching over her. And anyway, Coleman couldn't spare anyone else.

She picked up the phone and called Dinah. "I think we should get together, talk strategy. You call Bethany, I'll tell Loretta.

"Good idea. I have some thoughts. Why don't we—"

Coleman cut her off. "Let's meet in half an hour for coffee. Where should we go?"

"How about Hemrick's, the coffee shop across the street from the gallery?" Dinah said.

"See you there," Coleman said. The good news was that Dinah was galvanized. The bad news was that Hunt Frederick and DDD&W would destroy her if they could. They had to be stopped.

∽

Within the hour, the four women huddled in a booth at the rear of the coffee shop, leaning close to one another and speaking in low voices. "Do you think the gallery phones are bugged? Or the phone at home? Is that why you didn't want me to talk on the phone?" Dinah asked.

Coleman shrugged. "I don't know whether the Horrible Hulks could legally bug your phones, but I wouldn't put anything past them. Anyway, the last thing you should ever do is talk about anything possibly illegal on the phone. You *were* going to talk about something illegal, weren't you?" she asked.

"Maybe. I've been thinking about what you said about Patti Sue and Hunt Frederick's secretary lying to the police to keep their jobs, and I think you're right. I think Bethany and Loretta should wear wires, and we should put a bug in the ladies' room and one in the little office they gave me—the world should hear the way people like Patti Sue talk," Dinah said. "The people at DDD&W are disgusting and should be outed."

Bethany, her face glowing, said, "Go, girlfriend! Somethin' in the loo, in the office, on the phone—all that."

"Can you do it?" Coleman asked.

Bethany laughed. "Can a duck swim? After all that studyin' to be a detective last year when I was worryin' about money and my job and couldn't sleep, and the debuggin' of *ArtSmart*'s offices when we were tryin' to catch the person stealin' story ideas, I know *all* about it. The only tap that could be illegal is the one in the loo—it's illegal if one of us isn't in there and takin' part in the conversation. I'm pretty sure it's okay to record a call as long as one of the people bein' taped knows about it. If the bug is in our office and on our phone, one of us will always be part of the recordin', so they're just fine. But that's right about not discussin' anything important on the phone or in e-mail, even when it's totally legal. You never know who's listenin' or readin'."

"Well, we'll do the ladies' room, legal or not." Dinah decided. "Where there's one conversation worth recording, maybe there'll be more. I wish I had that catfight on tape. I'd turn it over to the *New York Post*."

"I'll be the photographer—did Lois Lane take pictures? I've got this great digital camera. This is *good*. It's been mighty quiet ever since I joined *ArtSmart*. Y'all had all the fun before I got here," Loretta said.

Coleman raised her eyebrows in mock disapproval. "Murder? Attempted murder? Me nearly getting killed once or twice? You have a weird definition of fun."

Loretta grinned. "But you can't say life was boring. Has anybody read those Women's Murder Club books? We can be like them."

"Except they're crime experts: a medical examiner, a police officer, a lawyer and such," Dinah said. "We don't know much about anything except art."

"That's okay, we have friends who know other things," Coleman said.

"And we can always round up some men if we need them," Loretta said, batting her eyelashes. "This is sooo exciting."

"I wish the excitement wasn't about me maybe being arrested for murder," Dinah said.

"Don't worry. It won't go that far," Coleman said, silently praying that she was right.

Twenty-Five

B ack on Cornelia Street, Dinah found Jonathan where she had left him, in the library, on the telephone. He told her that he was asking everyone he knew for advice, assistance, and favors. He had talked to Rob, to Greg Fry, and to the lawyers, as well as to numerous friends, and he was more than ready to take a coffee break. He listened attentively to her summary of her meeting with Coleman and the Byrds. He'd help with their plans, including enlisting Rob to assist them with listening devices at DDD&W. He returned to the library and the telephone, and she settled at the big table in the dining area to catch up on gallery paperwork. But she kept an ear tuned in his direction, and as the morning sped by, she could hear his growing frustration with the lawyers.

When she called him to lunch, he looked tired and exasperated. He relaxed a little after he'd eaten a chicken salad sandwich and sipped a glass of pinot grigio. But when she asked him how things were going, he frowned and shook his head.

"Too damned slow. The DDD&W people are sloths," he said.

"Anything new?"

"Greg Fry is putting together everything Rob's asked for—copies of the Fry Building lobby security sign-in and sign-out records for the last six months, the security camera's films for six months, the personnel department's files on the lobby guards, and the voice tape of the woman who called in the murder. And he's lending us a suite on the fifty-fourth floor where Rob's people can hang out, and where they can put the equipment to record your bugs. The suite is ostensibly rented to Rob. His name will be on the door."

"My goodness! That's a big help!" Dinah said.

Jonathan nodded. "Greg's a good friend. Those jerks at DDD&W are being obstructive, but we'll get what we want before we go to bed Sunday night if I have to keep them up all night tonight to do it."

∽

Dinah was worried about the Fry Building voice tape: Ellie's tape. She hoped the girl wouldn't get in trouble. She wished she could reach Ellie. But she'd done all she could until DDD&W reopened on Monday.

∽

While Jonathan was eating lunch, Sebastian Grant, the senior Hathaway lawyer—a.k.a. the Cobra—lost it. Sick of the complaints of the DDD&W lawyers, presumably echoing the protests of their masters, he shouted into his phone, "If the incompetent management at DDD&W *will* deliver imbecilic letters to the wife of Jonathan Cabot Lodge Hathaway the Third on a Saturday morning, they'll be bloody lucky if all they lose is a Saturday and Sunday on the golf course! For God's sake, get to work, or I'm coming over, and if I do, every one of you will regret it."

When a junior associate asked a more senior associate if Mr. Hathaway really answered to all those names, his senior snapped, "Of course not. But those dopes at DDD&W knew exactly what the Cobra meant, and so should you."

Grant, who overheard their conversation—he was thought to have supernatural hearing and eyes in the back of his head, and reveled in his reputation—agreed. An associate who said anything that stupid was probably too slow-witted to succeed in the realm of Sebastian Grant.

The DDD&W lawyers stopped whining and went to work. Maybe they hoped to spend a few hours with their families over the weekend. Grant smiled his serpentine smile, and everyone who saw it shuddered. They knew that not one person would see his home again until the Cobra had everything he wanted.

∽

Rob, struggling with jet lag, had a restless night, and as a result, overslept Saturday. He didn't arrive at his office until nearly noon, but even so, he found nothing about Dinah's situation waiting for his attention. The guys covering Cornelia Street must not have come up with anything, and his computer kids were silent. He sent a nudging e-mail to Pete, who was supposed to check on the Victor girls, asking him to get in touch as soon as possible.

Around two, information began to trickle in. The team questioning Cornelia Street residents had turned up a witness, the old lady who owned Carmine's, a wholesale bakery two doors away from the Hathaways' townhouse. The bakery was open all night baking bread and loading it on delivery trucks under Mrs. Carmine's supervision. She'd seen Dinah come home around one Friday morning, and her light go out at half past one. She swore Dinah didn't leave the house again until the driver picked her up a little before six, when the old lady was leaving the bakery to walk to her apartment down the block. The prosecutors would suggest that Mrs. Carmine had fallen asleep and missed Dinah's nocturnal wanderings, but her employees—including her live-in housekeeper—swore she never slept until after the last loaded delivery truck departed, and she was in bed in her apartment.

Not that Rob wanted Dinah on trial. But Mrs. Carmine's statement should give the NYPD pause. The police wouldn't find anyone who'd seen Dinah during the critical period, since she hadn't left the building, and if anyone—like Harrison—had planned to set her up with a lying witness, it was too late; everyone had been interviewed. One potential trap had been sprung. Rob didn't know for sure that Harrison was dirty, but his attitude was strange, and there was nothing to be gained by assuming he was clean. He'd have to check Harrison out thoroughly, but meanwhile, he e-mailed Mrs. Carmine's statement to his friend at One Police Plaza. He wanted it on record with a trustworthy person.

When the files from the Fry Building arrived, Rob turned them over to his assistant to organize and asked him to leave everything on his desk. He'd look at them on Sunday. At five he told everyone to go home and followed them out the door. Tonight he was cooking dinner for Coleman, and he needed to get started on the meal, and to make sure his apartment was in order.

Twenty-Six

At eight o'clock Saturday night, Jonathan told the lawyers that he'd be back on the telephone on Sunday at nine a.m. and signed off. He and Dinah ate lentil soup Dinah had made, walked Baker, and turned in early. Neither slept much, but they both pretended, lying apart and silent, wishing the night would end but dreading what morning might bring.

Loretta had a blind date with a young man who worked at an advertising agency, and she hoped he'd look like *Mad Men*'s Don Draper. She was meeting her date in the bar of the Algonquin Hotel, which she'd read about. On this, her first visit to the historic hotel, she planned to stand out. She was wearing a red velvet cocktail suit that looked more like Christmas than spring, but it was freezing outside and felt like Christmas. Anyway, it was Saturday night! At the Algonquin, she handed her black cape to the cloakroom attendant and leaned over to greet the magnificent cat napping on a luggage rack. Then she turned to face the room. She wasn't surprised to see that every eye was on her. She smiled at her admiring audience and waited for her date to step up and claim her.

Twenty-Seven

Coleman had accepted Rob's invitation to Saturday dinner at his apartment with trepidation, but so far he'd behaved. She was glad, because she wanted him to remain her friend, and this evening would determine whether that was possible. She mentally crossed her fingers.

She snuggled in the corner on the brown corduroy sofa, squashy pillows around her, Dolly in her lap, and sipped a Virgin Mary. Dinner smelled divine—basil, garlic, Parmigiano-Reggiano. "I like your open kitchen, so we can talk while you cook," she said.

He smiled over his shoulder. "Would you reconsider moving in with me? You have an open invitation."

She frowned. "Rob, you promised. For the hundredth time, I don't want to move in with you. I've told you over and over: I'll never live with anyone.

You know I love my apartment. I'll never move out of it—I expect to live there when I'm old and gray."

"I keep thinking you'll change your mind," he said.

"I'll never change my mind. I wish you'd stop bringing it up—you know I hate it. Let's change the subject. Did you see Heyward when you were in London?" The subject of her half-brother was uncomfortable but a lot better than Rob's trying to push her in a direction that didn't interest her.

Rob set the colander of cooked pasta in the sink to drain and turned to look at her.

"Yes, ma'am, I certainly did. He asked about you. I told him about *First Home*, and he asked me to congratulate you. It would have been nice if you'd told him about it, since his money enabled you to buy it." He poured the drained spaghetti into a big cream-colored pottery bowl, adding tiny steamed green beans and sliced boiled new potatoes from another pot. When he stirred in the pesto sauce, the scent of basil and garlic grew stronger.

Coleman's mouth watered. Rob's words had stung her conscience but hadn't cooled her appetite.

"I know. I'm embarrassed I haven't written him. I would have, if it weren't for Simon. I hate the thought of that creep reading my letters," she said.

"You're safe on that score. Simon's been in a Swiss clinic since a week or so after the night he was injured. Getting beaten with a baseball bat repeatedly by a lunatic is no joke. He had a lot of bones broken in his face—cheeks, nose, chin—and in both hands, and all his front teeth were smashed. Heyward says he'll be in the clinic for months. He's lucky to be alive. Meanwhile, Heyward's bought a house in London and visits Simon on weekends. He says he can't take Switzerland except in small doses, but it sounds to me like it's Simon he can't take. I think Heyward's lost interest in that jerk but feels obliged to help him."

This was welcome news, if true. "Do you mean Heyward may be breaking off his friendship with Simon?" Coleman asked.

"I think he would if Simon weren't in such desperate straits, both physically and financially. Heyward now knows how awful Simon is, and he's embarrassed that he was so taken in by him. When he apologized to all of us for defending Simon, believing we were wrong about that creep, I was the only one who responded. I feel sorry for Heyward—so smart about so much but completely fooled by Simon.

"I think Rachel has softened toward Heyward—he's helping her straighten out the financial mess Simon made. Simon owes Rachel a lot of money, which he has no intention of paying—probably doesn't have it. Meanwhile, they're still legally bound together in the ownership of the Ransome gallery, which means *she* still has to pay him," Rob said.

Coleman thought about the changes of attitude toward her half-brother. If both Rob and Rachel had decided to forgive Heyward, she should at least try. With Simon out of the way, maybe she and Heyward could be friends. "Is Heyward coming to New York anytime soon?" she asked.

Rob shook his head. "He's kept his house here, but he didn't mention plans to visit. I'm sure he'd come if you invited him."

"Is dinner nearly ready? I'm starved," Coleman said. More pressure. But maybe the pressure wasn't coming from Rob this time. Maybe her conscience—her own personal Jiminy Cricket—was telling her it was time to heal old wounds, to forget the past, and move on.

Heyward hadn't known of her existence until he was thirty-one and she was twenty-seven, but he *could* have known, if he'd bothered to look at the family papers. Coleman hadn't known family papers existed, let alone a half-brother. She'd learned Heyward was her half-brother only a few months ago. Her mother had given birth to a son before she married Coleman's father. Coleman had never had more than a few brief conversations with Heyward, but she couldn't help feeling angry knowing that when she and Dinah had been so poor, he was already a billionaire. He could have made their lives much easier.

She had to admit that after he moved to New York last year, he'd been more than generous to her, and he *was* her closest relative. Her only relative other than Dinah. Coleman didn't care if Heyward was gay, but she despised Simon, with whom he'd been infatuated. Maybe she'd write to Heyward and thank him for all he'd done for her, all he'd made possible. Right now, she'd concentrate on the pasta.

"Food's fabulous," she said.

He smiled. "I could be your full-time cook. Could start with breakfast tomorrow, if you'll stay over."

Coleman took a deep breath. She'd had enough. "Get off it, Rob. I don't eat breakfast. I sleep in my own apartment. Anyway, I have work to do—I'm leaving right after dinner," she said.

Rob sighed and poured himself another glass of Chianti Classico.

~

Back in her apartment, Coleman put aside the article she was editing and thought about Rob. Why *wouldn't* he be her friend? Until he'd started nagging her about staying over, living with him—all the stuff she'd told him she didn't want to hear—she'd planned to tell him about the letter offering to buy her magazines. She'd wanted to know what he thought about it. She *needed* him as a friend. He'd ruined this evening by his insisting on more than she could ever give him. Oh well, she hadn't heard any more from Colossus. Maybe Jonathan had persuaded them to leave her alone. Maybe she'd meet another man, a male friend to whom she could turn for help and advice, who didn't want to marry her, or change her into someone else. A mommy in Darien? Never. She had too much to do.

Twenty-Eight

Bethany and Zeke were celebrating Zeke's promotion at *ArtSmart* with a special Saturday night dinner at his apartment. Zeke had told her he'd arranged several surprises for her. Bethany loved Zeke's surprises and couldn't wait to see what he was up to. She had a surprise for him, too, but she was pretty sure he wasn't going to like it. She hated making him unhappy. Most of the time Zeke was the happiest person she knew. He was lucky and was grateful for his good fortune—his family, his financial security, and for Bethany's company.

Zeke lived alone in a big Central Park West apartment with a spectacular view of the park. He was the only child and grandchild of a well-off and doting Long Island family, who gave him everything he ever thought of wanting, and a lot he hadn't thought of. But he wasn't spoiled—far from it. He worked like a beaver, smiling all the time. He was sweet as strawberry shortcake, and lots of fun. Plenty smart, too.

Bethany was in love with him, although she certainly hadn't expected to be when she first went out with him nearly five months ago. She hadn't seen how anything permanent could come of their relationship then, and she still didn't, but she'd decided to enjoy being with him while it lasted.

She let herself in and hung her coat in the foyer. Surprise number one: the apartment was full of roses—white, pink, yellow, golden; large and small; buds and full blossoms; in vases and bowls and pots. Every room looked and smelled glorious. Something cooking smelled good, too. Roast duck? That meant Zeke's cook was here, although she didn't normally come in on weekends. Bethany had thought Zeke would have a restaurant meal delivered by one of those waiters in black tie from At Your Service. Wherever the food came from, Zeke didn't cook it; Zeke couldn't heat pizza in the microwave without burning it. Good in the kitchen he was not—but nearly everywhere else he was superb. She smiled, thinking about the many ways he pleased her.

Zeke emerged from the kitchen, resplendent in a brown velvet smoking jacket and a cream-colored silk shirt. Another surprise—he was a crewneck sweater and khakis kind of guy. He grabbed her and kissed her hard. None of those polite little pecks on the cheek for Zeke: he was a great kisser. When he came up for air, he said, "Like the roses?"

"Love 'em. Love your outfit, too. You look like you walked out of a Cary Grant movie. And what about those kitchen smells? What's cookin'? And who's cookin'? I thought Hattie was off tonight."

He grinned, his cute-ugly face lighting up. "Hattie came, cooked, and went. I wanted to be alone with you, so we're serving ourselves. Hey, I like what you're wearing. New?"

That was another good thing about Zeke: he always noticed her clothes. He loved her arty wardrobe, which she pieced together from ethnic shops and thrift stores and remnants. Her cloth-of-gold dress barely covered her long legs, and its halter neckline exposed a lot of bosom. The fabric was expensive, but she hadn't needed much, and Coleman had helped her make the dress. Coleman, who'd sewed since she was a child and began designing her own clothes and a lot of Dinah's when they were in high school, encouraged Bethany's experiments and helped with the tough parts. She and Coleman and Dinah were all clothes-crazy, and proud of it.

"I wanted to show off all the topaz and cat's eye and amber jewelry you give me. See, I'm wearin' the earrings you gave me for Christmas, and one of the necklaces. You keep tellin' me you're tryin' to match my eyes, and now I'm matchin' back," Bethany said.

"God, Bethany, what an opening! I planned to wait till after dinner, but I can't. I want to give you this." He took a black velvet box out of his jacket pocket and handed it to her.

She opened the box and stared at the ring inside. The metal was gold, the enormous stone a clear golden yellow, surrounded by lighter yellow stones.

"Good heavens, Zeke. I've never seen anything like this—it's gorgeous."

"It's a canary diamond, with yellow diamonds around it. It's an engagement ring. Will you marry me, Bethany? I love you so much."

Bethany had read that when a person was about to die, her whole life flashed before her eyes. She wasn't about to die, unless you could die of joy, but her head was spinning, and she saw pictures unreeling in her head. Herself as a child playing with her cousins and Dinah and Coleman in the clear brown shallows of the river that ran through Slocumb Corners, North Carolina, where they lived. The Byrd matriarch, Aunt Mary Louise: tall, ageless, benevolent, in a bright red caftan and turban. The family massed around her—cousins, aunts, her mother. The country school she'd attended. The simple white church where she and her family worshipped, and the lawn around it where they had picnics after Sunday services. The cemetery where her father was buried. The scent of the air—pine trees, honeysuckle, magnolias. The tiny cottage where her mother lived alone since Bethany left for college, and, later, New York.

"What is it, Bethany?" Zeke asked, his voice strained. "Please don't say no. Don't you love me?"

She looked up at him, her eyes wet. "Oh, Zeke, I do love you, you know I do. But we can't get *married*. It would never work."

He smiled. "Give me a list of all the reasons it won't work. I bet they're paper tigers."

"Well, there's your family—"

Zeke laughed. "Oh, they've known for months I was going to marry you, if you'd have me."

Her eyes widened. "They did? Did you ask them if it was all right?"

"No, idiot, I'm thirty-three, I don't need anyone's permission to get married. I told them almost as soon as I met you that I was in love with you, and after they met you, they were in love with you, too. They've been urging me to marry you, but I didn't want to ask you until I was pretty sure you'd say yes—don't tell me I'm wrong! My parents are wild about you, and thrilled their only son is finally ready to settle down. They have visions of grandbabies dancing in their heads."

She shook her head. "But you're white and I'm not. They can't like that."

"No, you're not white—you're an absolutely gorgeous shade of golden brown. My parents are leftover hippies, card-carrying liberals. They've marched for every cause, they've done their best to try to make things right wherever they've seen injustice, and they practice what they preach. They're thrilled at the prospect of a nonwhite daughter-in-law, especially if that potential daughter-in-law is wonderful in every way and named Bethany Byrd."

"You're Jewish, and my family has this unusual religion—"

"My family isn't religious, and they think your religion sounds interesting. They'd like to know more about it. Is it really based on some kind of voodoo, like Coleman says?"

Bethany laughed. "No, Coleman's teasin' when she says that. She loves my church; she tried to join it when she was five, and she's always been a tiny bit huffy she wasn't welcomed with open arms. They *would* have welcomed her if she'd been bigger and older—we admit members by Baptism—submersion—and she was way too little. We believe in old-time religion. Did you ever see Judith Jamison dancin' *Revelations* with the Alvin Ailey ballet? It's like that: music, clappin', lovin', weepin', dancin', swayin'. We eat a lot of meals together—picnics and potluck dinners at the church. We believe in faith, family, and miracles. If we got married, you wouldn't have to embrace our religion, just respect it. But you would have to change your name—you know that. You'd become a Byrd? Your family won't care?"

Bethany had described this family custom when they first met as a matter of interest, not with any thought that it would ever arise between them. The Byrds were matriarchal, and they believed that having the same family name bound them closer together. The custom originated in Africa, but it became a rule in the time of slavery, when slaves were named after their owners. Her female ancestors hadn't liked the takeover of their identities, and they'd adopted a secret name.

The name was originally an African word that meant Bird; it was a code name, as in "free as a bird." After the Civil War, their name was no longer secret, and they changed it to the more usual way of spelling a surname. To her family "Byrd" still meant freedom, and paradoxically, tied them closer together in a loving and loyal clan.

He grinned. "Mom and Dad don't care about that, either, and I'd be proud to be a Byrd. I've always wanted to be part of a big family, like the Waltons. I've watched a lot of reruns of that show."

"And you're rich, and I'm poor," she said, still tearful.

"My family isn't big rich like the Hathaways or Heyward Bain. We're comfortable, and we live well. But being rich isn't important to us, and the family has given away a lot of money to education and other causes. You and I and our children won't inherit a great fortune, but you don't care, do you? We'll both keep working, won't we?"

She stared at him. She almost believed that this could happen. "I'd never stop workin'—don't know how. That part's fine. But we'd have to go to North Carolina to ask Aunt Mary Louise's permission. And she'll want me to get married in our church in Slocumb Corners."

"I'd expected to ask somebody for your hand, I don't care where we get married, and I've been angling for an invitation to North Carolina to meet your family ever since we first went out in November. Anything else? If you'll just say yes, I can put this ring on your finger, we can eat the duck that's waiting in the oven, and then you can show me how you get out of that dress."

"Oh, yes—dear, dear Zeke." She held out her hand, and he slipped the ring on her finger.

❧

Later, she told him Dinah had confided that after the financial crisis was over, she planned to reduce the amount of time she spent at the gallery, and Bethany might be running the gallery a lot sooner than she'd anticipated.

Zeke looked surprised. "What's she going to do?" he asked.

"More research, more writing, look for a Midtown apartment. Jonathan's movin' his office to Midtown, and they both want to be able to walk to work," Bethany said.

"Do you think this mess at DDD&W has put her off corporate work completely?" Zeke asked.

"Absolutely. She says if we're ever offered another corporate art contract, she wants me to handle it, or we'll hire somebody. She hates DDD&W, and it got worse today. She's been thrown out of the place. Loretta and I are takin' over the print-hanging project."

Just as she'd expected, she could tell from his expression that he didn't like it a bit. He thought it was dangerous, but he'd never tell her not to do it. Zeke wasn't like that—if he'd been domineering and overprotective like Jonathan, she'd never have gone out with him more than once or twice, never mind living with him. She looked at her ring again and thought she was going to burst she was so happy.

Twenty-Nine

By late Sunday morning, Jonathan was exhausted, but he'd completed everything on his list: Bethany and Loretta had Greene Gallery identification cards and keys to the art storage room and the office assigned to Dinah at DDD&W. They'd start hanging prints Monday morning.

By special arrangement with the art movers, and after sending a couple of guys Rob hired to wait at DDD&W for their arrival, the prints Dinah had bought for the corridor walls had been delivered to DDD&W and were locked in the storage room. Two of the hangers who'd worked with Dinah in the reception and dining rooms would meet Loretta and Bethany at DDD&W at nine a.m. Monday.

A messenger had arrived with everything Jonathan had requested from Greg Fry, and another messenger had brought him Dinah's check from DDD&W's attorneys, along with the signed agreement covering all issues with DDD&W, including what DDD&W could say to the press and to their own staff about Dinah and the Greene Gallery. Jonathan had done all he could on his own and by asking favors from miscellaneous friends. He needed the big guns now.

He picked up the phone and punched in the number of Blair Winthrop, who'd been a boarding school classmate, his roommate at Yale, his closest friend at Harvard Business School, and best man at his and Dinah's wedding. Blair had stayed on at Harvard for a law degree and was now a rising star at the firm of Winthrop, Winthrop & Cabot, the lawyers who managed the Hathaway family's financial affairs. One of the most powerful law firms in the United States, where Jonathan would have worked if he'd decided to become a lawyer instead of an investment banker—Winthrop, Winthrop & Cabot was known by nearly everyone as "the Firm."

"Blair? You're not going to believe this, but Dinah's suspected of murder."

"Impossible," Blair said. "How could anyone think such a thing? Dinah's an angel."

"She *is* an angel, but she's being pushed into the frame by those bastards at DDD&W—you know them, or of them, I'm sure. She doesn't have an alibi for a murder that took place in their office, where she's been installing art, and the police don't have any other suspects, so they're after her."

"How can I help?" Blair asked.

"You can do a lot. The New York County District Attorney's office is investigating people at DDD&W for art tax evasion, and we need them to speed up their investigation. Several lawyers at the Firm know the DA, don't they? The SEC is sniffing around DDD&W, too—I don't know exactly what they're after, but they need to get moving. Both agencies may turn up other suspects for the murder, but it might be too late to help save Dinah's reputation," Jonathan said.

"I'll take care of them. What else?" Blair asked.

"Can you find out who's in charge of James Davidson's estate? He died in the 1990s. He had two daughters, who should have inherited everything. Apparently they didn't. I don't know why they didn't, and no one seems to know what became of them. Are they alive? If so, where are they? Davidson expected them to work at DDD&W, and if DDD&W refused them jobs, they should have come into a big art collection. We need to find them, talk to them. And do you know anyone at the Prince Charles Stuart Museum in Stuartville, New York? A trustee, maybe? The chairman of the board? The museum inherits Davidson money, too, and may have been cheated by the DDD&W crowd."

"I'll ask about the Davidson estate, and I'll find someone who knows that museum. I'll call you tomorrow. Don't worry. Give Dinah my love, and tell her she's not to worry, either."

❧

When Jonathan came into the living room, Dinah thought he looked less strained.

"I just talked to Blair. He and the Firm are going to help get things moving," he said.

"Oh, Jonathan, that's great. He's a good friend," she said.

"That he is, and he sent you his love, and said 'don't worry,'" Jonathan said.

"Good advice. I wish I *could* stop worrying. I need to tell you something, Jonathan. Promise me you won't get upset."

She described Oscar Danbury's behavior, how horrifying she'd found it, and why she hadn't told Jonathan. Then she held her breath, waiting for the explosion.

Jonathan frowned, but it was a thoughtful expression, not a signal that he was on the verge of a tantrum. "I've heard of someone else who did that—it was at a financial company—Steinbrew was his name. The people who worked with him thought he was wonderful, too. I could never understand it. In my opinion, he was disgusting."

"Could Oscar Danbury have known Steinbrew?"

He shook his head. "I doubt it—Steinbrew died a long time ago. But Danbury must have heard about it and imitated him. They don't teach that little trick in business school. I'm sorry you had to see it. Try and put it out of your mind, love. Danbury's just a filthy slob—one more bottom-of-the-barrel type in a rotten organization."

Dinah sighed. She should have known. Jonathan would never say a cross word to her when she was in trouble. She reached out and took his hand in hers. "Thank you," she said.

Jonathan, looking bewildered but ever polite, said, "You're welcome," and leaned over to kiss her.

"I wish we could take a day off from everything to do with DDD&W," Dinah said.

"Why don't I ask Tom to bring us the car and we'll drive north? We can take Baker and have lunch on the coast somewhere. The sun is out for a change. It's pale and uncertain, and it may rain again later, but for the moment, it's reasonably clear outside."

"Could we? That would be wonderful," Dinah said.

"Absolutely. We'll have to bundle up. It will be cold, but it will be a change, and I think it will do us good."

Forty-five minutes later, they were in the Lincoln, Jonathan at the wheel, Baker asleep on the back seat. She turned on the car radio and found a channel that played Golden Oldies music. She laughed out loud when she heard a male vocalist singing "Blue Skies."

Thirty

Loretta didn't like living alone. She'd had room-mates in college, and after graduation, she shared an apartment with two girls in Raleigh. She was bored and lonely in Bethany's one-room apartment. She'd been lucky to get it, with Bethany always at Zeke's, but the decorations, although attractive, made her homesick. The red-and-white quilt on the narrow bed had been pieced and sewn by Bethany's grandmother, who was also related to Loretta. The dried grasses in the big bowl on the table came from a North Carolina beach, and the room smelled of potpourri made from North Carolina roses. The cupboard in the kitchen was full of jam and jelly made by friends and neighbors of Bethany's family. Bethany's tiny nest was a constant reminder of home. She needed to get out for a while and get over feeling so bad. Today, like all the Sundays she'd spent in New York, were the worst days of the week. At home, Sundays after church were filled with family, friends, food. Here she had nothing to do.

The only good thing about the apartment was its location. She loved walking around Greenwich Village taking pictures. She sent most of them home to her parents, who were interested in everything she saw and did.

She pulled on an old duffle coat and tucked her camera in her pocket. She'd buy coffee, milk, and other necessities at the Food Emporium and pick up something comforting for supper. Maybe she'd go by the Chinese restaurant and get some wonton soup. She'd take a few pictures if she saw anyone or anything especially interesting. She ran down the stairs, but when she stepped out the door of the building onto the sidewalk, a toddler in a pink snowsuit careered into her and fell flat on her well-padded bottom.

Loretta leaned over and picked up the screaming child. She was a beautiful little girl with curly red hair and fair skin, although at the moment, her dimpled cheeks were nearly as red as her curls. Loretta didn't think she'd been hurt; her yells sounded angry, not as if she were in pain.

A man pushing a baby carriage reached out to take the little girl. "Here, let me," he said, cuddling the child, who stopped crying as soon as she felt his arms around her.

Loretta looked at the infant in the carriage. More red curls. What gorgeous children. The man was nice-looking in a Waspy way but a little old to be the father of these two. Grandfather? Uncle? They sure didn't look like him. He must have been blond once, but his thinning hair had turned gray. "Beautiful red hair," she said. "Do they take after their mama?"

The man grinned. "In more ways than one," he said. "I have a hard time keeping up with the three of them, and Mac—he's in the carriage—can't even walk yet. Kathy, my wife, is just like Kitty—always running, never walking, and doesn't always look where she's going. I hope Kitty didn't hurt you when she ran into you?"

"Goodness, no. I'm just glad *she* wasn't hurt. They're both adorable. Nice talking to you." She waved goodbye to the now-beaming Kitty and ran toward the Food Emporium, pausing to look back and take a picture of the gorgeous children and their doting father. They looked so happy together. Her parents would enjoy seeing their pictures, especially with the building where she was living in the background.

∽

Before leaving for the office, where she spent most Sundays, Coleman skimmed the newspapers. Still nothing about Dinah or any more about the death at DDD&W. That was good news, almost a miracle. She pulled on a red cashmere turtleneck, gray slacks, and boots. The rain had stopped, but the air was raw and chilly. She wrapped her ancient raccoon coat around her, grabbed Dolly, and set off at a brisk pace for her office.

She settled down at her desk and pulled out her to-do list. First, Dinah's problem: she'd done everything she'd pledged to do on the art side, except learn anything about the location of the Stubbs. Dinah was working on that.

As for the press, Debbi was doing an excellent job. Jonathan was working hard on other issues and getting good results. Rob seemed to be a little slow, but maybe he was having startup problems. Anyway, there was nothing she could do about that. Goodness knows, she had more than enough to do without worrying about Rob's work habits. She settled down at her desk and was soon absorbed in the demands of *ArtSmart* and *First Home*.

༂

Rob spent most of Sunday trying not to think about Coleman, reading the reports that had come in, and listing the information he had and what he still needed.

Pete had left Rob a summary on the Victor sisters. Born in a small town in southern Georgia. Struggled to finish high school. Made their way to Atlanta, then Chicago. Typists, then secretaries. Frances married and divorced in Chicago. Both of them worked for D&W in Chicago at the time of the merger—Patti Sue as a secretary for one of the accountants, and Frances as an assistant in the personnel department. When D&D merged with D&W, a lot of D&W people, including the sisters, transferred to New York. The Victor women landed at LaGuardia with higher-status jobs and better salaries. They weren't paid as much as the employees they had replaced, but those people had been well qualified, which the sisters definitely were not. Given their backgrounds, they were overpaid. They must have had pull. Or something on someone?

The sisters shared a Park Avenue condominium, which had to have cost at least a couple of million dollars. According to Pete, the maintenance was far more than they could afford on their salaries, even sharing. Each of them had five-figure bank accounts, too, and no debts. Where had the capital come from to buy the apartment? And how did they support their lifestyle? Money other than their salaries was coming from somewhere.

He'd assigned the guys who'd completed the Cornelia Street interviews to chat up the Victor sisters' neighbors, their doormen, the super of their building, trolling for information on friends, money, love life—whatever came up. He'd asked Pete to check out Hunt Frederick—finances, Texas reputation, the works.

He would also ask Pete to find out all he could about Harrison, but if the detective had gone bad, Pete wouldn't turn up much. Cops were good at hiding their skeletons in more secure places than their closets. The only way to get the facts would be calls to friends, and Rob would have to do that himself. He put it at the top of Monday's to-do list, along with making sure one of the investigators checked out the fight in the ladies' room.

He sighed. He had a long list of loose ends and not much time to tie them up. The story of Dinah's involvement in the murder was bound to break soon.

Fortunately, they didn't have to check out Great Art Management. The memo from the DA's office had explained exactly how GAM worked. They sold paintings to the not very knowledgeable who wanted something decorative or trendy or both to hang on their walls—definitely not in the Monet or Renoir class, but expensive enough to make avoiding taxes worthwhile. Great Art Management shipped the paintings to addresses outside New York—maybe even provided the buyer with the addresses.

But who at DDD&W was buying art? What, if anything, did Patti Sue Victor have to do with the racket? And did it lead to someone trying to kill her? If so, why?

Thirty-One

Coleman's week began well. When she read Monday's newspapers, she yelled "Yes!" startling poor Dolly; Debbi had struck again. From the *New York Examiner*'s "What's Happening" column:

> Is a blue-chip consulting firm at the center of the next art scandal? The will of James Davidson, who died in 1993, left a huge art collection to the firm he helped found—now Davidson, Douglas, Danbury & Weeks—as long as the firm employed a Davidson descendant. If a descendant no longer worked there, the entire collection was to go to the Prince Charles Stuart Museum in Stuartville, NY. There are no Davidsons at DDD&W today, and in December, the Prince Charles received 414 objects from the Davidson collection. Trouble is, James Davidson's will listed 1,049 works of art. What happened to the

missing items? Will "Bonnie Prince Charlie" rise again and force DDD&W to produce the missing art—or compensation to the Prince Charles Stuart Museum for what's missing?

The *Mirror*'s "Round the Town" column:

The word around town is that a renowned management consulting-accounting firm can't manage its own business, which should give its *Fortune 500* clients pause. Believe it or not, the firm—or two firms—let's call them "Upstairs" and "Downstairs"—which "merged" a few years ago, work on separate floors, and the twain rarely meet. Maybe that's why it's rumored that the SEC is investigating: are those Downstairs folks auditors or consultants? If auditors, isn't this the same kind of conflict the SEC found at Arthur Andersen? If the Downstairs crowd are consultants like their Upstairs partners, why aren't they working together?

And an e-mail from Amy:

I apologize for Hunt. He received a copy of our contract with you as soon as it was signed. The signing partners have let him know what they think of his inattention to DDD&W business and his rudeness to a client. He should apologize to you, but they say he never apologizes, never explains. Great attitude for the CEO of a service company, right?

Coleman laughed. She could hardly wait for her afternoon meeting at DDD&W. Would she run into the Cowardly Cowboy? She guessed not. He'd be lying low.

~

Hunt had just arrived in his office and hadn't had time to remove his overcoat, when Ted Douglas brought the column items into his office.

"We're being killed by the press," Ted said. "What are we going to do?"

Hunt read the clippings, his spirits sinking. "Is anything here inaccurate? Is there anything we can deny?" he asked.

"You know where the Stubbs are—you can respond to that one. I don't know anything about the Americana collection. There's nothing we can say about the split here—it's all too horribly true," Ted said.

"All right. Draft a memo to the staff for my signature explaining that the paintings are out for cleaning, and they'll be back Friday. Get whoever oversaw the packing of the stuff we sent to the Prince Charles to look at these lists—was it Patti Sue? See what she has to say, and get me a report on it. Maybe the missing stuff was stolen at the museum or by the movers," Hunt said.

"I hope you're right. Have you heard anything about an SEC investigation?" Ted asked.

"No, and I doubt if it's true. Even if it is, I don't think we have anything to worry about. None of those bean counters do audits, do they? They were supposed to stop after the merger. I *hope* they're helping Moose get business."

Ted shrugged. "I don't have any idea what they do. You'll have to ask Moose."

Hunt nodded. "I will. What's new on the murder? Have the police made any progress? Are they still convinced Dinah Greene is the killer?"

"Here's their case: the Greene Gallery is in financial trouble. Hathaway wants Dinah to let it go and become a full-time wife and mommy, so he's balking at continuing to prop it up. She needs our money desperately. She's not as ambitious as Cutthroat Coleman, but she wants the gallery to stand on its own feet before she steps aside as a career woman. Patti Sue, jealous and worried about her job, had been determined to get rid of Dinah and was agitated, complaining about her all over the office," Ted said.

"That's okay as far as it goes—she has a motive—but how did she accomplish the murder, if she did?" Hunt asked.

"Here's a possible scenario: suppose Dinah arranged to meet Patti Sue in this office—which I must say looks great, Hunt, the restorers did a good job and fast. Anyway, maybe Dinah told Patti Sue she'd share the job with her. Patti Sue is a dope and would have easily swallowed the bait, but instead of working with her, Dinah planned to get rid of her. For some reason, Frannie turned up instead. Anyway, Frannie supported Patti Sue's efforts, so maybe Frannie was the target," Ted said.

Hunt frowned. "How could a girl like Dinah Greene do whatever it took to make the cases fall? She looks too fragile to pick up a frying pan, never mind sabotage the office."

"That's the beauty part: Dinah Greene hangs art all the time, can handle tools with the best of them, and she has no alibi."

"Why haven't they arrested her?" Hunt asked.

"They need a little more." Ted counted his points off on three fingers: "What did she use to pull down the shelves? How did she get in your office? How did she get back and forth from their house in the Village to this building? I'm told that if they get the right answer to just one of those questions, they'll arrest her."

Hunt shook his head. "I still find it hard to believe. She doesn't seem like a killer."

Ted shrugged. "People have been convicted on far less. Even pretty people. Don't you watch *CSI*? Anyway, there's no one else. It has to be Dinah."

Thirty-Two

On Monday morning, when Loretta unlocked the door to the little office at DDD&W, she nearly stepped on an envelope lying on the floor. She leaned over and picked it up. Bethany, close behind her, whispered, "I bet it's another anonymous letter. Is Dinah's name on it?" She closed the door to the corridor.

"Yep, *Dinah Greene, c/o her friends.* It must be from somebody who knows Dinah's been banished from here," Loretta said.

"That could be anybody who came in last night or early this mornin'. Look what I grabbed from a desk we passed." Bethany handed Loretta an interoffice memo from Hunt Austin Frederick to all employees, dated and time-stamped the previous evening. Dinah Greene would continue to be in charge of the new art installation, but she would manage the project from her office at the Greene Gallery. Members of Ms. Greene's staff would complete the hanging of the prints. The Greene Gallery staffers working at DDD&W weren't named, and Dinah's absence wasn't explained.

Loretta and Bethany exchanged glances. "I bet Jonathan's lawyers warned those slugs that if there was a single negative word about Dinah or her business in this memo, he'd devote the family fortune and the rest of his life to ruinin' them. A lawyer wrote this," Bethany said.

Loretta nodded. "Yeah. But I reckon not naming us was Massa Frederick's idea. Dissing us, wouldn't you say? And he may not even know yet we's colored folks."

"Poor fool," Bethany said. "What's in the envelope?"

"A note telling us to look in all the drawers and cupboards in this office and in the store room ASAP, and make sure they're empty. It's typed, but there's a PS in tiny handwriting: *Look for the horses.* That doesn't make sense. No room for horses in here, not even room for mice. Could it be in code? It's signed *A Friend.*"

Bethany looked around the tiny room. "About the first part there's no problem: there's not much to search. The 'Friend' couldn't be talkin' about the horses in the Stubbs photocopies—they're at the gallery. Could there be other copies in here somewhere?"

"I'll check," Loretta said. "Look, all these desk drawers are empty, just a few supplies. I'll take pictures of the empty spaces. If some of the people here are as rotten as they sound, and if the cops on the case are crooked, they might try to plant something. The bookcase has nothing in it. Ditto the top file-cabinet drawer. Oh, look, there's a tool kit in the bottom drawer."

"That's Dinah's. She used it to hang the prints in this office. She must have forgotten it. Remind me when we leave, and I'll take it to her. We'll check the storage room later to see if anything's in there, but right now we should get down to business. I'll lock the door while we fix up the office," Bethany said.

They'd taped wires under their sweaters early that morning at the gallery, and one of Rob's men had hooked up the recorders in the suite provided by Greg Fry. On their way in, they'd installed listening devices in the storage room and in the restroom on thirty-two. All they had to do was put a listening device behind one of the flower prints Dinah had hung, and one in the telephone. They'd barely finished when someone banged on the door.

"Open up that door! We know y'all are in there!"

"I recognize Dinah's description of that dulcet voice," Bethany said. "It's the infamous Patti Sue." She folded the note they'd found, pocketed it, and unlocked the door.

Patti Sue, beet-faced, stormed in on a tidal wave of Jungle Gardenia. Detective Harrison, reeking of tobacco, loomed behind her, and further back, nearly hidden by Harrison's bulk, lurked a scrawny bald man in a short-sleeved white dress shirt. A big-haired brunette clasping a clipboard against her enormous breasts stood nearby. Detective Quintero, who appeared to be half-asleep, sat on an unoccupied desk across the corridor.

"What are y'all doin'!" Patti Sue yelled. "Why are y'all in here?"

Zeke had told Bethany when he'd dropped her off outside the Fry Building that morning that she looked like a princess in her bronze wool suit and the gigantic topaz earrings he'd given her for Christmas. Keeping his words in mind, and feeling his ring hanging on a chain under her blouse (she'd explained that she couldn't wear it openly until they'd received her Aunt Mary Louise's permission to marry), Bethany held her head high and tried to think like royalty. She proffered her Greene Gallery identification and a pass card signed by Hunt Frederick. Loretta took hers out of her bag and held it out, too, but Patti Sue ignored both of them, and kept yelling.

"Get outta here! You got no business in here!"

Bethany put her hands—one of them still clutching her ID—over her ears. "Please lower your voice. You're hurtin' my ears. Hunt Austin Frederick authorized us to continue the installation of the prints. We intend to do so. The hangers will arrive at eight."

Patti Sue and Harrison opened their mouths like a pair of goldfish, but before either could speak, the bald man pushed them aside and stepped into the room. "I'm Mark Leichter, office manager at DDD&W. I don't think we've met?"

"Bethany Byrd and Loretta Byrd from the Greene Gallery."

He raised his sparse eyebrows above rimless spectacles. "May I see your identification, please?"

Leichter examined their passes and smiled, his thin lips revealing pointed little teeth. "As you can see, your presence here is a surprise. Please be good enough to leave the premises while we verify these documents with Mr. Frederick and the lawyers."

Bethany shook her head. "Not unless you hand us a check for one hundred and eighty thousand dollars. If you force us to leave, you have to pay in full for the art project. I have a copy of the contract with me, and the appropriate page is marked. But if you're the office manager, I'm sure you know all about it?"

"I know the terms of the contract, but these are special circumstances, and asking you to leave while I check the validity of your papers with Mr. Frederick and the lawyers is a reasonable request," Leichter insisted.

Loretta handed him the memo Bethany had picked up. "We don't think so. I don't understand why you're surprised to see us. Here's Mr. Frederick's memo informing staff that Greene Gallery employees will continue to hang the prints. Surely this memo and our passes—signed by both Mr. Frederick and one of your lawyers—are sufficient 'validity'? Here are our business cards. Here's a copy of the Greene Gallery invoice for the earlier work, marked paid in full. Here's another for the balance of a hundred and eighty thousand dollars. Pay up and we're out of here. Otherwise, read my lips: we're hanging prints."

Leichter gritted his tiny teeth, glanced at the papers, and returned them. "Everything appears to be in order," he said. He marched away, his neck and back military stiff. The woman with the black beehive stuck her head into the office. "You should leave. No one wants you here," she screeched, and raced off to catch up with Leichter. She left a discount drugstore aroma in her wake—Listerine, cheap perfume, disinfectant.

Bethany turned to Patti Sue and Harrison. "Now, what can we do for you two?"

Harrison, his face nearly as red as Patti Sue's, flared his hairy nostrils. "I have a warrant to search this office," he said.

"May I see it, please?" Bethany scanned the paper he handed her. "Okay, get on with it. We have work to do."

He leered at her. "You'll have to leave, Mama, you and the other sister. You mighty fine women, but you in the way."

Bethany smiled. "One, I'm not leaving and neither is my colleague. Two, call me anything ever again but Ms. Byrd, and I'll have your—uh—large rear end in court so fast, your tiny brain may not catch up with it."

Loretta laughed. "'Mama!' My goodness, Detective, I think you should consider a little sensitivity training—you'll be saying 'Mammy' next, or 'Aunt Jemima.' You might want to do a calendar check, too. We're in the twenty-first century here."

Harrison flushed even redder and began opening the drawers and cupboards they'd just searched, slamming them closed when he'd looked inside. Then he spotted Dinah's tool kit lying on the desk and opened it, revealing her hammer, screwdriver, and the other tools she used for hanging prints. "Hey!

What's this? Just what I was looking for! It's even got Ms. Greene's initials on the lid of the kit. Now we know how she fixed the shelves to fall," he gloated.

Bethany and Loretta avoided each other's eyes. Hell's bells, Bethany thought, if only we'd come in over the weekend to clear out this room, or even an hour earlier. No way did Dinah kill that woman, but Harrison's discovery of the tool kit, and his take on it—well, it was definitely a situation. Why hadn't she thought of this when she'd seen the tool kit in the drawer? No point in grieving. Even if she had seen it, there was nowhere to hide it, and there hadn't been time to remove it before the arrival of the enemy.

Harrison searched the rest of the room, peering into every cranny. Was he looking for a place to plant something?

"You won't find anything else in here. We searched everywhere and photographed inside all the drawers and cupboards. The photos have the date and time on them. If somethin' new should turn up, we can prove it wasn't here earlier," Bethany said.

Harrison looked at her as if he'd like to hit her. Maybe he'd have tried, if Loretta wasn't watching. Bethany almost wished he *would* attack. She'd excelled in self-defense classes, and she knew every sensitive spot on the male body. She'd have loved kickin' the man in the googlies, maybe bashin' him in the ying-yang while she was at it. She bet his brain wasn't his only tiny organ. Her self-defense teacher had told her that even the smallest male body part could feel huge pain. *Ooh-eee*. What a temptation.

Harrison shoved Loretta out of his way and, with Dinah's toolbox in his hand, strode out of the office.

"If you're takin' that tool kit, I'll need a receipt," Bethany called after him. "In case you weren't plannin' to give me one, my colleague took a photo of you walkin' off with it in your hands."

He stopped, his back toward them, and scribbled on a scrap of paper he tore from his notebook. He passed it over his shoulder without looking back. Loretta, who had followed him into the corridor, took the paper and passed it to Bethany.

"Thank you," Bethany called after him, her voice syrupy. Harrison and Quintero disappeared down the corridor without a backward glance.

Patti Sue, who hadn't moved or uttered a sound while Harrison was searching the room, stared at them. "Are y'all Negroes?" she asked.

Bethany raised her eyebrows. "You could say so, although most people wouldn't," she said.

Patti Sue guffawed. "If y'all are Negroes, what'cha'll doin' in here? Why don't y'all go pick some cotton?"

"She'll sound good on tape," Loretta murmured.

Bethany nodded. She knew all there was to know about Patti Sue after seeing her and hearing her talk: white trash. Dinah had been too mannerly to say so, but that's what Patti Sue was. Vulgar, stupid, bigoted, and pig ignorant. Bethany had mostly been spared meeting the Patti Sues of the world, but she'd seen them on TV and in films.

"Neither of us has had to pick much cotton since we graduated from college," Bethany said. "Educated people don't need that kind of work these days. Those folks you see out in the fields are redneck crackers who barely made it through fifth grade." She turned to Loretta. "Didn't Dinah say she heard someone called a redneck cracker in the ladies' room the other day? I wonder who that might have been?"

Patti Sue, shrieking a mixture of obscenities and racial epithets, charged toward Bethany, who was standing behind the desk at the back of the room. Loretta, nearer the door and in Patti Sue's path, moved her foot slightly. Patti Sue tripped, crashing to the floor and hitting her head on the edge of the metal desk. Loretta smiled and said, "So sorry! It's hard to get out of the way in this tiny office."

Blood poured from a cut under Patti Sue's straw-like hair. She struggled to get to her knees but was handicapped by her tight pink leather skirt. Just as she pulled it up to her waist—exposing a purple thong with 'Monday' scrawled across the crotch—an enormous man in red suspenders appeared in the door, trumpeting like an enraged elephant.

"What the fuckin' hell is going on in here? Sounds like a goddamn riot. Patti Sue, what the hell are you doin' down there on the floor exposin' yourself? You ain't a pretty sight. Or sound. Shut up! Some of us are tryin' to get some fuckin' work done! I got four chocolate bars and six tea bags waitin' in a conference room, all dyin' to fork over some gold if they get a chance to hear me speak."

When Red Suspenders spotted Bethany and Loretta, his shiny full moon face lit up. "Hi-dee!

'Scuse me and my language. I din't know ladies were present. What are you Tootsie Rolls doin' here?"

"'Tootsie Rolls,'" Loretta repeated. "Excuse me, sir. Is that an allusion to our color?"

Red Suspenders howled, his big belly shaking. "No, Babycakes, I'd say that color-wise you're more like a Caramel Chew. I call all the girls Tootsie Rolls, like I call the Swiss chocolate bars, and that sure ain't an allusion to their color. They're white as snow, which ain't surprisin', seein' how as they live ass-deep in it. Who are you, anyway? You sure as hell dress up the place. For God's sake, Patti Sue, stop that caterwaulin' and go wash your face—you're bleedin' all over the effin' rug."

Patti Sue managed to stand up, pulled down her skirt, and fled, bawling like an abandoned calf.

Bethany contemplated their latest visitor. Coleman had described Harrison as a caricature cop; wait till she met this cartoon investment banker. "We're from the Greene Gallery, here to oversee the art installation. I'm Bethany Byrd, and this is Loretta Byrd."

"Greene Gallery? Bird gallery, I'd say—tropical birds. Parakeets? Love Birds? Lordy, Lordy, what a treat for these sore ole eyes. Say, Patti Sue dint attack you, did she? Her and one of the other dames here have fist-fights when they think nobody's lookin', mostly in the girls' privy. Y'all better watch out for her. Well, Love Birds, I gotta get back to work. My name's Michael Shanahan. Folks call me Moose. If you purty things need help, speak out. I'm a partner—I got pull here. Toodle-loo."

Loretta watched him lumber out and turned back to Bethany. "I took some terrific pictures of Harrison, Quintero, Patti Sue, that Leichter guy and his creepy girlfriend, and the Moose. The tapes will make great listening. If 'chocolate bars' are Swiss, 'tea bags' must be Brits. Do you think that makes him a 'hot dawg'?"

"I better call Rob and tell him about Harrison findin' Dinah's tool kit—he'll want to know right away. Another thing: I think Hairspray Woman is the other Amazon in the ladies' room. Did you hear her voice? Dinah said Patti Sue's rival's voice was shrill and piercin'. That hag's voice could break the sound barrier. She must be Leichter's assistant. Isn't there a staff directory in here somewhere?"

"In the top file drawer," Loretta said, taking it out and handing it to Bethany.

"Okay, got it. Her name is Naomi Skinner. I'll tell Rob about the tool kit, and what we suspect about Hairspray. Maybe he can confirm it."

Bethany made the call, while Loretta waited. When she'd finished speaking to Rob, Bethany said, "Let's hang prints. I agree with Dinah—this is a horrible place. The sooner we're done, the better."

Three hangers were waiting for them outside the print storage room. Two Dinah had hired; the third was Zeke, wearing jeans, a blue work shirt, and a big grin.

Bethany smiled. "I thought you'd turn up," she said.

She turned to her mail, including the latest missive from her secret informant, messengered over by Bethany. *Look for the horses.* Surely a reference to the Stubbs paintings? She pondered the note, frowning. If she needed to sell two stolen paintings by Stubbs, how would she do it? She'd have to think about that, but for now, she *must* speak to Ellie. She dialed DDD&W and asked for Ellie McPhee.

"There's no one here by that name," the operator said. Dinah hung up. They must have fired her. But wouldn't the operator have said "I'm sorry, she's no longer with us"? There was no point in calling Human Resources. With the department's manager dead, it would be in chaos. She'd have to turn the problem over to Rob. She couldn't shield Ellie any longer.

༄

After hearing the party line about Harrison—"good cop, nice guy"—from half a dozen acquaintances in the department, Rob knew he'd encountered the hard blue wall. He was wasting his time calling anyone on the job. He'd try an old friend who'd retired so recently he was probably still in the loop but might not have qualms passing on gossip about Harrison. Unless Harrison was a buddy? Unlikely. Nick looked like Santa Claus and had a similar personality; that was why his friends called him Nick. He would have nothing in common with Harrison. He was in luck. Nick answered on the first ring.

Thirty-Three

D inah was at her desk in the gallery by eight
Monday morning. She was determined to
complete the acquisition of the prints she
needed for the corridors at DDD&W. She'd call
every US dealer who might have the type of prints
she was looking for. Each print must be reasonably
priced, and be in stock, ready to ship. Thank goodness none of them needed special framing. She'd giv-
en the framing contract for all six hundred of the
corridor prints, in inexpensive wood painted black,
to a framer in Staten Island. In return for the big
order, she'd received a discount and a promise to
work around the clock to get the job done fast. Speed
was even more important now than when she'd made
the deal.

By one o'clock, she'd located the last of the
required prints. She breathed a sigh of relief. Every
purchase brought her closer to the end of her association with the loathsome crowd at DDD&W.

"Rob, hi, guy! Great to hear from you. How're things?" he said, sounding genuinely glad to hear from him.

"Fine, but busy," Rob said. "If you ever want part-time work, I can always use your help, Nick."

"Maybe I'll get bored after a few months of doing nothing, but it ain't happened yet. If you need me, though, I always have time for a friend."

"I'm not desperate, but thanks for offering. Say, what can you tell me about a guy named Ed Harrison? He's partnered with Joe Quintero. I've run into the two of them on a case."

"Yeah, I heard about that. Harrison isn't as bad as some—'course that's not saying much—but he shouldn't be on your case. I nearly called you about it. It's caused a lot of talk."

Rob frowned. "How's that?"

"Harrison moonlights for DDD&W. Security work. The guards at the DDD&W building—the Fry Building—are paid to call him on his cell phone about any problems at DDD&W. They phoned him when that woman was killed—that's how he got involved—he shoved his way in and grabbed the case. If anybody'd cared, maybe they'd have fought for it, but everybody knows it's nothin' but trouble, so he was welcome to it."

Rob could hardly believe what he was hearing. "You're right—he shouldn't be on the DDD&W murder case. Do you know who at DDD&W hired him?" Rob asked.

"A guy named Danbury—I remember it on account of my niece lives in Danbury, Connecticut.

I heard Harrison makes a bundle outta those DDD&W people. He needs the money bad—he's got a wife and kids, and he's also got a girlfriend. People say his sweetie works at DDD&W, and she doesn't come cheap."

"Oh, my God, worse and worse. Do the brass know about this?"

"Doubt it, but everybody else does, including Quintero. I'm amazed Harrison has got away with it as long as he has. Sorry for not calling to tell you about it."

"That's okay. You've told me now. Thanks, Nick. I owe you."

Rob put his elbows on the desk, his head in his hands. He had to report Harrison. And Quintero, who, at best, was guilty of helping Harrison cover up his tie to DDD&W. But unless it was handled exactly right, the disclosure could make Dinah's situation worse. The department didn't take kindly to being told one of their own was crooked, and they'd be furious if the story got leaked to the press. This was politics, and not his kind of thing. Jonathan was the client. Let him decide what to do. He picked up the phone, called Jonathan, and told him everything he'd learned.

"That certainly explains Harrison's hostility toward Dinah, and his determination to pin the murder on her," Jonathan said. "He's a henchman for DDD&W, paid to take care of damage control, even if it means hurting an innocent person. I don't think you should be the messenger on this, Rob. I'll call Sebastian Grant and get him on the case. I'll tell him about the fight in the ladies' room, too. He should know that somebody was quarrelling with Patti Sue over a partner who's apparently seeing both of them."

"Good plan," Rob said, with an inward sigh of relief. The brass wouldn't shoot the messenger, but they wouldn't like him much either, and Rob needed to stay on their good side. They were often his clients, and even more often, an important information source. Sebastian Grant was the perfect choice to pass the word. At One Police Plaza, they already detested the Cobra, who was indifferent to their opinions.

Thirty-Four

Jonathan had been so busy Monday morning, he'd forgotten to eat the lunch he'd ordered hours earlier. He was struggling to choke down a dried-out roast beef sandwich with room-temperature milk when Blair Winthrop phoned. Winthrop had spoken to William Tolliver, the SEC chairman, who would see that the SEC made their investigation of DDD&W a top priority. Tolliver had said that DDD&W was on their list, but the company was small and an oddity, so they'd put it off while they dealt with larger and more typical organizations.

"Why is it odd?" Jonathan asked. "I mean, other than the obvious? Like the split in the company, which the SEC probably doesn't even know about."

"Tolliver says most firms that are accountants and consultants were originally accounting firms that expanded into consulting because consulting is a lot more profitable. DDD&W is the opposite—a consulting firm that acquired an accounting firm, much less profitable than their existing business. Their strategy doesn't make financial sense, and even more peculiar, they acquired D&W after it was obvious that firms consulting for the clients they were auditing faced legal problems. Nobody could understand the merger when it took place, and they still can't."

Jonathan drew a big question mark on the pad in front of him. "Coleman's friend Amy, who works at DDD&W, told Coleman the firm needed lots of quants to analyze the financial services industry in which they're trying to be a major force, and a lot more to deal with the taxation issues in their merger and acquisitions practice. They hired a big hitter from Bache, Gold & Glatz—a man named Michael—uh—Moose Shanahan to run those areas, and he claimed you couldn't get anywhere without an army of numbers guys. She said that was the justification for the merger. Does that make sense to you?"

"No. I've never heard of a consulting company acquiring a company to get a bunch of accountants. Tolliver thinks DDD&W should be investigated, and so do I," Blair said.

"Good. What about the district attorney? About the art sales tax?" Jonathan asked.

"The people in the DA's office will begin questioning people at DDD&W this week. Somebody at Great Art Management ratted them out. Patti Sue Victor will be the first person they interview—she's Great Art Management's contact. GAM spotted her as a patsy at a conference of art dealers and corporate collectors and hired her on the spot. The DA's people have identified about twenty people at DDD&W guilty of tax evasion on not terribly expensive art they bought through Great Art Management. None of the senior management at DDD&W is among the twenty," Blair said.

"Twenty? Good Lord, the mind boggles," Jonathan said.

"Indeed. I read in the *Wall Street Journal* that the New York DA had nearly a hundred people under investigation for this type of crime. That sounds like a lot, until you hear there are twenty at one firm," Blair said. "Anyway, that's it for the SEC and the DA's office.

"For everything else, you have to come to Boston. I've set up several appointments for you tomorrow, starting with lunch at the Firm with Ned Carville. He can tell you everything you need to know about the Davidsons. He knew them well, and since we have no legal connection with the family, he's free to give you the background you'll need for your afternoon appointment with Lucas Parker, the attorney in charge of the Davidson estate. Parker's the son of Davidson's executor, who was a friend of Davidson's. Parker Sr. lived in New York and died soon after Davidson did. After his father died, Parker Jr., who lives in Boston, took over the management of the estate. The father was highly regarded, but I don't know anything about the son," Blair said.

Jonathan drew another question mark. Blair knew all the A-list lawyers in Boston, and nearly everywhere else. If he didn't know Parker, the lawyer was at best a nonentity. A second-rate lawyer handling Davidson's affairs? Odd, except that nepotism got him the job. If Parker Jr. were incompetent or a crook, that could explain a lot.

"Finally, we're having dinner with Ian MacDonald, the chairman of the board of the Prince Charles Stuart Museum. I'm told he's eccentric, but a decent chap. He can't get to Boston from Stuartville until nine or so, so dinner will be late—we'll dine at the Century Club—and you should plan to stay over. I'll put you up, of course."

"Thanks a million, Blair. I'll see you tomorrow."

Thirty-Five

At three o'clock Monday afternoon, Coleman, wearing a lightweight wool suit the color of early spring leaves and a silk blouse a shade darker, arrived in the thirty-third floor reception area at DDD&W. The day was again rainy and cold, and she'd nearly frozen, even with a lined raincoat over her suit. She gave her coat to the receptionist, who seemed flustered when she heard Coleman's name but kept her head long enough to call Amy's assistant. The young woman ushered Coleman into a conference room where two clean-cut young men and Amy waited.

"Coleman, these are my associates, Michael Gerstner and Terry Howard. They'll be working with me on your project. They'll take you through the numbers, especially on the production side, since that's where you said you need the most help."

The presentation was clear and succinct. *First Home* was overstaffed, a little on the editorial side, a lot in other areas—accounting, finance, marketing, production. Amy and her team would interview and evaluate everyone in those departments and suggest which employees should be kept, and which terminated. Coleman knew a fair amount about most of the editorial staff and hoped to retain about half of them. She would talk to those who interested her right away.

Amy's team had checked on the two magazines' office leases. Coleman could get out of *First Home*'s lease—the building had a tenant who wanted to take it over. *ArtSmart*'s landlord would let Coleman have additional space. There'd be substantial cost reduction from the relocation of the reduced *First Home* staff; their offices were glitzy and overpriced.

Coleman could cut costs by using a single printer and a single paper supplier for both magazines. Amy gave her a binder summarizing their findings to date. They'd have additional recommendations by Wednesday.

No one mentioned Hunt Frederick's attempt to bar her from the office, and since in Coleman's mind the Cowardly Cowboy was toast, she didn't give him a thought until she was back in her office and saw the column items she'd left on her desk that morning. She'd love to know how he was responding to the press. Maybe Bethany and Loretta would have heard about his reaction. The Byrds should be e-mailing a report on their day's activities anytime now. Rob had cautioned them not to put anything in print that they didn't want the world to know or to see produced in court—their reports should be short and cryptic. She checked her e-mail. Oh, good, there it was.

> To: Dinah, Coleman, Jonathan, and Rob, from Bethany and Loretta.
> Subject: A day at the office
>
> Hairy Ferocious found the Angel's bag of tricks, says he knows how the Angel magicked the trap. Cowardly Cowboy wrote the troops that the rhino heads were at the cleaners, home Friday. Dried Peach had a hissy fit, and a horny animal chased her off. We hung 150 prints. Lots of bystanders, questions, interruptions.

Coleman smiled. She'd probably have to translate the letter for Jonathan and Rob, but she understood every word. The Byrds were in fine fettle, their senses of humor intact. But she sobered when she thought about "Angel's bag of tricks." What had Dinah left behind? How could Harrison possibly "know" Dinah "magicked" the killing trap—when she hadn't? Were the Stubbs *really* out being cleaned? Or was that a cover story, cooked up by the Cowardly Cowboy?

Thirty-Six

Coleman had agreed to meet Jonathan, Dinah, and Rob Monday night for an early dinner at a small Lexington Avenue bistro, well known for its cassoulet. She was reluctant to pair up with Rob again, but she had to support Dinah, and for that, she needed to be a part of this investigation. She'd do her best to keep Rob at a distance.

The restaurant was warm and redolent of garlic and roasting meat, appealing on this chilly night. They ate cassoulet, and everyone but Coleman drank a young red wine from Cahors, while Rob updated them on his investigations. The big news was about Harrison: Rob was sure he'd be removed from the case. Maybe Quintero, too.

To Coleman's disappointment, Rob's investigators had turned up nothing against Hunt Austin Frederick. He'd sowed some wild oats in college but had, like other famous Texans, been born again in midlife—didn't smoke, drink, do drugs, or gamble.

He was a regular churchgoer and donated money to charity, especially education and his church. After an expensive divorce from a feather-brained Texas deb who'd amused herself with her tennis pro while her husband was traveling for DDD&W, Hunt Austin Frederick was said to have been grateful for the chance to move to New York and take on a challenging new assignment. He'd kept a low social profile since his arrival in Manhattan.

Rob's people had done a quick check on DDD&W management. The founding Davidson was dead, of course, and Rob assumed his stock was tied up in his estate. Based on shares owned, the organization should be called Davidson, Frederick (who had acquired a healthy chunk of stock when he became managing director), Douglas, Danbury & Weeks.

Ted Douglas, descendant of the original Douglas and inheritor of the Douglas family's stock, lived in a magnificent apartment on Sutton Place with his wife of many years, Glenda Gould, heiress to a Pittsburgh fortune. They owned a weekend house in East Hampton, and a ski house in Vail. They had no children. They belonged to the right clubs, attended the most prestigious benefits, played tennis, and skied. They lived a typical well-off Manhattanite life. Neither money nor social position was an issue in a world governed by Glenda the Gould, as Coleman had long ago christened her.

Since Leichter had been made a partner at Weeks's behest, Rob had also had him investigated. After the merger, when Weeks and Leichter moved east from Chicago, Leichter bought a small house next door to the one his father-in-law had chosen in Teaneck, New Jersey. Leichter, his wife, and their four daughters were said to be firmly under his in-laws' thumbs. Leichter worked long hours and played golf every weekend with Father Weeks. His wife was preoccupied with the house, the children, and her mother. Their social life appeared to be totally child-related. Their expenses, like his income, were modest, but no one interviewed thought Leichter aspired to more.

Oscar Danbury had bought a town house in the East Nineties when he moved to New York. He lived there with his wife, who'd been his high school sweetheart. They had two sons away at school. Work was apparently his only interest, and his wife volunteered at a nearby hospital. Danbury was rumored to be a miser, with a great deal of money tucked away in conservative investments.

The detectives investigating the Victor sisters had discovered a neighbor who lived across the hall from them and hated them. The neighbor, an ancient crone with little to do but spy and gossip, reported that both sisters had mysterious boyfriends— criminals, she was sure. She said one of the men looked like a TV mobster—she'd seen him with Frances twice—and Patti Sue's beau was "weaselly like." Age? Couldn't say. Color? Not black; she'd have noticed. But the men were "real ugly." She swore she'd recognize them if she saw them again. She claimed she always knew the sisters would come to a bad end.

No one else in the building admitted meeting the Victor sisters, or knowing anything about them.

"They've always kept themselves to themselves," one of the doormen said. None of the doormen was willing to comment on their gentlemen friends. "Lotsa people come in and outta here," one of them growled. "We don't keep track." The detectives doubted they'd learn more.

"Too bad neither of the boyfriends sounds like Harrison," Coleman said. "I was sure his girlfriend at DDD&W would turn out to be Patti Sue or her sister."

"Me, too," Rob said. "Next on the agenda is Great Art Management. Their name has been linked to antiquities smuggling, fake art, bogus antiques. They have a stable of artists capable of faking on demand—Impressionism, Realism, Picassos, copies of works by Frank Stella, Roy Lichtenstein, and other contemporary artists. Whatever the client wants. In fact, Coleman, one of your favorite artists is represented by them."

"Who?" Coleman asked.

"Crawdaddy," Rob said.

"Oh, that creep. That's the kind of place where he would be involved," Coleman said.

"Crawdaddy?" Jonathan asked.

"The photorealist who crashed Coleman's party, and had his picture taken with Coleman and me," Dinah explained.

"Oh, him. He was a nasty piece of work," Jonathan said.

"Anyway," Rob continued, "apparently whenever a client is unhappy with a purchase, GAM reimburses his money and takes back the object, probably selling it to a greater fool. Nothing negative has been published about them, there's no record of anyone suing them, and nothing has ever been proved against them."

"Something's about to be proved," Jonathan said, explaining that a Great Art Management employee had confessed and named Patti Sue as the contact at DDD&W. The DA's office would strike this week. The SEC was also on the move.

"That's great news, Jonathan," Rob said. "I wish mine was. I still don't have a line on the Davidson girls, and it's wait and see on the Stubbs portraits. If they turn up at DDD&W on Friday, I guess we've been on the wrong track there."

"I've been thinking about the latest anonymous note," Dinah said. "Our informant tried to let us know about the office search, although we didn't get the note in time to remove my tool kit. I'm sure the portraits won't be back on Friday, and I have an idea about how to find them."

"Go to it. I wish you luck," Rob said.

"What about the stuff you got from the Fry Building?" Coleman asked Rob.

"None of the security guards has a criminal record, but they're sloppy. If someone they know comes in, they might not sign him or her in; the same if a person they know leaves the building. Their sign-in and sign-out books aren't as full as they should be, given the number of people on the videos. The videos show what you'd expect—lots of people coming and going, mostly the same people over and over. The DDD&W people are in and out constantly."

"Did the audio tape of the girl calling in the murder tell you anything?" Jonathan asked.

Rob shook his head. "You can barely hear her. I'd think it was a hoax except that there *was* a murder."

Dinah, looking worried, spoke up.

"Uh—I have something to tell everyone about that. I know who the girl was—her name is Ellie McPhee. She was Patti Sue's assistant. She turned up right after I discovered the body, and I asked her to call the guards downstairs," Dinah said, looking at Jonathan's astonished expression. "I know I should have told you. But she's a sweet little thing, and I didn't want to hand her to the bullies at DDD&W, or the police. I thought they'd learn she was in the building from the security people—or the tape—or she'd come forward, and I wouldn't have to tattle on her. But the thing is, I tried to call her, and she's not there."

Coleman sighed. Just like Dinah to try to protect someone, even when it wasn't in her own best interest. She'd done that sort of thing as a child. When a little vase on her grandmother's dressing table was broken, everyone thought Dinah was the culprit, because dusting that room was her responsibility. Dinah hadn't told anyone that she'd seen Morton, a neighbor's child, looking scared, tiptoeing out of the room. Weeks later, Morton, overcome by guilt, had confessed.

"What do you mean 'she's not there'?" Rob said.

Dinah shrugged. "Just that. The DDD&W operator said she's gone."

"Do you think she was fired?" Rob asked.

Dinah shook her head. "I haven't a clue."

"Has Dinah broken the law by not reporting this woman to the police?" Jonathan asked Rob.

Rob shook his head. "I don't think so. She hasn't lied to the police. I'll put one of the detectives on Ellie McPhee right away, see if we can find her. I don't think we should wait too long before we tell the police about her, and it would be good if we can give them more than the name of a missing girl. Of course, she's not the only one missing. As I said, the Davidson heiresses are in the wind, too. I've got people looking for them. They can try to find the McPhee woman as well," Rob said.

"We're not getting very far, are we?" Coleman said.

Jonathan shook his head. "No, but I think we'll know a lot more when I get back from Boston. I'm looking forward to meeting the chairman of the Prince Charles. I've faxed him Dinah's analysis of the collection—what they have and what's missing. I'll be interested to hear his reaction. And I'm sure I'll learn a lot from the Davidsons' lawyer," he said.

"I hope you do better than I have," Rob said. "I have nothing but bad news. As you guessed, Coleman, Patti Sue denies any fight in the DDD&W ladies' room, and Mrs. Thornton says she can't talk to us unless Hunt Frederick clears it, which he isn't going to do. We'll have to try to get the police to investigate the fight. Maybe the Cobra can make it happen. Patti Sue's lying, of course. It's apparently known inside DDD&W that there was at least one, maybe more, fight between her and another woman.

Listen to what the Byrds picked up today." He clicked on a tiny tape recorder.

Say, Patti Sue dint attack you, did she? Her and one of the other dames here have fist-fights when they think nobody's lookin', mostly in the girls' privy. Y'all better watch out for her. Well, Love Birds, I gotta get back to work. My name's Michael Shanahan. Folks call me Moose.

"Will he tell us more?" Dinah asked.

Coleman nodded. "Sounds like he will. I doubt if he'd talk to the police, but I bet Bethany or Loretta can chat him up and get what we need. He's susceptible to beautiful women."

"Do you know Moose Shanahan?" Rob asked. His tone made the innocuous question sound like an accusation.

Coleman was irritated by the question but kept her response civil.

"I know *of* him. Big-deal college football player, big-deal investment banker, big-deal ladies' man. I don't know if he's currently married. He's a serial marryer," Coleman said.

"Well, whatever he is, he knows what's going on at DDD&W," Jonathan said. "Can Bethany and Loretta find out from him who the other woman in the catfight is?"

"They think they know. They think it's Naomi Skinner, Mark Leichter's assistant. But it would be good if they can pin it down, and I'm sure they'll try. If they don't get anywhere, we'll try another approach," Rob said.

He turned toward Coleman. "While we're on the topic of people at DDD&W, how do you know Theodore Douglas, Coleman?" Rob asked.

Coleman thought he was more interested in prying into her past than in the case they were discussing, but there was no reason she shouldn't answer him.

"Teddy? I've seen him around town for years. Decent manners, pleasant, inoffensive," she said.

"I've known Douglas a long time, too," Jonathan said. "I've always thought he was insignificant—nothing like his father and grandfather. They were both very intelligent, and very successful. Ted barely made it through any of his schools. I was surprised to learn he'd done so well at DDD&W. His wife's family's influence and money must have helped."

"Getting back to my problems: how bad is it Harrison found my tool kit?" Dinah asked.

Rob looked at her, his expression grave. "I won't lie to you: I'd rather he hadn't, because it gives him more ammunition against you. Unless they can prove your tools were used to loosen those shelves, finding them doesn't help make their case, but it's another smear opportunity. I keep thinking everything—including the tools—is going to show up in the tabloids."

Dinah looked so miserable, Coleman changed the subject. "How are the hangers doing, Dinah?"

Dinah's face brightened. "They're doing fine. We're speeding along. By the end of the day Tuesday they'll have completed the corridors on thirty-three and be halfway through what's left of the job. The rest of the prints are already coming in. Today I had a batch picked up in the New York area—from New Jersey and Connecticut dealers as well as in the city—and they're already at the framer's. They'll arrive at DDD&W ready to hang Wednesday. If all goes well, Bethany and Loretta will have finished the job by the end of the week."

∽

They finished dinner a little after nine, and Rob, feeling terrible about Coleman's coldness and his own less-than-stellar performance on Dinah's case, returned to his office. Shortly after he arrived, Pete, looking puzzled, appeared in his door. "May I speak to you for a minute?" he asked Rob.

Rob looked up from his papers. "Sure. What is it?"

"I've got a weird one: I checked the Internet, didn't turn up anything on Ellie McPhee. No address in the US, no social security number, nada. Called DDD&W's human resources department, and the snippy woman who answered the phone says no one named Ellie McPhee has ever been employed by DDD&W."

Rob frowned. "That's ridiculous. Dinah knows her. She saw Ellie McPhee often—the woman was Patti Sue's assistant," he said.

Pete shrugged. "I hear what you're saying, but I'm telling you, everybody I talked to said she doesn't exist."

"Have you asked Coleman's friend, Amy Roth-man?"

"Did that. Ms. Rothman has a vague memory of a girl sitting outside Patti Sue's office, but she never met her, and can't remember what she looked like. She phoned a few others at DDD&W she thought might know her, but no one did," Pete said.

"Have you asked the lobby guards?"

Pete nodded. "Checked the books. No one by that name has ever signed in or out of the building. The guards never saw anyone like Dinah describes, never heard the name."

"Oh, God, I hate this case. Nothing ever gets resolved, nothing's simple. Let's get Dinah in to look at the security tapes to see if she can spot her friend. But even if she does, I don't know where that'll get us," Rob said. He decided to go home and not think about business until Tuesday.

༄

Rob was reading in bed when the phone rang at eleven thirty. It was his friend at One Police Plaza.

"Bad news for your client, Rob. We examined Ms. Greene's tools. Her screwdriver and the claws on her hammer were used to bring down the shelves. The scars on the wall and on the wood matched."

"Oh, hell. Will she be arrested today?" Rob asked.

"No, they still haven't figured out how she got in the office, and the building has no record of her returning after she left at midnight. They haven't found a cab driver who took her uptown between one a.m. and five a.m., or anyone who saw her on the subway. They're still being super careful. But if they get either of those two pieces of the puzzle, they'll arrest her."

Rob got up and paced. He wouldn't sleep tonight. He dreaded telling Jonathan and Dinah about the tools. He'd let them sleep while they could.

Thirty-Seven

First thing Tuesday morning, Dinah watched the Fry Building videotapes. Ellie McPhee did not appear in the tapes for the two weeks before Dinah was given the contract, nor had she appeared since. Dinah told Rob she felt like Ingrid Bergman in *Gaslight*. Mystified, she gave up and took a taxi to the gallery. After she'd settled at her desk, she put Ellie out of her mind. She had a theory about the location of the Stubbs paintings, and she was anxious to check it out. She put in a call to Rachel Ransome at her London gallery. She and Rachel had become friends when they met in London last year, and they spoke often.

"Dinah? How lovely to hear from you."

"Thanks, Rachel. How are you?"

"I think my problems with Simon are about to be resolved, thanks to Heyward Bain," Rachel said.

Rachel sounded happier than Dinah had ever heard her. Simon Fanshawe-Davies had been a thorn hedge in Rachel's side. He had been Rachel's protégé and employee. She'd given him 20 percent of the Ransome Gallery as a reward for what she'd thought was his loyalty and hard work. He'd repaid her generosity by stealing from her and betraying her in every possible way, even trying to implicate her in his unscrupulous transactions. But the legal agreements making him her partner were so binding, she couldn't free herself from his clutches. Because he'd been seriously injured earlier in the year, he wasn't around to annoy her. But no matter where he was, he was legally entitled to 20 percent of everything the gallery made, while Rachel struggled to recover the vast amounts of money he owed her. If Rachel had rid herself of that bloodsucker, it was terrific news.

"Wow! Tell me all about it."

"I cannot yet tell you all the details, but as soon as I can—perhaps later this week—I shall, I promise you. What is your news?"

Dinah had decided not to tell Rachel about her own predicament. Her friend could do nothing to help, unless she could solve the mystery of the missing Stubbs. Given Rachel's connections as a highly respected dealer and scholar, Dinah hoped she'd be able to discover their whereabouts, if they, as Dinah suspected, were on the market in London.

"Rachel, can you find out if two important Stubbs portraits are for sale in London? Or have been sold recently?"

"Of course, my dear. What are the paintings?"

"*Portrait of Lady J* and *Portrait of Lord J*. They were left to DDD&W, a US company, by one of its founders. But we think someone may have stolen them. The logical place to sell them is England—Stubbs is so much admired there, and if they were sold privately, people in New York might never hear about the transaction."

"How very interesting. I shall make inquiries immediately and telephone you when I know anything."

୬

Rob reached Jonathan on his cell phone, on his way to the airport, and gave him the bad news about Dinah's tools.

"When did Dinah take her tools to DDD&W?" Jonathan asked.

"They were messengered to her last Tuesday—a week ago today. She used them that afternoon to hang prints in her office and left them in a locked file drawer, behind a locked door. As you know, Frances Johnson was killed between two and four Thursday morning."

"Someone had to know they were in that office, and was able to get past the locked door and the locked cabinet to borrow and use them. Now we know for sure that someone at DDD&W is trying to pin Johnson's murder on Dinah. We have to catch whoever it is before he—or she—hurts Dinah more than she's already been hurt. I hate seeing her so miserable."

Thirty-Eight

Jonathan's flight to Boston was on time. He met Blair Winthrop and Ned Carville in one of the small private dining rooms at the Firm. Carville, a specialist in corporate law, was a senior partner. He was prominent in his field and rumored to be in line for something big in Washington the next time the Republicans were in office. He sounded like a Kennedy when he spoke—he had that ghastly accent. His brown hair was graying at the temples and his hairline was receding, but his light brown eyes were as bright and clear as a boy's. His face was lightly tanned and healthy looking, and he was thin as a whip.

They chatted about inconsequentialities while the grilled Dover sole and green salad were served, but when the waiter left the room, Carville turned to the subject that interested Jonathan. "Blair tells me you want to know about the Davidsons," he said. "It was a tragic family. James and his first wife, Sally, were childhood sweethearts who married young. The marriage was fine until their teenage son was killed. Sally never got over it—took pills, was in and out of clinics, became a zombie. James withstood it as long as he could—he'd always adored her—but he was lonely. He had an affair with his secretary, who became pregnant with twins." He paused and took a bite of his fish.

Jonathan was making notes on the pad the waiter had left near his right hand. Affair? Illegitimate twins? Very un-Boston.

Carville sipped his Evian and continued. "The divorce was amicable since Sally neither cared what James did, nor what happened to her. She died in an assisted-living home a few months after the divorce—heart failure, they said, but it could have been a drug overdose. No one wanted to blacken her name; there was no autopsy, and she was buried quickly.

James insisted that his secretary take a paternity test to make sure the little girls were his, and demanded a rigid premarital agreement. He'd never have married the woman if she weren't pregnant, and she knew it. He didn't treat her very well, and she left him. She soon found another husband, less suspicious and more loving than James. She vanished from his and the girls' lives. I think she and her husband live in Italy. I'm not sure the girls ever knew her; I'd guess that was part of James's arrangement with her." He took another bite of fish, while Jonathan waited for the next installment.

"James was crazy about the twins—Elizabeth and Margaret—but they were only three when he drowned while swimming. He probably had a heart attack. There was nothing suspicious about his death, and again, there was no autopsy. After that, the girls lived with James's sister and her husband in Virginia, who were their only relatives, and they died in a plane crash when the girls were in college. Tragedy of tragedies.

The odd thing is, nobody seems to know where the girls are now. Lucas Parker, the lawyer you're seeing this afternoon, might know, but he and I don't travel in the same circles, and I don't like him, so I've never asked him about the twins."

"Do the girls have money?" Jonathan said.

"James left some money for their education, but it couldn't have been much. They went to Miss Mitford's, a boarding school near Richmond, from the seventh grade through high school, and Witherspoon College, in Summerville, Virginia. Inexpensive schools. He must have settled only a modest amount on them, because he didn't believe in leaving kids a lot of money—he thought it spoiled them. He wanted them to work for a living. He tied up most of his money in a trust for DDD&W, which, except for the twins, was his only love. He expected the girls would work at DDD&W, but I gather they didn't?"

Jonathan shook his head. "No, and I don't know why. It's hard to believe they could just disappear."

Carville shrugged. "Girls get married and change their names—or change their names, period. They may even get new social security numbers, if they're trying to hide."

Blair, who'd been listening attentively, frowned. "Why would they hide?"

"I don't know that they *are* hiding," Carville said. "But the researchers at the Firm tried to find them, and they didn't turn up under the name of Davidson, dead or alive."

When the meeting broke up, Jonathan was even more puzzled than he'd been earlier. Not only did it seem impossible that the girls could have disappeared, but their schools were surprising. Why did the only children of the wealthy and socially prominent James Davidson attend such obscure schools? Why didn't their father leave enough money to give them a decent education? Were they perhaps backward? Slow? Did that explain why they couldn't get jobs at DDD&W? Maybe this lawyer, Lucas Parker, could supply some answers.

But Jonathan's three-thirty meeting with Parker was not only uninformative, it turned ugly.

Parker was a Pillsbury doughboy with an unpleasant personality. His skin was flour paste white, and his plump form was held in place by a sausage-casing vest, but he wasn't cheerful and smiling, let alone giggly like his doppelganger. *Stubborn* and *obtuse* were the words that came to mind: he simply could not—or would not—understand why Jonathan was concerning himself with something that Parker did not think was Jonathan's business. He insisted that anything to do with the Davidson estate was his affair, and he intended to keep it that way. He said so several times, in an unctuous voice that set Jonathan's teeth on edge.

"I agreed to this meeting because Blair Winthrop asked me to see you," Parker said, looking down his nose at Jonathan. "But you have given me no reason why I should discuss the Davidsons' financial affairs with you."

Jonathan tried to contain his exasperation, but he felt like screaming at the idiot. "As I've said repeatedly, but perhaps too subtly, I've encountered some irregularities concerning the Davidson estate, and I'd like to talk to the girls about them."

Parker's body, froglike, seemed to swell. "*I* am the only person with whom you should discuss the Davidson estate. As for 'irregularities,' you are insulting. The estate was in my father's hands, and it is now in mine."

Jonathan stood up. "Parker, I've heard about attorneys like you, but it's been my good fortune never to have met one. I haven't asked you for anything confidential. I simply want to talk to James Davidson's daughters. You won't tell me if they are alive or dead, let alone how I might reach them. The irregularities to which I refer are about to turn into a public scandal. You should inform yourself by reading these." Jonathan dropped a set of the photocopied clippings from the columns that mentioned DDD&W on Parker's desk.

Parker curled his lip. "I've seen those articles," he said. "They're ridiculous. I'm told that this nasty press campaign is a personal vendetta engineered by you, because your wife is suspected of murdering someone who worked at DDD&W."

"You're a pompous jerk, but you're also a fool. Your saying that proves it. Say it again in front of a witness, and I promise you, you won't practice law again in the United States. In fact, you'll be lucky if you can earn enough to *live* in the United States."

Jonathan strode to the door, but before he departed, he turned back and glared at Parker. "When I find those young women, I'm going to tell them that you are so bullheaded, so stupid, you wouldn't take steps to protect their assets. Some people would describe your behavior as criminally incompetent—or just criminal. I'll advise the young women to take legal action against you, and I'll represent them at no expense. You're a disgrace to the legal profession. The next time you hear from me, it will be through the Firm."

In the car on the way to the Century Club to meet Blair, Jonathan telephoned Rob to ask if he'd had any luck tracing the Davidson girls.

"Not yet," Rob said. "Have you learned something about them?"

"Their lawyer wouldn't tell me anything. But I have the names of their schools: Miss Mitford's and Witherspoon College, both in Virginia. Maybe the schools have addresses for them."

"I'll put a guy on it right away," Rob said. He sent an e-mail to Pete explaining his request, adding that if Pete was too busy, he could farm it out to one of his friends. It was a simple request; anyone could handle it.

Thirty-Nine

Jonathan recognized Ian MacDonald's kilt as the red plaid of the MacDonald clan. With it he wore a black velvet jacket ornamented with silver. He should have looked elegant, but MacDonald was a big craggy man, with tree-trunk legs and receding reddish-blond hair. His fair skin was ruddy and freckled, marking him as a man who spent more time out of doors than at formal dinners. He had laugh lines around his pale blue eyes, but he wasn't laughing tonight; he looked like a volcano on the verge of erupting.

When Blair asked what he'd like to drink, he asked for Scotch whisky, and swigged it throughout the meal, rejecting the excellent wines Blair had selected to drink with the smoked salmon and roast beef. Even with enough whisky in him to float a yacht, MacDonald was a man of few words. "I ken the Davidson family well. All the Davidsons I ever heard of did good. They go all the way back to the Bible. But the Douglases are a treacherous lot. I know naught of Weeks nor Danbury." He repeated the speech several times.

Jonathan, bewildered, turned to Blair for enlightenment.

Blair, grinning, explained that the first David in Scotland was the son of Malcolm III, king of Scotland, and Margaret, the much beloved queen of Scotland, a devout Christian. Margaret and Malcolm died in 1093. The Earl of Douglas was said to have deserted the Scottish cause in the fifteenth century. "Scots have long memories," Blair added.

Jonathan nodded. This one certainly did.

When coffee was served, MacDonald spiked his with more whisky and took a big gulp. The steam rising from it proved it was scalding hot, but the inside of his mouth was apparently as immune to heat as his blood was to whisky. Jonathan took advantage of MacDonald's mouthful of coffee to ask what he planned to do about the missing art. MacDonald glared at him, his bloodshot eyes the only sign of his alcohol intake.

"I'd like to kill the buggers, but I cannae. I'll have to beat the bloody bastards with the law."

"Can the museum afford a prolonged court battle?" Blair asked.

"Nae, the museum cannae, but I can. I got all the siller I'll ever need, and more besides. But I dinnae ken a lawyer for this. My lawyers deal with the land and such."

Jonathan and Blair exchanged glances, and Jonathan said, "We already have a lawyer and a detective working on this problem—we think some of the people at DDD&W have committed other crimes. We could probably save time—and money—by joining forces."

MacDonald's eyes gleamed. Within twenty minutes a deal had been struck, and MacDonald departed for Stuartville in the back seat of an ancient Rolls Royce, with a young, presumably sober, driver at the wheel.

Jonathan went to bed Tuesday night exhausted but satisfied. Adding MacDonald and the defrauded museum to those prosecuting DDD&W greatly strengthened their position. Eccentric as he was, MacDonald would still make a good ally.

৵

Rob was trying to decide which of the vast list of things to do he should tackle first, when Pete appeared in his office door. "I got a pal to call Miss Mitford's, the Davidson girls' school. He spoke to the registrar. Margaret Davidson was married and divorced. She kept her married name, Galloway. She died last summer—suicide, people say, although her sister Elizabeth insisted it was an accident. Ms. Galloway was buried in the family plot in Connecticut with her father and brother, but because of the way she died, the funeral was private, and there were no articles in the local paper. Most people around there don't even know Margaret's dead."

"What about Elizabeth?"

"She was at the funeral, but nobody's seen or heard from her since, and neither of her schools has a current address for her."

Rob frowned. "Too bad, the schools were our best hope. See if you can think of any other approach to locating Elizabeth, or her mother."

Pete, looking dubious, nodded, and departed. Rob put a big question mark by Elizabeth Davidson's name and returned to his list.

Forty

"Did you see this?" Loretta held out Tuesday's *Daily Reporter*, open at the gossip page.

"No, I haven't seen the papers. What's happenin'?" Bethany asked. She took another sip from the paper cup of Starbucks's strongest and blackest she'd picked up on her way to the office. She'd decided not to eat or drink anything prepared at DDD&W. The people were so hostile toward the Greene Gallery they'd probably poison anything that came near her and Loretta. Anyway, everything here had sugar in it.

"Another story about DDD&W," Loretta said. "Listen:

Jonathan Hathaway, the scion of one of Boston's most established families, is dining tonight in Beantown—not on beans, we hasten to add—with Ian MacDonald, chairman of the Prince Charles Stuart Museum, of Stuartville, New York.

Under the late James Davidson's will, the Prince Charles recently received the multimillion-dollar Davidson Americana collection, from DDD&W, the New York–based consulting firm. But somebody grabbed all the goodies before shipping the bequest to the museum. According to sources who've seen what arrived in Stuartville, the museum got only scraps and bobtails, a fraction of what they'd expected.

Hathaway's wife, art dealer Dinah Greene, and her cousin, Coleman Greene, editor of *ArtSmart*, discovered that the collection had been stripped of its most valuable objects. Hathaway is the bearer of the bad news to the museum. (See *Arts Section* for a related article.)"

Bethany nearly spilled her coffee. "Wow! They know everything, don't they? What's the related article?"

"They printed the list from the will beside the list of the things that went to the museum. Is Coleman giving this stuff to the columns?" Loretta asked.

"I'm sure she's responsible for the earlier pieces, but not this one. Jonathan won't like havin' his name or Dinah's in a tabloid, and Coleman wouldn't ruffle his feathers. I'm guessing the *Daily Reporter* picked up the story from the *New York Examiner* and did its own research," Bethany said. She dropped her empty cup in the trash basket and sighed. "Okay, let's hang—but first, who's going to chat up the Moose?"

"I'll do it. I don't mind," Loretta said.

She'd tackle Moose right now. But first she'd stop by the ladies' room to check her appearance. She needed to look her best for this little job. Every time Moose had seen her in the corridors he'd complimented her clothes. He was a noticing man.

The Joan Crawford–cut turquoise suit and matching platform shoes were just right. The rosy lipstick was perfect, too. She touched the hair sticks she'd tucked into her chignon. Well, knitting needles really, left over from unsuccessful attempts by her great-aunt to teach her to knit. But they'd be sold as expensive hair sticks if she'd had to buy them at Bloomingdale's. They were hot. She'd buy some more when she'd saved a little. She enjoyed the admiring stares of the DDD&W men, and she looked forward to interviewing the Moose. This was a chance to strut her stuff. She knew what to do; she'd been watching TV detectives for years.

Moose, his brow furrowed and a pencil behind his ear, sat behind an enormous desk littered with paper. He looked up and grinned. "Well, howdy, Love Bird! You here for help? You got the right guy. What can I do for you?"

Loretta leaned against the wall inside his office door and considered Moose. Despite his compliments, she didn't think he was interested in her sexually, or that talking trash with him would get her anywhere. Today he looked really busy. His eyes were cold, and his jaw looked tight—she'd cut to the chase. She could flirt anytime; this was business.

"You talked about Patti Sue fighting. We know the other woman was Naomi Skinner. Who's the partner they were fighting over?"

"You got the women right. Forget about the partner, Sweetie. Don't go there. And stay away from those women. Trust me. Patti Sue's a mean, ugly bitch, and so is Skinner. Messin' around with them is dangerous. Don't get involved. Forget it."

Loretta, thrilled with having their suspicion of the Skinner woman confirmed, tried again.

"So you're not the partner Patti Sue and Naomi Skinner are fighting over?"

Moose guffawed. "Get real, Love Bird. The DDD&W women are bow-wows. I take out models and stars—at least, I did before I got married. Lemme show you a picture of my wife." He picked up a silver-framed photograph from the array on his desk and handed it to her. Loretta recognized the exquisite face, the perfect body, the de la Renta ball dress. She'd seen that lady's photograph in fashion magazines. Moose must be loaded big-time. Maybe even a billionaire. Dressing the way she did cost plenty.

"Wow! Isn't she on the best-dressed list?"

"That's my girl," he said, his round face glowing with pride.

"I can see why *you* wouldn't be interested in Patti Sue or Naomi Skinner. But can't you tell me who is?" she begged, her tone as persuasive as she could make it.

He shook his head, and no matter how she wheedled, he wouldn't say another word. She gave up and rejoined Bethany and the hangers. When she repeated the conversation to Bethany, Loretta added, "But he knows who the partner is. He just didn't want to tell me."

"You think he's involved with those women?" Bethany asked.

"No, I believe him about that. Anybody married to that Nicole Kidman look-alike wouldn't go out with what he calls bow-wows. But I think he knows all about it, just won't talk." She shrugged. "Boy stuff. Loyalty to the other boys above all. Anyway, we know for certain who the other woman is."

"Good. I'll send Rob an e-mail. Let's hang prints."

༄

Bethany was standing on a ladder in the hall hanging a print when her cell phone rang.

"Bethany, it's Rob. We have a problem."

When he explained that Dinah's tools had been used to sabotage the bookshelves, Bethany groaned. "Got it. What do you want me to do?" She climbed down the ladder and moved out of earshot of the other hangers.

"See if you can open that file cabinet without a key. Try a nail file or a letter opener. Find out who has duplicate keys to your office and the print storeroom. Someone must. And Bethany, don't tell anyone about this. Jonathan doesn't want Dinah to know until she has to."

"Okay, done." Zeke, who'd followed her down the hall, raised his eyebrows. She climbed down and smiled at him. "I'll tell you later, lover. I'm going back to the office for a minute," she said and hurried down the hall.

When she and Loretta had arrived yesterday, the metal file drawers were locked, and the key had been where Dinah said she'd put it, taped to the bottom of the stapler in one of the desk drawers—not findable without a time-consuming search. Seemed unlikely that whoever used Dinah's tools would have wasted time looking for the key, and since the killer wanted people to believe Dinah did it, he or she wouldn't have forced the lock. So how did the killer open the file, and relock it?

Similar cabinets in her high school had interchangeable keys. She bet these did, too. She walked around a couple of corners and stopped at an assistant's desk. The young woman looked up. "May I help you with something?"

"I hope so. I can't find the key to the filing cabinet in my boss's office. But it looks like it's one of those cabinets where one key fits all. May I borrow yours to see if it works? I'll bring it right back."

"Sure, here it is," the woman said, handing her the key.

Five minutes later, Bethany returned the key. "Just as I thought, your key fits my boss's file cabinet," she said. "Thanks."

The young woman shook her head. "Don't mention it. Some security, huh? I'll remember not to leave my wallet in there."

Bethany grinned. "Me, too. Thanks again."

Now for the other keys. Dinah said that Ted Douglas's assistant had arranged the installation of the locks. She was Bethany's next stop.

"Hi! I'm Bethany Byrd, Dinah Greene's assistant. We've begun hangin' prints, and I wanted to introduce myself. But I also wanted to ask you something."

"What's that?" The woman was so colorless, she was nearly invisible. Grumpy, too. The corners of her mouth turned downward. Douglas's wife must have hired her.

"The doors to the office and the storage room were open when we got here—I guess Dinah left 'em that way 'cause there weren't any unhung prints lyin' around. But we've had some prints delivered, and we're expectin' a whole lot more, and we need to be able to secure 'em," Bethany said.

The woman frowned. "Where are the keys I gave Dinah Greene?" she asked.

"I don't know, ma'am," Bethany lied. "Maybe she took 'em with her?"

The woman nodded, her face sour. "Typical. No one here can keep up with keys." She opened her middle desk drawer and pulled out a large ring holding thirty or more keys, each labeled. She removed two from the ring and handed them to Bethany. "Don't bother to return them," she said. "I have several more sets."

"Thank you so much," Bethany said. Another moron. Anyone could have taken those keys. She called Rob and reported what she'd learned.

"Thanks, Bethany. That helps. I'll tell Jonathan, and he can give the information to Sebastian Grant. The whole office had access to the tools and to the chairman's office. That doesn't clear Dinah, but it could mean reasonable doubt. I'm still trying to figure out how to make the police investigate Naomi Skinner. I've told several cops about how she had good reason for wanting Patti Sue out of the way, but they've ignored me."

⁓

Ted hovered outside Hunt's office until Hunt couldn't stand it any longer and called him to come in. "The police are closing in on Dinah Greene," Ted said. "They found her tool kit in her office here, and her tools were used to loosen the shelves."

Hunt, astonished, turned to look at Ted. "And after she loosened the shelves, she left the tools here?"

Ted shrugged. "The office was locked, and so was the cabinet where the tools were kept. But that's not all: Naomi Skinner cleaned out Frannie's office, and Frannie had twenty or thirty master pass cards in an unlocked drawer. Anyone could have taken them. Anyone could have gotten in this office."

"What an idiot that Johnson woman was. Are you saying Dinah Greene might have taken one of those cards?"

"Yep. The police now have two more pieces of information they needed. They've identified the tools that were used to loosen the shelves and learned that Dinah Greene not only had access to them, she used them all the time. Her tools are definitely the murder weapons and they know how she could have got in your office. I bet there's an arrest soon, maybe as early as tomorrow," Ted said.

"Maybe so," Hunt said. But the story didn't make sense. Dinah Greene was smart. If she'd used those tools to kill someone, surely she wouldn't have left them behind. If they didn't belong to her, he'd think they were planted, that someone was trying to frame her. But they *were* hers. She'd brought them in herself. On the other hand, if Dinah had access to the master pass cards, so did everyone in the office.

Forty-One

When Rachel telephoned Tuesday afternoon, Dinah almost failed to recognize her voice: Rachel, the most controlled person she knew, sounded excited.

"The Stubbs paintings are here! They are for sale in the Dulaney Gallery on Cork Street. My friend at the British Portrait Gallery has an appointment to look at them, and I invited myself to accompany him. I inquired about their history, and the story is rather odd: the seller prefers to remain anonymous and will supply provenance only to the purchaser. But Dulaney is a respectable gallery and would not knowingly handle stolen goods. The gallery received the paintings in January but was asked not to show them until March. My friend thought perhaps it had to do with taxes. If I sense a quick sale in the offing, what should I do?"

"If you think they're about to be sold, do anything you can to stop it, and call us. But otherwise, don't do anything. We don't want to spook the thief. Thank you, thank you, thank you, dear friend," Dinah said.

"I am enjoying being involved. You must tell me more. I am very curious about those paintings. And Dinah, you are the first to know—except for Heyward Bain, who is an angel—I am free of Simon. I now own 100 percent of the Ransome Gallery."

Dinah congratulated Rachel and called Coleman. After exclaiming over the discovery of DDD&W's Stubbs paintings in London, Coleman wanted to know how Bain had freed Rachel from Simon, but Dinah didn't know the details.

"I'd never have believed it," Coleman said. "I bet it cost Heyward plenty."

"But even with a lot of money to pay him off, getting rid of Simon was a miracle. He's a parasite—he's fed on Rachel for years, he'd be hard to detach. Rachel says Heyward is an angel. I am so embarrassed when I think how much I disliked him when we met..."

"I know," Coleman said. "And I still haven't thanked him for helping my dream come true." Or almost come true. She longed to tell Dinah about her difficulties with Colossus, but Dinah's problems were so much more serious, Coleman couldn't bring herself to add to her cousin's worries.

Forty-Two

Sebastian Grant was in a state his associates rarely saw: stymied. He was also in a tearing rage. He'd telephoned everyone he knew in the higher ranks of the NYPD, repeating what he'd heard about Harrison. To a man, they'd said "Got proof?" But the incriminating information had come from a retired cop. He couldn't give them the guy's name. His fellow officers would annihilate him for ratting out another cop.

He started over, calling everyone again. This time, he insisted that the *department* investigate Harrison. "If he turns out to be corrupt, and you haven't even bothered to look into my allegations, I'll see you all over the front page of the *New York Times!*" he shouted into the phone.

"You're making up this stuff because he's gonna arrest your client," said one of the cops he was threatening. "We'll investigate, but it'll be so slow, your client will be in jail long before we've made the first call."

Grant slammed down the phone and called the deputy mayor he knew best. But city hall wasn't buying it either. "We can't look like we're yielding to pressure because Dinah Greene is connected. The mayor's had a dozen calls about her—they all say she's a saint, first cousin to the Virgin Mary. Maybe so, but she's also a murder suspect. Get her out of the frame, and I'll see that Harrison is investigated. But that's the order it's got to happen in—clear her, and we'll check him out." The deputy mayor hung up before Grant could reply.

Grant left for the gym to work off his fury. He'd get that bastard Harrison yet. When he'd cooled down and his mind had cleared, he telephoned Jonathan. He had a plan. They didn't call him the Cobra for no reason.

"Why don't *we* investigate Harrison?" Grant said. "The police should clean up their own house, but to hell with them. We'll do it for them, and get plenty of proof. We won't tell the bureaucrats until we have everything we need on Harrison and can nail him to the wall. We probably should have done it earlier, but I don't think we could have turned up anything without the tip from Rob's buddy about Harrison's moonlighting at DDD&W. Who'd have thought it? Let's start with the Fry Building and persuade the guards to tell us what they know."

Jonathan didn't hesitate. "I'll call Greg Fry, and get Rob's people on it right away."

At last, a breakthrough and much bigger than Rob had anticipated: the lobby guards admitted that they knew Harrison worked for DDD&W and reported to Oscar Danbury. Yes, they'd agreed to call him about any incidents involving DDD&W. Yes, they'd called him when Frances Johnson was killed. They didn't see anything wrong with it; still didn't—until Fry's head of security set them straight. Two guards were fired and the others were left wiser and more attentive to their duties, which included discretion.

The men had often seen Harrison with his sweetie, Trixie, who worked in the DDD&W cafeteria and dining room. She'd been tight with Frannie Johnson and Patti Sue Victor. Because of Trixie, Harrison spent a lot of time with the sisters. Another piece of the puzzle fell into place: the sisters had blackened Dinah to Harrison even before he met her—Dinah was the enemy, and Harrison's expensive girlfriend was Trixie of the large bosom and fat-making food.

Now the brass would *have* to act. Rob faxed his notes to Sebastian Grant and called his friend at One Police Plaza and explained about the keys to Dinah's office and file cabinet. Rob went on to tell his friend about the key cards found in Johnson's desk during a DDD&W cleanup. Anyone could have borrowed Dinah's tools. Anyone could have unlocked the managing director's office. His friend agreed. The search was wide open. He'd alert the police.

"If Ms. Greene is innocent, I'm beginning to doubt we'll ever get the murderer. Everybody in the place could get in everywhere. Their security is nonexistent," Rob's friend said.

"What about alibis?" Rob asked.

"Harrison and Quintero say your client is the only person without an alibi. They say that's what's keeping Ms. Greene in the frame."

"I see," Rob said. But he didn't believe it. After they replaced Harrison, everything would have to be rechecked—this time, he hoped, by unbiased detectives. With the information on the easy access to both Dinah's and Hunt Frederick's offices, the search for the killer would have to be broadened. But a cloud still hung over Dinah's head. If only they could discover the identity of the killer before everyone in town heard that she was—or had been—a prime suspect in a police investigation.

Forty-Three

Early Wednesday morning

Rob had been awake for hours, tossing and turning—worrying about Dinah, about his business, his workload, and Coleman—when the phone rang. He had the sinking feeling that late night or early morning calls always inspired: the news was bound to be bad. When he heard the voice of his friend at One Police Plaza, he was sure of it.

"Rob, there's been another murder at DDD&W."

"Oh my God," Rob groaned. "Who was killed? Don't tell me it was one of the Greene Gallery women?"

"No, Patti Sue Victor, the sister of the first victim. They found her body an hour ago. She died around midnight Tuesday. She'd been hit on the head and then shoved down an elevator shaft. She might have died from the fall, but in any case, when the elevator went down again, it crushed her. You better hope Ms. Greene has an alibi for late last night. If she doesn't, the DDD&W crowd will be sure to say Greene shoved Victor down that elevator shaft."

"Okay. Thanks for the heads-up. I won't forget it."

When Rob called Jonathan at home, the answering machine picked up. He left a message for Jonathan or Dinah to call him and tried Coleman, who was instantly awake and horrified by the news of a second murder at DDD&W.

"Oh, no. I can't believe it. Jonathan stayed in Boston last night—he's probably still there. I don't think the first morning shuttle to New York leaves Boston until six. Dinah was alone again. It was another setup. Who knew Jonathan would be in Boston overnight?" she asked.

"I don't know. *I* didn't. I knew he went to Boston, but I assumed he came home last night. Will you call Dinah? I didn't get past her answering machine. And see if Loretta and Bethany have alibis, will you? I want to make sure they don't come under suspicion. I have to call Sebastian Grant, and I'll try to reach Jonathan on his cell phone," Rob said.

Coleman dreaded telling Dinah about Patti Sue's death and discussing her lack of an alibi. She put off calling her and tried Bethany, who was at Zeke's. Bethany was stunned to hear about Patti Sue's death. She had an alibi: she'd been with Zeke since the previous afternoon.

"Zeke and Loretta and I left DDD&W around four thirty. We had a quick drink at Hennessey's on

Lexington at Sixtieth. That's where we parted company. We put Loretta in a taxi—she was headed uptown to visit friends. I think she planned to stay overnight. I have their number; she's been stayin' there a lot. Zeke and I ate dinner here at the apartment—his cook was here. She'll alibi me. I spent the night. Zeke can vouch for me. The doormen, too, I guess," Bethany said.

Coleman reached Loretta at her friends' apartment, where she'd been since she left Bethany and Zeke. They'd watched videos and ordered pizza, and everyone was in bed by midnight. Loretta had slept on a bunk bed in a room with three other girls. Her alibi, like Bethany's, was solid. Coleman e-mailed the information to Rob, and, bracing herself, called Dinah.

Dinah, in tears, was incredulous. "*Why* is this happening? I'm almost never alone at night, and this has happened twice when Jonathan was away. They'll never prove I did it, because I didn't, but I can't prove I didn't do it. I was home. It's just like before: I walked the dog about nine o'clock, came in, locked up and was in bed by nine thirty. But there was no one here to swear I stayed in," she said.

Would Dinah feel worse or better if Coleman told her what she was thinking? Maybe Coleman should have mentioned her suspicions earlier, but suspicions were all she'd had. She still had no proof, but she had to speak up. "I'm sure someone knew Jonathan was away, and used that information to implicate you," Coleman said. "Who knew Jonathan was spending the night in Boston?"

"I didn't tell anyone but you," Dinah said.

"Would anyone at Jonathan's office have known?"

"I doubt it. Jonathan left Blair's number with me in case of an emergency. I don't think he'd have told anyone else he planned to spend the night in Boston, leaving me alone. He's very security conscious."

"I've been trying to figure out who could have known you were alone the night Frances Johnson was killed," Coleman said. "I've hesitated to tell you what I concluded, because I know how much you like and trust the person I believe is responsible for leaking the information. One person who knew Jonathan would be away both times was your driver."

"Oh, Coleman, don't be ridiculous," Dinah said. "Tom's totally trustworthy. He's a former policeman."

"Exactly," Coleman said. "*Because* he was a cop, he may know Harrison and Quintero, or talk to people who know them. Where's Tom now?"

"Probably waiting for Jonathan at the airport. You want me to call and ask him? I will, but it's a waste of time."

"Humor me," Coleman said.

"I'll call him, but you're wrong," Dinah insisted.

೧

Five minutes later, Dinah, sobbing and nearly hysterical, reported that Tom *was* the leak about Jonathan's overnight absences. "He hangs out at a cops' bar in the West Forties—sees Harrison and Quintero there all the time. They introduced themselves. They were together almost every night. They could tell cop stories. And, Coleman, I think I'm responsible for their looking him up. When they first interviewed me, I told them our driver was a retired policeman, gave them his name and number. Tom didn't know Harrison was after me or that he moonlighted for DDD&W. He says he can't swear he told them about Jonathan's travels, but he 'probably' did. He didn't have much to talk about. He didn't realize there was anything secret about our activities."

"Did the police interview Tom about your comings and goings?" Coleman said.

"He says he was interviewed over the phone by somebody he didn't know. He doesn't remember the man's name."

"I bet they had someone he didn't know talk to him so he wouldn't connect Harrison and Quintero with the DDD&W investigation," Coleman said.

"Maybe so. I'd never have believed Tom could be so indiscreet," Dinah said.

"I'm sorry, Dinah. I was pretty sure it was going to work out this way. I thought about it a lot, and I couldn't see how anyone else would know Jonathan's plans."

"Well, I thought Tom was totally trustworthy. I thought he was my friend. Just one more blow. Like I thought Hunt was a nice man—a gentleman," Dinah said.

"We all make mistakes about people. What are you doing today?"

"I don't know. Wait for Jonathan to come home. Mope."

"Would you like to do some sleuthing? I have an idea I planned to discuss with Rob but I haven't wanted to call him. I'd rather have you check it out.

"Really? What is it?" Dinah had stopped crying.

"We've been assuming the killer at DDD&W is a man. But there's no reason it couldn't be a woman. What if it's one of the creepy females we've encountered there?"

"How would I check on them?"

"Start by calling Rob. Ask if anyone has checked on the hairspray woman. Or that skeleton who works for Ted. Or even the Gray Lady. Just because she looks like everyone's ideal grandmother doesn't mean she isn't a baddy. Rob should suggest some ways of finding out about them."

"Oh, Coleman! That's a great idea! I'll let you know later today how I'm doing."

∽

But when Dinah called several hours later, she reported that Rob was sure all the DDD&W women had been cleared of suspicion. None had records, and all had alibis. She sounded more depressed than ever, and Coleman was sorry she had suggested that her cousin try to help with the investigation. She wished she was confident that Rob had done a thorough check on the women at DDD&W. She no longer trusted Rob's investigative work.

Forty-Four

Coleman stared at the letter. As Jonathan had prophesied, the would-be buyers of *ArtSmart* and *First Home* hadn't given up. The second letter was signed by Roger Black, Executive Vice President, Mergers and Acquisitions, Colossus Publishing. He described the disadvantages of being small: Coleman's two "little" magazines had no purchasing clout for paper, or printing, or anything else. When her "little" company was part of Colossus, she would be able to get anything she needed. He used the word "little" in every sentence.

The threat was obvious. If Colossus Publishing owned her magazines, management would make sure she got the supplies and services she needed. If she tried to remain independent, they'd see that she faced shortages, even cutoffs from suppliers. She might be forced out of business. Before that happened, she'd *have* to sell, and probably at a rock-bottom price. She was certain Colossus had the power to do what they threatened. But why would they? Surely she was too small a fish to warrant so much attention from the biggest shark in the publishing world.

She put her questions to Jonathan in a cover note when she faxed the letter to him. When he called back a few minutes later, he sounded even more worried than he had been when last they spoke.

"I'm so sorry about this. I thought they might come back, but the threatening tone of the letter is unusually unpleasant. You threaten them—they think if they let you reject them, they'd set a bad precedent. All they do is take over organizations like yours. Very few of their serious targets have escaped. They're a monster merger machine. They're in the bully pulpit, and intend to remain in it," he said.

"But I don't want to sell. How did the few that escaped do it?" Coleman asked.

"You won't like the only possible solution. You'll have to find another powerful organization—what's called a 'white knight'—and sell to them. You'll still lose control of your magazines, but to somebody who is more congenial, and who'll let you keep a minority share. But they'll definitely be in charge," Jonathan said.

"Either way I lose my magazines," Coleman said. She'd never felt so helpless, so trapped.

"You know what you should do? Ask Heyward Bain for help," Jonathan said.

"Why him? What can he do that you can't?" Coleman said, annoyed. Was this another ploy to make her get in touch with her half-brother? Jonathan avoided his own ghastly relations whenever it was possible, but like everyone else, seemed determined to see her involved with Bain. She already owed so much to Bain, she felt awkward about asking him for help.

"He can do plenty. This is not my kind of banking, Coleman. A battle to fight off a hostile takeover is a specialty. Bain's a billionaire with an international reputation for winning any battle he enters. Colossus might back off just knowing he's involved."

"I can't call him. He gave me all this money, and I've never even thanked him properly. Can't you find someone else?" Coleman asked.

"I'll try, but I doubt if I can get you a deal you'll like," he said.

When Coleman hung up, she was near despair. She'd been so thrilled with the acquisition of *First Home*. Now it seemed she might lose everything. If Jonathan was right, she'd have to beg her half-brother for help. She'd never had to beg; she'd always managed to take care of herself. And she'd lose her magazines anyway—Heyward would be in control. For the moment, all she could do was wait to hear from Jonathan. She didn't do waiting well.

Forty-Five

London

Heyward Bain's library was the first public room the decorators had completed. He'd asked for an oasis where he could work while the rest of the house was finished, and the decorators had selected the library because they could complete it quickly. The walnut paneling had needed only polishing; the Oriental rugs and the furniture were antiques, requiring cleaning and minor restoration. The scent of the blue hyacinths in the blue-and-white Chinese pot on the coffee table added the perfect final touch. But the room's serenity and beauty seemed to increase his restlessness.

When he'd moved to London, he'd thought that after his busy and stressful months in New York, he'd enjoy a quiet life. He'd lived as a recluse for many contented and productive years. But now that he had the peace he'd sought, he couldn't seem to concentrate. Simon's incarceration in the clinic in Switzerland was part of the problem. Not that he missed Simon—far from it. Living with Simon would be intolerable. But Heyward felt duty bound to visit the poor wretch every weekend, and the tedium of those weekends was beyond belief. Simon was a bore, with no interests except himself and money. Why he hadn't seen that sooner was a mystery. Heyward's brief infatuation with Simon had been expensive in ways more important than money. Simon had cost Heyward the esteem of people he admired.

He wanted Simon out of his life, but he couldn't abandon him in his current physical condition, nor could he ignore Simon's financial situation. Simon had been beaten badly by a lover he had cheated and, because of his battered hands, couldn't even sign a check. He had given Heyward power of attorney, probably thinking Heyward would pay all his debts. Not a chance. He was paying Simon's expenses in Switzerland, but when he emerged from the clinic, Simon would have almost nothing left of the small fortune he'd illegally amassed. Simon had owed every penny of that money and more to Rachel Ransome, for whom he had worked. He'd repaid all she'd done for him by stealing from her. Of course, Simon had also treated Heyward badly, but Heyward, unlike Rachel, could afford the losses, and Simon's perfidy had set Heyward free. Or nearly free. Heyward was taking steps to rid himself completely of Simon, but it was slow going.

Heyward had settled Simon's debts to Rachel, partly with his own money, and partly by arranging for Rachel to buy back Simon's interest in the Ransome gallery for almost nothing. Because of what Heyward had done to make amends both on his own and on Simon's account, Rachel and he had come to an understanding, perhaps the beginning of a friendship. If so, Rachel might be his only friend in London. Maybe his only friend anywhere.

Of the others to whom he'd insisted that Simon was a good person, and that everyone who disliked and mistrusted him was wrong, only Rob Mondelli seemed willing to forget Heyward's mistakes. Heyward had enjoyed his recent London dinner with Rob. It had been good to have news of Coleman, Dinah, and Jonathan. He wished *they* were his friends. But he didn't see how he could do more than he had done to win them over.

He walked to the window and stared out at Zachary Square. The mild weather, the yellow daffodils and pale pink and white blossoms on the fruit trees in the square should have cheered him, but all he felt was an unfamiliar emptiness. Could he be lonely? Surely not. He'd always been alone and had long ago come to accept it. When he felt sorry for himself, he had worked: inventing, investing, writing. He'd published six successful books, fiction and nonfiction, under pseudonyms, and by the time he was twelve, he'd made millions from his inventions, mostly devices to help people stop smoking, or to improve the quality of air corrupted by cigarette smoke—air cleaning filters and the like.

His empire was far larger and more diversified than anyone knew, and his riches far greater, even after he'd settled a fortune on his half-sister to try to atone for her impoverished childhood, a childhood he could have made better, if he hadn't been so self-centered. He sighed. He neither needed nor wanted more money, but until recently, he'd found intellectual challenge in making it. For the first time in his life, he couldn't think of anything he wanted to do.

The intercom buzzed. He frowned. He'd asked not to be disturbed. It was unlike his staff to ignore instructions. "Yes, Hicks? What is it?"

"Jonathan Hathaway is calling from New York. He says it's an emergency."

He grabbed the phone. "Jonathan, what is it? Has something happened to Coleman?"

"Coleman is okay, at least physically. I apologize for bothering you. I wouldn't have called if I could have figured out anything else to do. Colossus Publishing is trying to take over Coleman's magazines—she asked me to find a white knight, but her two magazines are fairly small, and no one's interested—"

Heyward interrupted. "I understand. I'll come at once. Coleman is my sister, and this is my fight."

"I have to warn you: I couldn't persuade her to ask you for help. She's embarrassed because you've done so much for her, and she hasn't thanked you properly—"

"Never mind all that. Will you have someone e-mail me everything you have on her magazines and Colossus's approaches?"

"Of course. But Heyward, another thing—I might have been able to help Coleman more if I hadn't been preoccupied with another problem: Dinah's been accused of murder, and I've been told she could be arrested. But even if she isn't arrested, her reputation could be ruined."

"Nonsense. That's ridiculous," Heyward said.

Jonathan sighed. "You sound like my friend Blair Winthrop. That's almost exactly what he said."

"I know Blair. He's nearly always right. For that matter, so am I. On Dinah, we agree—anyone who thinks she's a killer is insane. As for Coleman, I'll be in New York tomorrow morning. You can dismiss Coleman's problems from your mind; consider everything taken care of. And I will do all I can to help Dinah," Heyward said.

"Do you know anyone at DDD&W? I think they're trying to frame Dinah," Jonathan said.

"I know of them. At one time they had a good reputation, but in the last few years, it's declined. While your office is e-mailing, ask them to send me everything you have on DDD&W."

"Rob's done a lot of investigating—"

"Send me whatever he's turned up, too. You never know—I might know someone, or think of something. I'll see you tomorrow, Jonathan."

Heyward was rarely angry, but this was too much. Damn those pirates at Colossus. They'd rue the day they attacked his sister. And what were those idiots at DDD&W thinking? Dinah Greene was incapable of taking home an office-owned pencil, let alone murder. His family and friends were in trouble. But not for much longer.

What an extraordinary feeling: his sister needed him. Well, Coleman didn't know it yet, but she could relax. He'd deal with Colossus. He'd wanted a project that intrigued him, and this one certainly did. His mind was already working overtime.

He pressed the intercom. "Hicks? Come in, please. I need to speak to every executive who works for HB Enterprises. Set up a conference call, and ask your assistant to make our travel arrangements. Get the two of us on a British Airways flight to New York tomorrow morning—the one that leaves around eight or nine and gets in before lunch."

Hicks tried to speak, but Heyward didn't have time for questions.

"Ask Mrs. Carter to pack for me. Tell her I don't need much—I have clothes at the house in New York. She hasn't been my housekeeper long, but she's sensible, she'll know what to pack." He was making notes on the pad on his desk while he talked.

"Yessir," Hicks said.

"We have a crisis on our hands. Colossus Publishing is attacking Coleman. They're after her magazines. They'll do their usual—strip them, destroy them, keep a few people, a few ideas, ruin the magazines and expand their reach a little. We'll get rid of Colossus and make sure she's armed against any other pirates.

"You and nearly everyone else in the London office will come with me to New York. Leave a skeleton staff here to answer the phones, deal with the mail, or any emergency. I want you on the plane with me, but scatter the others around—no more than two on the same flight, this afternoon or tonight, or at the latest tomorrow. Put everyone up at the Sherry Netherland or the Pierre—I want them within walking distance of my house. Ask your assistant to call the house, and let Horace know I'm coming so he can prepare for my arrival. They'll need to order food, and get some additional help—we'll have a lot going on. And I want our real estate people on the phone—I don't care what time it is. I want to buy a building in New York, and I want to do it fast."

Forty-Six

When the plane took off from Heathrow Thursday morning, Hicks was still trying to talk Bain out of his plans. "Mr. Bain, I can't understand why you want to enter the publishing business. It's an unattractive industry—low margins, highly competitive, many failures, in consolidation. Book sales are declining, bookstores closing, and publishers are laying off employees. Magazines disappear daily. And you want a vertically integrated company? There are difficulties with that strategy—at least one major company, Carsen Publishing, apparently went under trying it—"

"Yes, I know," Heyward said. "We'll do it differently. Coleman will be in charge of publishing the two magazines, which she already owns. I've investigated them and I'm confident about their future. She has two perfect niches: *ArtSmart*, the top magazine in the art world, and *First Home* is perfect for her talents—its mission is how to save money without sacrificing style. I'll acquire whatever's needed for the manufacturing side of the business and run it myself until I can find a CEO to take over. Or maybe I'll enjoy running it and decide to continue as CEO."

Hicks shook his head. "Where's the growth? Where are the profits? I don't see the advantages of integration."

"The problem with a fully integrated publishing company is that the tail wags the dog: so many people work in manufacturing, data processing, and so on, and so much money is tied up in equipment that manufacturing overpowers the creative side and eventually runs the magazines into failure. We won't make that mistake. The two sides of the publishing business are totally different and require different talents. Production can't be dominant. As I said, we'll run the two parts of the business separately. I'll take over the production side of Coleman's business with a company I'll control with 51 percent ownership, and my sister will own 49 percent. That will give her plenty of incentive to use our paper and other materials and services. She'll keep her magazines and concentrate on what she does best: hiring writers, selecting articles, writing and editing, dealing with the art world, and the decorating and homemaking worlds. It's her talent that will make the magazines a success."

Hicks nodded, but he didn't look happy.

"As for the other side of the business, we'll buy a paper mill and a printer, and modernize them. I have ideas for improving the papermaking system, raising the standards for air and water purity, and making paper mills more attractive to nearby communities.

My work in cleaning up tobacco smoke will be useful in dealing with the sulfurous smell of the fumes the paper industry produces. Every time I've been on the coast of North or South Carolina or Louisiana or Mississippi, I've encountered that repellent odor, blown by the wind to the beaches. It's a problem in a beach resort like Kiawah, South Carolina, where people come to play golf and tennis and relax. They want to lounge on the porches of their multimillion-dollar houses, swim in their pools, and breathe in the salty scent of the ocean, the green smell of newly cut grass, and the sweetness of the honeysuckle and magnolias, not rotten eggs."

Hicks perked up. "You'll invent again?"

Heyward smiled to himself. Hicks knew how much money Bain's inventions brought in, and he'd been trying to persuade Bain to return to inventing. "Why not? There's not a lot of scope for my antitobacco activities these days. Most developed countries have stopped their citizens from killing themselves with cigarettes, and there's very little I can accomplish in the countries that still permit smoking.

"I've been thinking about testing some of my ideas on a new industry, and this is the perfect opportunity. We'll own and run everything, from the forests through the printing, and we'll be able to study the industry from every perspective. We'll cut costs while we make everything greener. Coleman will always be our most important client, but we'll take on others, too. I'm sure we can make a success of it, but we have to move fast. Pay what you must, but get what we need as quickly as you can. I don't want to give anyone time to get in my way."

Heyward sipped the black coffee the flight attendant had brought him, while serving huge English breakfasts to most of the other passengers. "The most important technical developments in paper manufacturing in the late twentieth and early twenty-first century have occurred in Asia and Europe. Put together a team to research major breakthroughs abroad. Hire the people to do the research, or work with an investment banker, or a consultant—I don't care—just get me information on what's going on where. We may have to hire some overseas paper-making experts to help us get started. Find out who's good and who might be available. Don't worry about the cost."

Heyward took several magazines from his brief-case and handed them to Hicks. "Here are the most recent issues of *ArtSmart* and *First Home*. Ask someone to analyze them for their physical properties, paper size and quality—that kind of thing. What do Coleman's magazines have in common physically? Page size? Paper quality? How do they differ? Can we standardize them? You know what to look for. I think magazine publishing should be a real business—one that makes money. Remember all those stories about this or that magazine that burned money until the owner closed it down? Ridiculous."

"This project will be expensive," Hicks warned. "You may end up burning money, too."

Heyward laughed. "Not a chance. I promise you: in time, we'll coin gold."

"What about this building you want to buy?"

"That's a top priority. I've asked our real estate people to contact the Fishley Brothers' office, and ask Reuben Fishley to sell me the Third Avenue building where *ArtSmart*'s offices are. It's not much of a building, so I doubt if the Fishleys will care; it's probably scheduled for eventual demolition and replacement. When we get to New York, I want you to make the sale happen. Tell the Fishleys I'll be grateful if they'll let me have it—explain that I want it for family reasons. I'll pay their asking price, and I'll also owe them a favor. We should be able to work out something about demolition and replacement when the time comes. If it's going to take long to finalize the sale, ask if I can lease the building immediately. Check on available office space in the building, see if I can move in fast. I want to take possession as soon as possible. We'll work out of my house till we have office space.

"Now to the entertaining part: my other priority is taking out Colossus. I don't think that will be difficult," Heyward said.

"Got it. Which banker will deal with Colossus?" Hicks asked.

"Jeb Middleton—my friend, Jeb the Reb—I don't think you've met him. I called him and put him in touch with Jonathan. We're going to lock in supplies for Coleman, to make sure Colossus can't shut her down. Jeb's a South Carolina Middleton, but he was a poor relation and went through Harvard with scholarships and a lot of hard work, including waiting on tables and bartending. He graduated from Harvard Business School at the top of his class, and he's one of the best bankers I've ever met. He's also got deep-South manners, and could charm a mockingbird out of a tree.

"When you meet him, don't let his low-key style deceive you. He can come across as half-asleep. When the opposition relaxes, he pounces. He worked for Morgan & Morgan until he went out on his own. As soon as I heard he was available, I retained him. There's no one I'd rather have on my side. I'll ask him to help with the paper and printing businesses, too."

Heyward took some more papers out of his brief-case. "Now for a new topic: Coleman's cousin Dinah is suspected of murder. Have a look at these and see what you think."

Twenty minutes later, Hicks looked up. "I don't see how we can help, do you?"

"Maybe. I'll have to think about it a little more, talk to Jonathan again. I'm intrigued by the missing Stubbs paintings, and the missing heiresses."

Forty-Seven

Thursday

Coleman had put aside her own and Dinah's problems and was reading an article submitted by a decorator for *First Home* when her private line rang.

"Coleman, this is Heyward. Your white knight has arrived," he said.

"Oh, I'm sorry Jonathan bothered you—I asked him not to—I already owe you so much—"

"You mustn't think I'm doing this just as a favor to you. I've been looking for a new project, and this one fascinates me. We'll get rid of Colossus, and then we'll get to the interesting part."

Yeah, right. What was interesting about the magazine business, except her job? Did *he* plan to take over her magazines, too? "Which is the interesting part?" Coleman asked.

"I'm interested in the manufacturing part of the business—the printing, the papermaking, the physical side of putting it all together. If you're free, Andrew Hicks—he's my assistant; I don't think you've met him—and I can brief you on what we plan to do. We'll come to your office, if that's okay with you?"

Two hours later, Coleman escorted her brother and Hicks to the elevators, her head spinning. Tree plantations. Odorless paper processing. New technology imported from Europe. Restoring the US paper industry. When she'd realized that Heyward had no desire to be involved in the creative side of the business—*her* business—she'd relaxed and listened. She didn't doubt he could do what he said he could. She'd seen Heyward the Genius at work, and she was awed. He was Jack the Giant Killer; George the Dragon Slayer.

When he'd completed his explanation, Heyward suggested that she let him take charge of everything to do with Colossus. When she hesitated, he said, "In your next letter, they'll tell you your paper supplier will no longer sell you paper. Don't panic: we've locked up enough paper to keep your magazines supplied for years. Same with your printers. You'll have to trust me, Coleman. Think of it as a chess game. I'll anticipate their every move, and I'll always be ahead of them, no matter what they do. Ignore their letters. When you get mail from Colossus, don't open it—have it delivered to me or Hicks. Your messenger won't have far to go. I've taken over the penthouse in this building."

"You have? Wow! That was quick. Okay, Colossus is all yours. If I can forget about those creeps, I can concentrate on revamping *First Home*—which is what I want to do more than anything. Thanks again, Heyward."

She didn't much like the idea of letting Heyward fight her battles—she'd expected that they'd work together to defeat Colossus—but another letter from Colossus had arrived today, and if she read it, she'd worry instead of work. She knew she didn't have the expertise or the money to take on a huge, rich predatory company. Letting Heyward deal with Colossus was comparable to trusting Jonathan with financial matters. She was confident Heyward was at least as knowledgeable about whatever he undertook as Jonathan was in finance.

She might as well turn over Amy's reports to Heyward, too—no point in reading that stuff if Heyward or one of his people would do it for her. She packed the gray binders Amy's team had put together with the letter from Colossus and asked a passing intern to take the box upstairs to the penthouse.

She called Dinah to tell her Heyward was in town, and asked if Dinah would invite him to dinner, too. The more the merrier, Dinah said—or at least, the more distracting. She'd phone him herself. She'd already spoken to Rob, and he was coming.

Coleman's phone rang again. This time it was the receptionist.

"Coleman, something's going on in the lobby. One of the guys downstairs called to say the building's been sold. People moving everything, changing signs. Do you know what's happening?"

Coleman was horrified. Colossus must have bought the building—Heyward was too late. She and her magazines were about to be evicted! She dialed her brother. "Heyward? This building's been sold—what? You did? I do? Good Heavens. I can hardly wait to see the sign."

She hung up and spoke to Dolly. "Guess what? Heyward bought the building. The new sign downstairs reads CH Holdings. The C is me! Can you believe it? Let's go look at it." She grabbed Dolly's leash, and the two of them rushed to the elevator.

She stared at the sign, trying to let it sink in: she was part-owner of a Manhattan building. Back upstairs, she called Dinah to share the news.

"*Who-oo-ee.* You are some lucky girl," Dinah said.

Coleman agreed (although she feared there was still a long way to go before Colossus gave up and went away). She asked about the progress of the print hanging.

"They could have finished today, but they're dragging things out so they can be around Friday morning to see the so-called Stubbs," Dinah said.

"After they see them, I hope they'll pick up the check and run," Coleman said.

Forty-Eight

As soon as he looked at the binders Amy gave Coleman, and compared them to his study of Colossus's activities, Hicks realized what was going on: the DDD&W team recommended this or that supplier to Coleman, but before she could evaluate their suggestions, let alone implement them, Colossus took the recommended suppliers out of play. If Amy and her associates listed "must hires" in *First Home*'s accounting or marketing departments, Colossus hired the stars before Coleman received the relevant DDD&W reports. Someone at DDD&W was leaking information to Colossus.

Hicks took his evidence to Bain's office, where Bain and Jeb were discussing the paper business. After he'd described his discovery, Hicks added, "Miss Coleman may be missing out on some good people, but what's more important is that what they're doing is illegal—DDD&W is supplying, and Colossus Publishing is using, inside information.

Somebody ought to put a stop to it. What I don't get is why Colossus is being so obvious about it."

"I think they want Coleman to know that they have access to her consultants, to information that should be privileged. They think they can undermine her confidence, and she'll crumble, give them what they want. They want to make her believe she can't even trust an old friend like Amy Rothman," Heyward said.

"*Can* Amy Rothman be trusted? Maybe she's supplying Colossus," Hicks said.

"What do you think?" Heyward asked Jeb. "You know a lot of Wall Street people. Do you know her?"

Jeb nodded. "Yes, I know Amy, and she's a straight arrow, never heard a bad thing about her. I reckon Moose is the mastermind of this little scheme. He left his last job because he wasn't made head of investment bankin'—he wanted more status, and a lot more money. He needs money bad. Keeps gettin' married, keeps gettin' divorced. Expensive hobby. His new wife is a spendin' champion. She pays more for clothes in a year than Portugal's GNP. He was promised big money at DDD&W, but it was all on the come. He's entitled to a hunk of the profits, but the business hasn't gone nearly as well as he expected, and there *are* no profits. Poor ole Moose must have needed money bad, and spotted a way to get some. What a dope."

Heyward looked amused. "Do you know everyone's secrets?"

Jeb laughed. "Pretty much, if they're players. It goes with the game. You got to know street gossip. Who're you interested in?"

"What about Hunt Austin Frederick?" Heyward asked.

Jeb shrugged. "Hunt Austin Frederick's richer than most people on the Forbes list—he's got a lot of cattle to go with his hats. All those names he's sportin' are tellin' us he's kin to every millionaire in Texas, and he's got a piece of ever'thing that makes money in the whole dang state. If he's into wrong-doin', it sure ain't cause he needs money. He ain't been in New York long, which prob'ly means he's innocent of anything at DDD&W in New York, but what with phones and e-mails and such, I reckon he could have been runnin' things from anywhere. Only why would he steal? What's his motive?

"Back to Moose; I reckon he is usin' one or two of those little pissants that tote his briefcase to do the dirty work."

"Are they likely to be using inside information for stock trading, too?" Hicks asked.

"I wouldn't be surprised. Moose has always been a speculator. As for who else is mixed up in his rack-et, I think we can eliminate some of 'em," Jeb said.

"Who?" Heyward asked.

"That creep Leichter is so beat down by his father-in-law, he can barely breathe. I hear he's one for the ladies, but since he couldn't afford to buy a woman a hot dawg off a street cart, he's said to stick to the company ink, so he can pay off his girlfriends with office favors. He's prob'ly stealin' paper clips, and messin' around with any female that'll have him, but that's it.

"Oscar Danbury is a genuine lunatic. He could be up to anything, includin' this. He'd steal if he got a chance. He thinks somebody's going to kidnap him or somethin'—got bars in every window of his house, and a bank vault full of gold in case of the revolution. You've heard about his parlor trick?" Jeb asked.

Heyward held up his hand. "Yes, yes, spare us. I already know too much about that disgusting creature. Who else?"

"No other big-time players at DDD&W. Featherweights. Paper pushers. Small-town boys who should have stayed there," Jeb said.

"How do you think the information is transferred?" Hicks asked.

"Nothin' easier. I'm bettin' every word DDD&W produces is computerized, and that there's no security. One of Moose's Merry Men digs into any files Moose is interested in, gives the information to Moose, and Moose takes it to Colossus, and they pay big for it," Jeb said.

Hicks raised his eyebrows. "That simple? I'm surprised it doesn't happen more often."

Jeb shrugged again. "Maybe other DDD&W clients are also buyin' inside information from 'em. But it don't happen in most companies cause you can go to jail for it. The feds and the New York Attorney General have been puttin' away a lot of folks for insider trading, and they'll be glad to catch a few more. I'm sure Moose will end up in jail, and he'll take a bunch of others with him, includin' his helpers at Colossus," Jeb said.

"What do we do about it?" Hicks asked.

"We-ell," Jeb drawled. "I think I should have a chat with Rick Oliver. Remember him? The banker who first contacted Miss Coleman? I reckon he's a pawn, but I'll make sure he's out of the game, and that he tells Colossus all about us. It's time to let the pirates know who the good guys are, and just how much we've got in our arsenal."

"Good plan. I'm going to talk to Hunt Frederick tomorrow. I think it's the courteous thing to do, given Coleman's connection with his company. Maybe I'll learn something about him—figure out what he's up to, for better or worse. But before I do, tell me what you think about what's going on at DDD&W. Is there a master criminal at work?" Heyward asked.

Hicks shook his head. "I don't think so. People are taking advantage of slack management who've given them a license to steal. I see it as a collection of individual rackets."

Jeb nodded. "Right. Mold grows in dark dank places. Maggots turn up in rotten meat. Same thing at DDD&W. Nasty scams sproutin' up all over the place."

"So how do we handle it?" Heyward asked.

"Sniper attacks. Sharp shootin'. Take 'em out one at a time," Jeb said.

"I agree. We'll go after each one as soon as we can prove something against him, her—or them," Heyward said.

"We've proved that someone at DDD&W is using inside information but not that it's Moose," Hicks pointed out.

"If we tip off the authorities that Colossus is usin' inside information they're gettin' from DDD&W, with what we give 'em, they'll get a warrant and go into the DDD&W computers, and see who's been messin' around in Miss Coleman's business. When Moose's lackeys are caught, they'll talk, and Moose will fold. I know—I've played poker with him," Jeb said.

Heyward nodded. "Right. Jeb, please give copies of everything we have on this inside information lead to Rob so he can pass it on to his friend at the SEC. Hicks, you take everything we know to the DA. We might as well get them involved. Make sure you let Jonathan and Dinah and the lawyers know what's going on. I'll call Coleman. When I talk to Hunt Frederick, I'll warn him about Moose. Coleman says they're friends. If so, this will hit hard, unless Frederick already knows about it, which I doubt. But if he does, we'll turn him in, too."

Forty-Nine

Determined to dazzle Bethany, Coleman, and Dinah with her detective work, Loretta took a taxi from her apartment to the Park Avenue building where Patti Sue Victor and Frances Johnson had lived. She expected to flirt her way past a doorman, so she had put on a sexy black suit and white blouse similar to the outfit Bette Davis wore after her makeover in *Now Voyager*. But her blouse was tighter and lower cut, and her skirt shorter than Bette's. She had to make concessions to twenty-first century male tastes. She carried the black leather briefcase her roommates had given her for college graduation. She wanted to look like the reporter she'd pretend to be.

She chatted up the pony-tailed doorman, who gave as good as he got. When she was sure he was sufficiently smitten to gossip about the tenants, she asked about the lady who lived opposite Victor and Johnson.

"Orlando. She's an old crow. She keeps her door open twenty-four seven so she can watch the hall action. She knows plenty about them two—they were her hobby. I swear to God she din't think of nothin' else," he said.

He walked Loretta to the elevator and pressed the button for the seventh floor, still talking. "The old lady was divorced maybe seventy years ago. She's ninety if she's a day and mean as a snake, but she's got all her marbles. She'll talk your ear off if you give her a chance," he warned.

When Loretta told Mrs. Orlando that she planned to write an article about Frances Johnson and Patti Sue Victor, the old lady welcomed her with an open door and a great gush of words. She talked so fast Loretta had difficulty understanding her, but when she calmed down, Mrs. Orlando made a vitriolic kind of sense.

"Both of them floozies had boyfriends," she said. "Nasty fellas. They sneaked around like thieves—night crawlers, both of 'em—didn't ever take those women out. Only who could blame 'em? Mutton dressed as lamb, and neither one had morals as good as an alley cat. What do you want to know?"

"Do you recognize any of these men?" Loretta fanned out the photos she'd taken of Harrison, Quintero, Moose Shanahan, and Mark Leichter.

Mrs. Orlando pointed a claw at Quintero. "That's one of 'em. He's the one looks like a goombah, greasy hair an' all. He was courtin'—if you can call it that—Frances. And this one"—she pointed to Leichter—"he's the one sniffin' after Patti Sue. Ugly old thing! Neither one of them men would win a beauty contest, but then, them floozies looked like dog's dinner."

Loretta, on cloud nine, thanked Mrs. Orlando, tucked the photographs back in her briefcase, and floated to the elevator. She could hardly wait to call Coleman.

Fifty

The Cobra was in his element. He'd enjoyed telling the suits at One Police Plaza that Harrison and Quintero had been investigated by private detectives when the NYPD refused to do it. He loved giving them a summary of the cops' misdeeds. When the bureaucrats sputtered that the investigation was retaliation for Harrison's focus on Dinah Greene, and that they didn't believe a word of it, he faxed each of them the Fry Building guards' sworn statements about Harrison's second job and his girlfriend. He gave them time to read them and called again. He listened with silent joy to their heavy breathing and their abrupt hang-ups. There'd be a crisis at One Police Plaza today, and maybe at city hall.

When he'd wrung every drop of pleasure he could from razzing the top cops and the pols, he telephoned DDD&W's senior lawyer to enlighten him about Harrison and his relationships with Oscar Danbury and Trixie. He explained that with the departure of Harrison and Quintero, new detectives would be appointed and the case reinvestigated, broadening the list of possible suspects. He reminded him that the Greene Gallery's assignment would be completed by noon on Friday; the check must be ready and waiting.

He finished with the announcement that he also represented the Prince Charles Stuart Museum, which was suing DDD&W for the recovery of the works of art missing from the Davidson Americana collection. The relevant documents would reach Hunt Austin Frederick today. After he'd completed that call, leaving a shattered lawyer to spread the news inside DDD&W, he leaned back in his chair and sighed. What a great morning.

∾

When Rob called his friend in the DA's office, he was assured that Patti Sue's death had nothing to do with their sales tax investigation. "The people at Great Art Management say Ms. Victor was a moron. They're not sure she knew that she was involved in anything illegal," Rob's friend explained. "The DDD&W guys who were sending empty boxes to addresses out of state knew what they were doing, but they say all that Victor did was introduce the greedy louts to Great Art Management. This is how it worked: GAM had a program promoting art for young collectors. When the young collectors Victor introduced to GAM balked at the prices, GAM showed 'em how to save

money through tax evasion. But it was small potatoes—cheap art, and not much tax money involved."

"What will happen to them?" Rob asked.

"The stupid little thieves will pay their taxes and
penalties and go about their business, but if
DDD&W management has any brains, they'll fire
'em. Cheat once, they'll cheat again, and maybe bigger. As for Great Art Management, it's history."

Rob hung up and thought about what he'd heard.
He had no reason to doubt their assessment of Patti
Sue—except that she'd been murdered. If every
brainless pawn was killed, the planet would be a lot
less crowded. Only it didn't happen. She must have
done something to make someone kill her. But what?

The SEC investigator called while he was still
thinking about Patti Sue. "I heard about the roundup
of the DDD&W tax dodgers," he said. "I wish I could
say I've nabbed twenty bad guys. But no one at
DDD&W is doing audits. They stopped as soon as
the merger went through."

"Do you mean they're not doing anything illegal?
I can't believe it," Rob said.

"I didn't say that. We think they're up to plenty,
just not auditing. We think you should talk to the
New York Attorney General. That woman makes
Giuliani and Spitzer look like plump house cats. She
goes after corporate corruption like a starving leop-
ard after a gazelle. This could be her kind of thing.
She can't move without hard information, but you
should tell her all you know and suspect about these
people so she can investigate. We'll do the same."

Rob couldn't see himself calling the AG with optimism based on no evidence. She'd bite his head off. He was trying to decide what to do when Hicks called with the information about insider information at DDD&W. When Hicks heard what the SEC investigator had advised, he volunteered to talk to the AG. Rob sighed with relief. He didn't mind calling the SEC, but he was terrified by the AG.

Rob's friend at the SEC was grateful for Rob's information, and Rob was feeling good about having done a colleague a favor. He was also looking forward to dinner at Dinah's, where he'd see Coleman, when Coleman called.

"Rob? I just heard from Loretta. She talked to the Victor sisters' neighbor—the one your guy found—and would you believe the woman identified a photo of Quintero as Frances's lover? And Leichter as Patti Sue's? So Leichter is the guy Patti Sue was fighting over. Can you imagine? No wonder Quintero looks so ghastly. Johnson was his sweetheart, and he had to investigate her murder and keep their relationship a secret. I wonder if he really thinks Dinah killed her. He's not the brightest guy I ever met. Anyway, Loretta did good. I have to hand it to her—she's enterprising. Oh, and I figured out it was Tom, Jonathan's driver, who was leaking information about Jonathan's whereabouts to Harrison and Quintero—he's admitted it. He told them when Dinah was alone, and they could have told anyone."

"Oh, God," Rob groaned. "How the hell did we miss all that? I should fire my guys and hire you and Loretta. Would you ask her to write up her interview with the neighbor and include the time and date, too? And make some copies of the photos? And would you write up how you found out about Tom? The Cobra will want to pass everything on to the police."

Fifty-One

"Those arrests for tax evasion aren't going to do us a lot of good," Ted Douglas told Hunt. "Twenty guys...can you believe it? That will make headlines. Thank God all the crooks are from downstairs. That fool Patti Sue really got us into it this time."

Hunt nodded. "Got herself killed, too. Her death must be connected to the tax fraud, although the DA's office thinks not. Any ideas about who killed her and her sister, if Dinah Greene is innocent?" he asked.

Ted shook his head. "I still think Dinah did it. But both Patti Sue and Frannie came in with the D&W merger—that was a mistake. We shouldn't have let it happen."

"No point saying what we should have done *then*. The question is, what do we do now? Did you get that report from Patti Sue about the Americana collection?"

"No. I asked her for it, but I guess she didn't have a chance to do it before she was killed," Ted said.

"Is there any way to get a paper trail on the shipments? Anything we can follow up?" Hunt asked.

"Not that I know of. Ms. Skinner cleaned out Patti Sue's office when the police said it was okay, just like she did Frannie's. Says she didn't find anything useful."

Hunt sighed. "That lunatic Scot from the museum and the Hathaway lawyer they call the Cobra are going to take us to the cleaners over the missing stuff from that damn collection. One of the lawyers talked to an old biddy who works at the museum, and she told him the name of the shipper, and how many crates they received, and get this: they videotaped the two museum guys unpacking the stuff, said it was standard museum procedure to prevent theft and to verify what arrived. Nothing could have been stolen at the museum. And the shipper videotaped the sealed cartons when they picked 'em up, and again when they delivered 'em. They're in the clear, too."

Ted frowned. "What could have happened to the missing art?"

"Patti Sue must have packed up the good stuff and sent it somewhere—maybe to a dealer—by a different shipper," Hunt said.

"Patti Sue? I always thought she made a pine tree look like a genius. She must have had a boyfriend who pulled the strings," Ted said.

"Somebody who works here?" Hunt asked, startled.

Ted shrugged. "There's a rumor that Patti Sue and another secretary had a fistfight in the ladies' room over one of the partners. I thought it was a joke, but maybe it's true," he said.

"Oh, hell. Who'd know?" Hunt asked.

"Moose, maybe? I heard a couple of those kids who work for him talking about it in the men's room," Ted said.

"I guess I better check out the rumor, and question the Victor woman's boyfriend, if he exists. Unless we can find the missing art, the partners will have to pick up the tab."

"Oh, God," Ted groaned. "I hadn't thought of that. Will it be a lot of money? Won't insurance cover it?"

"I think it'll be a huge number, and I can't see insurance covering the disappearance of the art unless we can figure out when and how it disappeared. For all we know or can prove, it's been missing for years, and no one noticed. We'll call the insurance people, but I doubt if they'll turn up anything we've missed."

"What a mess," Ted said.

"You're telling me. You know they're pulling off the two cops who were on the case? Starting the murder investigation all over with a new team? Everyone will be questioned again, and all because Danbury hired that ape Harrison as a bodyguard or something. Paid him with DDD&W's money, too," Hunt said.

Ted nodded. "Yeah, I know. What a screwup. I'll be surprised if they ever arrest the person who killed those women."

❧

Jeb Middleton poked his head in the door to Heyward's office. "I just talked to Rick Oliver, the guy who wrote Miss Coleman the first letter? He swears he got out of the Colossus business with Miss Coleman the day Jonathan called him. He told Colossus he had a conflict because of a long-standin' relationship with Jonathan: they went to kindergarten together—it happens to be true. But he hadn't known Miss Coleman and Jonathan's wife were related. Colossus didn't force Oliver to keep botherin' Miss Coleman, because that fool Black—the guy who writes Miss Coleman the nasty letters—was pantin' to take over. Sounds like he gets off on beatin' up their targets, and 'specially scarin' ladies. And speaking of scarin', Oliver sounded scared out of his britches when I told him I was actin' for you, and that Miss Coleman is your sister. He asked if Miss Coleman had any more kin he ought to know about."

Heyward smiled. "Will he tell his friends at Colossus?"

"Oh, yes. I asked him to. I said they shouldn't communicate with Miss Coleman unless they're apologizin', and that if they kept on botherin' her, you'd retaliate. I didn't tell him that the SEC and the New York Attorney General were prob'ly about to put 'em out of business," Jeb said.

"When are you going to contact Colossus directly?" Heyward asked.

"Friday. I'm givin' them time to reflect on their sins. Then I'll tell 'em what happens to bad boys."

Fifty-Two

Coleman, with Dolly in her carrier, was the last to arrive for Dinah's dinner. She was surprised and pleased to see a good-looking stranger with Heyward. Heyward introduced her to Jeb Middleton, and after they'd chatted a while, he seemed even more attractive. She was sure she saw an answering gleam in his eyes.

But she was shocked by Dinah's appearance. Always slender, Dinah had lost weight she couldn't spare, and despite an unusual amount of makeup, Coleman could see dark circles under her eyes. She hadn't realized what a terrible toll the DDD&W problem was taking on her cousin. Annoyed with herself, she vowed to talk to Dinah alone after dinner and try to find out how she could help.

When introductions were completed, and Dinah asked Heyward what brought him to New York, Coleman thought he might talk about her struggles with Colossus, but he raised another topic.

"Oh, this and that. Since I arrived, I've been trapping vermin. Everyone here knows about the inside information crimes at DDD&W, and Colossus, but I've also been on the trail of the Stubbs. I had the same thought you did, Dinah, that whoever had stolen the paintings would try to sell them in London. I called Rachel this morning, and when she said the only way to learn the identity of the Stubbs' seller was to buy them, I bought them. The seller is the Davidson Estate, Lucas Parker Esq., Executor. He has no more right to sell the paintings than I do. I'm sure we'll be able to have him arrested. And, of course, the sale to me won't go through. The paintings will be held in a London bank while ownership is determined," he said.

"Parker! I knew he was a bad lot," Jonathan exclaimed. "Wait till you hear about my discussions with him, and the story of the Davidson family."

When he'd repeated everything he'd learned, Dinah was the first to speak.

"I don't believe it," she said.

Jonathan, frowning, stared at her. "Don't believe what?"

"The story about those girls never seeing their mother. They had no one. Their father, the only person who didn't want them to talk to their mother, died when they were little. I think that as soon as they were old enough to use a phone, they called her, long distance. I would have," Dinah said.

Rob rubbed his head. "You may be right, Dinah. I should have thought of that. But I learned today that one of the girls is dead. Margaret killed herself last July. And we still can't find her sister."

"Oh, how terrible," Dinah said. "That poor girl. And her poor twin."

༄

Dinah went into the kitchen to serve the soup, and Jeb and Coleman followed her to help. But before Coleman left the room, she heard Heyward ask Jonathan how he wanted to handle the problem of Lucas Parker.

"Turn him over to the Firm," Jonathan said. "They like to handle any Boston legal misdoings. They'll make sure that Parker gets what he deserves. Do you mind if I call now? The Firm never closes, and some say never sleeps. They'll take care of Parker, and they'll do it fast."

"No, go ahead," Heyward said, and joined the others in the kitchen.

Jeb, pouring champagne, offered Heyward a glass when he came in the kitchen.

"No, thanks, but I'd like some water," he said. Coleman brought him the water, and Heyward raised it to toast the group.

"Jonathan is making the call to pull the plug on Lucas Parker. He said he wouldn't be long. Let's drink to Justice," he said.

"And so say all of us," Coleman murmured.

After delicious turkey stroganoff that everyone but Dinah gobbled up, Coleman turned down Jeb's, Heyward's, and Rob's invitations to ride uptown. She thanked them but insisted on staying to help Dinah clean up. Dinah demurred, but Coleman ignored her and banished Jonathan with a roll of her eyes.

Fifty-Three

"What is it, Dinah? Tell me everything," Coleman said, loading plates into the dishwasher.

"I feel awful," Dinah said. "At first I was angry. Like at our meeting, when we made the plans—putting in the bugs and such.

"But my anger kind of burned out—I tried to pretend everything was all right—but it didn't work, and I began to be really scared. I know I may get arrested, may have to go to jail. Maybe worse. I've been praying, of course, but I feel like maybe I could have done things differently and none of this would have happened.

"I've finished hanging the prints we need for DDD&W, and I don't have anything to do. I can't sleep. I worry all the time. I wish I could do something to help find the murderer, and clear up my situation. Everybody is trying to help—Jonathan's not even doing his own work, he's so busy helping me. But I don't know how to *act*. I feel like I have to keep up a good front for Jonathan—he's so worried. And I don't know how to *do* anything. You've always been the activist, the one who gets things done. I've mostly had my head in books."

Coleman thought fast. Dinah was her best friend, and as close as a sister. She, Coleman Greene, who prided herself on her loyalty to her friends, had been so preoccupied with her magazines, with the attempted takeover, and with her brother's rescue program, she'd let Dinah down. That had to be rectified.

"I'll give you a list of things you can do by yourself, and we'll do some together. Remember how we worked together to solve the Print Museum murders last year? We'll do it again. We make a great team," Coleman said.

Dinah's eyes brightened. "What can I do right away?" she asked.

"We have to find Ellie and Elizabeth. You could start by calling Elizabeth's schools, or visiting them, or looking at their yearbooks, maybe getting photos like Loretta did."

Dinah nodded. "I can do that. I've wondered—two young women with similar names—Ellie and Elizabeth—vanish. Could they be the same person? Is Ellie Elizabeth and hiding for some reason?"

"I've thought about that, too. Maybe the school or the minister of the church where Margaret's funeral service was held can tell us what Elizabeth looks like," Coleman said.

Dinah nodded. "Right. I'll start with the schools. What else?"

"Find out what you can about the girls' mother. Who'd she marry? The minister might know that, too. Or neighbors. Or the local paper. Somebody's got to know what her name is, right? If you find out who she is, you can find out where she is," Coleman said.

"Okay, what else?"

"If Ellie isn't Elizabeth, we have to find both of them. Who is Ellie? Why is she involved? What does she know about the murders? And why did she disappear? And where is Elizabeth?"

"What else?"

"We all agree the Stubbs they'll exhibit at DDD&W on Friday will be forgeries—copies. How many people in New York could make copies so good they can fool the crowd coming in to look at them? Can you get a list of the possibilities? When we have a list, we'll start calling or visiting them. I don't know if anyone will admit to copying them—that depends on why they thought they were doing it—but it'll be a start."

"I'll try," Dinah said. Some of her normal color had returned.

Coleman sighed inwardly. Her magazines—her business—would have to wait while she helped Dinah. She'd explain to Heyward tomorrow: he was family; he'd understand.

"Jonathan?" she called. "Will you see me to a cab?" She leaned over and kissed Dinah on the cheek. "We can do this. I promise," she said. Dinah needed exoneration. Being cleared of suspicion. Not having her reputation marred. Not giving Jonathan's ghastly family another opportunity to disapprove of their precious son's wife. Coleman didn't know how getting Dinah out of the frame could be made to happen, but it had to be done. She feared Dinah was on the verge of a breakdown. She'd never seen her sound so down. And, of course, she *would* pretend everything was all right—she would smile no matter what. That's the way they were brought up.

Fifty-Four

Thursday morning Loretta awoke at five and couldn't go back to sleep. She tossed and turned for more than an hour, thinking about her Quintero and Leichter discoveries. At a little after six, she gave up and went into the kitchen to make coffee. She was still on a high about her successful detection, and she had an idea about how to hit another home run. Should she go in early this morning and implement her plan? She wasn't supposed to be alone at DDD&W, but there was never anyone around before nine. Anyway, she thought Coleman and Bethany were crazed on the topic of security. Except for Monday, when she and Bethany had their unpleasant encounters with Harrison and Patti Sue, no one had ever looked cross-eyed at Loretta, let alone threatened her. She made up her mind. She'd go.

After a quick shower, she dressed in her dark green suit, the white ruffled blouse that went with it, and dark green shoes—she wouldn't leave the house looking less than her best, no matter what—and took the subway uptown to the Fry Building, stopping at a deli to pick up coffee and a bagel before riding the elevator to thirty-two. She put her breakfast bag on the desk and hung her jacket on the back of her chair before sticking her head out the door and looking up and down the hall.

Not a soul in sight. She tiptoed across the hall. She didn't bother trying the door to Patti Sue's office. She'd seen Leichter and Skinner boxing up everything in that office and locking the door behind them. That office was squeaky clean, not a scrap of paper left behind.

But no one had searched the desk outside Patti Sue's office, where Dinah said McPhee had worked—at least, not since Loretta had been at DDD&W. Loretta didn't give a hoot about the girl who came and went like a spook, but Bethany, Coleman, and Dinah did, and Loretta wanted to impress them. Not that she thought that what she was about to do was so brilliant. But everyone else had overlooked the obvious: Ellie's desk.

It was unlocked, and a glance in the cluttered top drawer proved it had never been cleaned out.

She went through every drawer. If anyone appeared and asked her what she was doing, she'd say she was looking for a book Dinah had lent Ellie. But no one turned up, and she removed everything from the desk except office supplies and stuffed all the papers and files into her big tapestry carryall. There was a lot of paper, but even stuffed, the carryall didn't bulge. If someone saw her, she wouldn't look suspicious. She tried to look casual while crossing the hall.

After locking herself in the tiny office, she glanced through Ellie's papers. One thing was for sure: Ellie was Dinah's Deep Throat. That tiny writing was unmistakable. She'd seen it on the "Look for the Horses" note that she and Bethany found the first day at DDD&W. But even if Ellie delivered helpful little messages to Dinah, she could still be a killer. Her disappearing act proved she was hiding something.

Most of Ellie's papers looked like trash, but Loretta found one treasure: a pass card with Frances Johnson's name on it. If no one had thought to cancel it, it would open any door at DDD&W. Wonder how the Ellie girl got it? Never mind. Loretta now had access to the managing director's office to photograph the Stubbs paintings, even if she couldn't get in officially. One big problem solved. She put the card in her wallet and looked at her watch. She could take everything to Coleman's office and still be back in time to meet Bethany to hang a few more prints.

❧

Coleman's office phone rang while she was reading and answering her e-mails. She glanced at her watch. Not many people called her before eight. When she answered, she was surprised to hear Loretta's voice.

"Coleman? Sorry to call so early, but I'm on the way to DDD&W to meet Bethany. We're trying to hang prints early in the morning when there aren't so many gawkers. But I need to drop some papers off for you—I'm near your office. I went through Ellie McPhee's desk, and I've got everything that was in it. There's some interesting stuff."

"Good Lord!" Coleman exclaimed. "You mean nobody ever looked? I can't believe it."

"Since nobody here admits she existed, I guess no one bothered to search her desk. Anyway, may I bring them by?"

"Absolutely. Come ahead."

Loretta arrived a few minutes later, and she and Coleman laid all the papers on the big table in the conference room. Coleman congratulated Loretta and complimented her on her ingenuity and enterprise. "You're going to make a great investigative reporter, but please don't go back to DDD&W alone," Coleman said. She didn't remember until much later that Loretta hadn't answered. She'd just smiled, and waved goodbye.

⌒

Loretta saw Bethany in line at the Starbucks near the DDD&W building and hailed her. Seemed like a long time since she ate that bagel.

"How about buying me a small black coffee and a low-fat cranberry muffin?" she called.

"Sure will," Bethany said. "Wait for me by the door and we'll go up together."

The elevator was crowded. She recognized some of the passengers who worked for DDD&W. She saw another vaguely familiar face, but she didn't associate him with DDD&W. She'd probably seen him at Starbucks or on the subway. She nodded to him, but he ignored her. Maybe she'd seen him some time when he hadn't seen her.

Should she tell Bethany about her early morning activities? She thought not. Bethany would rant about her being in the building on her own, and she didn't feel like hearing it.

"Let's hang prints," she said.

~

After Loretta left, Coleman telephoned Dinah and described Loretta's discovery of the files in Ellie's desk. "I'm bursting to look at the papers, but I haven't glanced at a single sheet—I'm saving them for you. One thing Loretta told me: Ellie was your Deep Throat. When you get here, come to the *ArtSmart* conference room, where we can spread it all out and organize everything. Remember how we figured out things in there last year? Maybe working in there will bring us luck."

"Wow! I can't wait—I'll be there in half an hour."

Fifty-Five

Dinah felt much better. She had something to do that might make a difference. True to her promise, Coleman hadn't touched the papers. Ellie was Dinah's mystery, not Coleman's.

The material was already partially organized, because Ellie had kept groups of related papers in neatly labeled file folders. Loretta was right. Ellie *was* her anonymous correspondent—Dinah recognized the writing, too. Maybe the files would reveal her whereabouts and why she sent Dinah the notes. And why she disappeared. Dinah had a bone to pick with that girl—leaving her like that.

The file labeled "Publicity" contained the article with the photo of Coleman and Dinah with Crawdaddy, but nothing in the files touched on the problems at DDD&W or provided clues to the whereabouts of Ellie McPhee, until Dinah looked at a file entitled "House Cleaning." Had Ellie given it that boring label to deter snoopers?

In it were sheets of paper covered in Ellie's tiny writing: a diary. She had noted that a few weeks before Christmas, Frances Johnson had wrapped the Stubbs paintings in heavy brown paper, tied them with thick cord, and left the office carrying them to a car driven by Harrison. Ellie had heard Johnson tell someone the paintings were going out for cleaning but wrote that she didn't believe it. She'd examined them when they were still on the wall, and they looked to be in superb condition. They definitely didn't need cleaning. Could Johnson be stealing them? She'd followed the car in a taxi and watched Harrison drop Johnson at a narrow building on Broadway in the Twenties. The sign over the revolving glass doors read "Artists Only." Johnson entered the building, and Ellie watched her take the elevator to the fourth floor.

Ellie couldn't follow Johnson without being spotted, but when the woman emerged empty-handed from the building and got back in the car, now headed uptown, Ellie went into the lobby and looked at the directory on the wall. She made a list of the occupants of the six offices on the fourth floor, but she hadn't recognized any of the names. Neither did Dinah. That was no surprise. If the artists weren't famous and didn't make prints, Dinah wouldn't necessarily have heard of them. But Coleman probably would know him.

Sure enough, Coleman, who had finished looking through the "Publicity" file, leaned over her cousin's shoulder and scanned the list of names of artists in the "Artists Only" building.

"James Turner, Daisy Kelling, Charles Krishner, Jasper Redding, Hester Peabody, and Newt Orleans," she read aloud. "Everyone has a good reputation—except Newt Orleans. Not that his reputation is bad—he's just a pushy creep, and I don't like him. That's one of Crawdaddy's names. He's a photorealist, so he definitely could have made the copies. I bet he's the one who did it."

"Ellie had that newspaper picture of him with us in the file, too," Dinah reminded her.

"Right," Coleman said. "Hey, here's an idea. Maybe when Frances Johnson took the paintings to that building, she thought she was taking them to be cleaned, and that Newt Orleans was a professional conservator. Then she saw his picture in the paper with us. The paper described him as a well-known photorealist, with a different name, Crawdaddy. She'd realize he wasn't a conservator and that something was wrong—"

"Yes!" Dinah interrupted. "Everyone thinks Parker, that horrible Boston lawyer, must have had an accomplice at DDD&W. Maybe it was Frances Johnson, and she called Parker to ask about Crawdaddy and why was he doing the cleaning. Parker told his partner in crime that Frances Johnson was snooping, and her questions got her killed. Or maybe Johnson knew the accomplice and called him directly."

"And the killer figured out a way to throw suspicion on you by using your tools. I think we've figured out why Frances died. But why kill Patti Sue? And who is the killer?" Coleman said.

"Both thefts—the missing work from the Americana collection, and the Stubbs—had to be about money, didn't they? Could the bad guy be one of those people downstairs? Like the disgusting Oscar Danbury? Or that awful man Patti Sue was fighting over?" Dinah asked.

"I think it is about money, and your guess is as good as mine as to the identity of the murderer." Coleman said. "I tell you what—let's go downtown and see Crawdaddy. I'll phone him and tell him I want to interview him. He's always after me to write an article about him. I'm sure he'll see us. We could go right now, if he's available."

But an assistant in Crawdaddy's studio said he wouldn't be in until after lunch. She could give Coleman an appointment at two. Would that work? Concealing her impatience, Coleman confirmed two o'clock and turned to Dinah. "What do you want to do now?"

"I want to make those phone calls we talked about. Is it okay if I make them here?"

"Sure. I'll be in my office. Unless you need me?"

"No, I'll be fine."

Coleman disappeared down the corridor, and Dinah took a pen and a lined yellow pad out of her bag. Five minutes later, she was speaking to a friendly assistant in the headmistress's office at Miss Mitford's in Virginia, where the Davidson girls had gone to high school.

"My name is Dinah Greene. I own the Greene Gallery in New York City, and I'm helping the lawyers locate and evaluate art inherited by Elizabeth

Davidson. As it turns out, there are lots of Elizabeth Davidsons. We're sure the one we're looking for went to Miss Mitford's. Can you tell me what she looks like?"

"No problem," the secretary said. "Elizabeth is nearly six feet tall, and beautiful. She played basketball here—she was a great player. She became a model after college. I wasn't surprised. She looked like a model."

Dinah couldn't believe it was so easy. "Do you have a current address for her?"

"No. She had an apartment in New York, but we heard she gave it up after her sister died. Somebody said she moved abroad—to France? Or maybe England. We haven't received a change of address from her."

"One more question—do you know the church where Margaret's funeral service was held? Or the name of the minister?" Dinah asked.

"Yes, of course. We sent the details of the service to Margaret's classmates. It's the New Salem Presbyterian Church in New Salem, Connecticut, and the minister is named Goodfriend. Unforgettable name, don't you think, for someone doing the Lord's work?"

"Uh, yes. Very suitable. Well, thank you so much. You've been most helpful." Dinah ran down the corridor to Coleman's office.

"Guess what! Ellie and Elizabeth are definitely different people. Elizabeth is very tall, and as I've told you, Ellie is a tiny little thing. So we're looking for

two people. The school people think Elizabeth is living abroad."

Coleman looked up, smiling. "Go, girl! Keep calling! Find the girls' mother!"

❧

Mr. Goodfriend answered his own phone and was
quick to respond when Dinah asked about Elizabeth's mother.

"Oh, Barbara. We still miss her. She's a lovely person. She remarried years ago. Her husband's name is
Lawrence Athos—they call him Larry. They live in
London. Do you want her address and phone number? I'm sure it's current because we've had some cor-
respondence since Margaret died. You know about
poor Margaret?"

Dinah was stunned by the flood of information.
She'd braced herself to drag facts out of the man. She
took notes as fast as she could, and when the minister paused to breathe, she leaped in.

"Yes, I heard about Margaret's death. I am so sorry. I would like to have her mother's address and
phone number. Tell me, do you know where Elizabeth can be reached?"

"She lives with her mother and stepfather. She's
doing very well as a model in London." He rattled
off the London address and telephone number of the
Athos family, while Dinah took it down.

"Thank you so much. I really appreciate your
talking to me," Dinah said.

She hung up and sat back in the chair, rubbing her forehead. She couldn't believe it had been so easy. Why hadn't Rob found Elizabeth and her mother? Too distracted by Coleman's breaking off their relationship? Not paying attention to his business, and leaving too much to subordinates? Jonathan would be furious when he heard that Dinah had learned in minutes what Rob and his associates had failed to discover. So would Coleman. Come to think of it, *she* was angry. The cloud hanging over her might have disappeared days ago if Rob had been doing his job.

She dialed the number Mr. Goodfriend had given her and waited for what seemed a long time before a soft voice answered. "Athos Residence, Barbara Athos speaking."

"Mrs. Athos, this is Dinah Greene calling from New York—"

"Oh, Dinah—I've heard so much about you from Ellie! You won't mind if I call you Dinah, will you? I feel as if I already know you—please call me Barbara."

Dinah shook her head, disbelieving. How did Ellie fit in?

"Uh—you know Ellie?"

"Of course. She's my husband's niece. Her last name is Athos, too. Eleanor Athos. She lives in Los Angeles, but she worked at DDD&W for a bit. I told her to get out when that woman died—I was afraid for her. The police would have discovered her identity, and what she was doing might have been illegal. She was spying, you know. She was supposed to have written you to explain. She said she would—I'll send her an e-mail, and give her a nudge."

"Uh—Barbara—I'm confused. Maybe you could give me some background?"

"I'm sure you *are* confused. Ellie was supposed to write or call you when she got back to LA and explain everything. Well—you know about Margaret's tragic death?"

"Yes. I'm so sorry for your loss," Dinah said.

"Thank you. I'll never get over it, nor will Elizabeth. We blame that horrid Lucas Parker. I'm sure he prevented Margaret and Elizabeth from getting work at DDD&W as their father wanted. It was not getting the job that was the final blow—Margaret left a note saying so. She felt hopeless: her marriage didn't work out, she didn't have the money for law school, and then DDD&W turned her down. I'd have liked to go after Parker and DDD&W legally, but frankly, we don't have the money for lawyers. Larry teaches, and I work three days a week at the library and give piano lessons at home. We don't have much spare cash, although we tried to help the girls when they were younger. Goodness knows what became of their father's money. I know he would have made sure they were taken care of. They never had anything. And they had to go to those awful schools. It was a shame."

"You're right to blame Lucas Parker—he's a terrible person. But tell me more about Ellie. I've been so worried since she disappeared. I think she knew I didn't hurt anyone, and I'm suspected by the police of murdering that poor woman," Dinah said.

"Oh, my dear, I'm so sorry. We didn't know the woman was murdered, or that they suspected you. Ellie didn't know anything about her death. She called me right after you told her the woman was dead—what you told her was all she knew. She went to DDD&W after Margaret died, when Elizabeth was also turned down for a job at DDD&W. Elizabeth is a successful model, but she doesn't enjoy it. She's brilliant, and wants to go to business school. I wish you'd talk to her. Why don't you call her? Anyway, Ellie took a job at DDD&W to try to find out what was going on. But you should get the story from her. It's easiest to reach her in the evening between five and seven California time, or seven and nine in the morning, also Pacific time. She'll want to tell you the story. If you'll excuse me, my doorbell is ringing—my next pupil has arrived. I'm so sorry for your troubles. Ellie will help if she can, I know. Let's talk again soon."

Dinah could hardly wait to tell Coleman all she'd learned. As much as she wanted to talk to Ellie, she was glad she could rest for a while before speaking to the girl. Her head and her writing hand hurt, and she was tired of listening and taking notes. She looked at her watch—nearly noon. Maybe she and Coleman could go somewhere for lunch and discuss everything before their two o'clock appointment. But first she had to write up a report on her conversation and e-mail the information to Coleman, Jonathan, Rob, and Heyward. They always wanted everything in writing. She was glad she had something to report—even if nothing she'd learned would help clear her. The black cloud still hung over her head.

Fifty-Six

As soon as it was over, Blair Winthrop called Jonathan to describe Lucas Parker's collapse. The Firm's partners, irate at Parker's plundering of the Davidson estate and abuse of the Davidson girls, had sent three of their best, including Blair, to confront him.

When his pompous façade was punctured, Parker burst into tears. After he managed to control his sobbing, he whined about his bad luck: he'd done poorly at the obscure college he'd attended and worse at his even more obscure law school. He'd failed the bar exam three times before he passed. Unable to find a job, he'd set up a practice on his own, attracted few clients, and was forced to live on handouts from his exasperated father. He'd hated his father. Why should the old man have success, money, respect, and admiration, and Lucas nothing? It wasn't fair.

His father's fatal heart attack had rescued him. Parker inherited his father's money, and more importantly, he'd grabbed the Davidson estate. He'd looted it ever since, sharing his plunder with the girls' aunt, Davidson's weak younger sister, and the ne'er-do-well she married. After the girls' aunt and uncle—their only relatives—died in the plane crash, the Davidson estate became Lucas's private playground.

He educated the twins as cheaply as possible and gave them meager allowances. They'd wanted to go to graduate school—Margaret planned to be a lawyer, and Elizabeth had counted on going to business school—but he wouldn't allow it: too expensive, and they'd learn too much. For the same reason, he wouldn't permit the girls to work at DDD&W. He told them the estate couldn't afford graduate school, and he'd blocked their employment at DDD&W.

How had he managed to prevent their being hired? He'd called Frances Johnson, DDD&W's head of human resources, told her that the girls were unstable, spoiled, and lazy. If hired, they'd damage DDD&W's reputation. Frances made Margaret's application disappear and told the girl there was no job available. It wasn't his fault the girl killed herself; she was always unstable. Later, Frances handled Elizabeth's application the same way. When he gave Frances five thousand dollars for her help, she'd asked if she could do anything else for him. He was fairly certain she'd meant services of a personal kind, but he'd pretended not to understand and engaged her and her sister for the art projects.

Patti Sue had packed the Americana collection, working from two lists he'd drawn up after researching prices. She shipped the trash on List A to the museum, and the valuable items on List B to a storage facility in Boston. Everything was still there. He'd waited to see if anyone at the museum complained, but no one did, and he'd planned to start selling the Americana collection that summer. Did Patti Sue know what she was doing? No, she hadn't a clue. She was stupid. Frances was smarter, but she was also more demanding.

How had he managed the removal of the Stubbs? Frances Johnson took them to be copied, telling people at DDD&W they were out for cleaning. When the copier had made the photographs to work from, Ms. Johnson shipped the original paintings to Parker. Parker had sent them to England to be sold.

Who made the copies? He had no idea. Frances Johnson had handled that. All he'd provided was the cash to pay for it. How had the copies come back to DDD&W? He had no idea. Where was Elizabeth Davidson? He hadn't heard from her since Margaret's funeral. He had no reason to be in touch with her. Who else did he deal with at DDD&W? Just the Victor sisters. How did he know them? He didn't, not really. When he called Frances Johnson, she was impressed because he was a lawyer and the executor of the Davidson estate. She'd smelled money and made it clear she expected to be well paid. After she'd received the first package of cash, the art projects were easy to arrange. He'd never met either of the sisters. But they both had become greedy, and he'd stopped speaking to them. He insisted he hadn't killed them—he claimed he thought their deaths were accidental.

"Do you believe he was in this by himself?" Jonathan asked Blair.

"No, none of us does. Someone at DDD&W must have been working with him, someone who oversaw, at least from a distance, what the Victor sisters were doing. But Parker insists he was alone—it's his story, and he's sticking to it," Blair said.

"Why do you think he's protecting his accomplice?" Jonathan asked.

"Because his accomplice is almost certainly a murderer. As long as Parker pretends he doesn't exist, and he can't be identified, Parker can't be accused of being involved with the murders. Parker hasn't left Boston since Christmas," Blair said.

"What will happen now?" Jonathan wanted Parker behind bars. He pitied Elizabeth Davidson and her even more unfortunate sister.

"We've informed all the appropriate authorities, and everyone has agreed that the Firm will take over Parker's assets—all of which were stolen from the Davidson heirs—and everything to do with the Davidson estate, including the stored Americana. Parker isn't married, and he's in practice by himself, so we don't have anyone to contend with, except him, and he's a wet rag. The Firm has asked me to form a committee to recover all we can for Elizabeth, to settle the Davidson estate, and to oversee management of her money. I hope you and Heyward Bain will serve on the committee. Will you?" Blair asked.

"Of course. I'm sure Heyward will, too. What happens to Parker?" Jonathan said.

"Jail and ruin. He'll get all the law allows," Blair said.

"Rob thinks maybe some of the deaths in that family are suspicious—too much bad luck. What do you think?" Jonathan asked.

"We've considered that. All the early deaths were investigated, but if there was a crime involved, no one could discover it. I don't think anything new could be turned up at this point—everything happened too long ago. Anyway, Parker was too young to be involved. There's little doubt he's responsible for Margaret's suicide, but unfortunately, I don't think he can be charged with it. Too bad. I'd like to see him tarred and feathered."

Jonathan wrote up a summary of what Blair had told him and e-mailed the information to Rob, Coleman, Heyward, and Sebastian Grant. Then he called Dinah.

Dinah was glad that the despicable Lucas Parker was going to jail. When Jonathan had completed his story, they discussed Loretta's and her own discoveries. As she had thought, he was furious with Rob and planned to have a word or two with him about his failure to get the information Loretta and Dinah had turned up so easily. When he finished fuming, Dinah told him that she and Coleman were going downtown to see an artist. He assumed they were looking at prints and sounded pleased that she was taking an interest in her business again. She didn't explain who they were seeing and why. She was sure he'd have forbidden her to go. He suggested that they take his car, and she accepted, although she was still furious with Tom.

A subdued Tom drove them downtown. Jonathan had warned him that another indiscretion would mean dismissal, and Dinah, normally softhearted, had agreed. She was almost as annoyed with Tom as she was with Rob.

She and Coleman settled at a table at BLT Fish, and after they'd ordered, Coleman took out her pocket calendar and the little notebook she always carried.

"I've been thinking about our theory that Frances Johnson caught on to what was going on with the Stubbs when she saw that newspaper article picturing Crawdaddy and learned he was a painter and not a conservator. Maybe a newspaper article tipped Patti Sue off, too. The missing Americana story appeared in the paper on a Monday, with a follow-up on Tuesday. Patti Sue died late Tuesday night. We now know from Parker that Patti Sue packed that collection from two lists he sent her—the good stuff to his warehouse, and the junk to the museum. Everyone said she didn't understand about the tax dodge she helped with. What if she didn't know she was doing anything illegal with the Americana either? Maybe she found out when she read the story in the paper about the works that should have gone to the museum, just like we think Frances Johnson learned about Crawdaddy not being a conservator when she read about him in the paper. Maybe she called Parker, asked for more money, maybe threatened to expose him—"

"I bet you're right," Dinah said. "Should we call Rob or Jonathan? Tell someone?"

"Let's wait till after we see Crawdaddy. We might learn more. Right now, let's eat. I'm starved, and we're running out of time."

~

Crawdaddy greeted them at the door. "I finally gotcha here," he crowed. "I knew you'd see the light." He tried to embrace Coleman, but she ducked and squeezed past him, holding Dolly's carrier in front of her like a shield.

He looked and smelled as disgusting as he had at Coleman's party. She didn't think he'd washed his hair since then, and the shirt and jeans were the same—or identical to—those he was wearing in the newspaper photograph. To her surprise, the studio was clean and neat. She'd thought it would be a pigsty. She glanced around. A small tidy woman wearing glasses sat behind a desk in the corner. She must be the assistant who answered the phone. And cleaned the place?

Coleman turned to the painter. "Okay, we're here. Show us your work."

She followed him around the room, ignoring his patter, examining the paintings. They were realistic landscapes with bright blue skies and brighter blue water. Yellow sunlight on the green grass and trees.

"Okay. Got it. Anything with living creatures? Sheep? Cows? Horses?" she asked.

He stared at her, frowning, his eyebrows in a tangle. "This is my best work. Don't you like it?"

Coleman shook her head. "This is not what I'm looking for. Not enough life, action—"

He interrupted. "But I've seen work like mine in *ArtSmart*."

"That was then, this is now. I'm working on summer and early fall issues, and I want outdoor life—animals, children, the beach, swimming, tennis, golf—all styles—abstract, realist, whatever. And I'm looking for autumn themes: back to school, football, foxhunting—"

He scowled. "I don't do that kind of work."

"Right. And that's why I haven't written about you. *ArtSmart* is about trends—what's new, what's hot, what's about to happen. We don't show yesterday's work."

Dinah spoke up. "Sometimes you do. If you see art that looks like what you have in mind but was done much earlier, you run it and call it influential, or seminal."

"That's true, but I don't see it here," Coleman said.

Crawdaddy stared at the floor, his face sullen. "I don't think I've ever done anything like what you want."

"Have you made any prints?" Dinah asked.

"Yeah, but with this same kind of image. If you don't like the paintings, you won't like my prints, or anything I do," he said sadly.

Coleman, who felt she'd done her duty by looking at his art, was ready to come to the point. The man was such a liar, it might be a waste of time to question him, but she had to try. "Do you ever make copies of paintings?"

Crawdaddy looked up and grinned. "Sure. All the time. Copying is how I make a living."

Coleman nearly gasped. *He was the one!* "Did you copy a pair of paintings of horses for a company?"

"Yeah, for DDD&W. Beautiful paintings—Stubbs. This guy called me, said they were too valuable to hang in the office. They were putting the originals in a bank vault and hanging the copies. Nobody would know the difference."

"What guy? What was his name?"

"Uh—wait a minute—Betsy? What was the name of the man from DDD&W who called about the Stubbs?"

The woman looked up. "Parker. The woman who delivered the paintings was Johnson. Another woman, somebody Victor, picked up the paintings and the copies, and brought the money. Cash. I didn't have any conversation with either of them." She looked back down at the papers on her desk.

Coleman exchanged glances with Dinah. Dead end.

"Thanks, Crawdaddy. You've been very helpful."

"But you're not going to put me in the magazine?" he said.

"No, but I promise, if we're ever doing an article on your kind of work, I'll call you," Coleman said. "Thanks for seeing us."

When they were in the elevator, Dinah asked, "Why do you dislike him so much? You know other artists that are dirty and smelly and poor, and you don't hate them."

"Because he's a liar and a cheat. His family is super rich. He just pretends to be poor to try to sell his art, thinking no one will buy if they know his father is a multi-millionaire. His dirt and his thrift-shop clothes are an act. Meanwhile there are genuinely poor artists out there who are clean and decent and don't lie. Besides, Crawdaddy has no talent, and someone should tell him so. He should try another career. Maybe go to work for daddy in the waste management business."

Dinah nodded her understanding. She and Coleman had been poor and knew what it was like to struggle. They had no sympathy for a person who faked it. "Do you think Parker made that call?"

"Maybe, but who knows? He'll say he didn't, that Johnson must have persuaded someone to call Crawdaddy. Or even if he confesses he made the call, we won't have learned much. This is so frustrating. We keep filling in pieces of the puzzle, but we don't get any closer to knowing who the killer is," Coleman said.

"Nor to clearing my name," Dinah said, her voice barely audible.

Coleman looked at her. "Maybe Ellie can help. Are you going to call her?"

"Yes, I'll start trying to reach her as soon as it's five p.m. in Los Angeles. But I don't think she can help. Her aunt says she doesn't know anything."

Coleman could see Dinah was on the verge of tears and rushed to reassure her. "Look how much you've discovered in such a short time. Keep trying. Someone out there knows what happened."

Fifty-Seven

Heyward Bain looked around the infamous office. It didn't look like a murder scene. The dark wood gleamed. The bookshelves were intact. The books had been replaced. Even the rug, which Dinah had described as soaked in blood, looked pristine. "I've heard a great deal about this office," Heyward said.

"Yeah, it's plenty ugly, and now it's probably haunted. I'm sure you know a woman was killed in here—everyone does," Hunt said. "Unfortunately, I'm stuck with the office. What can I do for you, Mr. Bain?"

"I understand you plan to clean up some—uh—misbehavior at DDD&W?"

Hunt stiffened. "Excuse me, Mr. Bain, I can't see how our affairs concern you."

Heyward smiled. "I'm already involved in your affairs. You are perhaps unaware that Coleman

Greene is not only Dinah Greene's cousin, she is my sister?"

Hunt sat up straight. "I did *not* know that. So you're our client's brother? I hope she's pleased with our work?"

Heyward shook his head. "I didn't come here to talk about Coleman. We ran into some problems at DDD&W, and were obliged to disclose them to the attorney general. I'm guessing the AG's people will be all over DDD&W soon. Maybe the SEC, and the DA's office, too."

Hunt paled. "What are you talking about?"

Heyward handed him the copies of Coleman's DDD&W reports and the corresponding information about Colossus's activities. "Our lawyers think these are enough to warrant the agencies' investigations. This is a clear-cut case of DDD&W's providing inside information to the people at Colossus Publishing, who promptly acted on it."

Hunt, skimming through the reports and letters, seemed to age as he read. "Do you think Amy Rothman is responsible for leaking the data?" he asked.

"No, Amy Rothman and her team are honest and reliable. We think Michael Shanahan is the mastermind. If I were you, I'd confront him as soon as you can. I wanted to warn you before you hear about all this officially," Heyward said.

"Thank you. Please apologize to both Dinah and Coleman Greene for me. Tell Dinah I never thought she did anything wrong. My actions about the two of them coming to the office were based on the advice of our lawyers—we were trying to protect DDD&W. As for our internal problems, rest assured I'll put a stop to them, and I'll certainly cooperate with the authorities," he said.

"It's hard when friends are involved," Bain said. He couldn't help feeling sorry for Hunt. The man looked as if he'd been run over by a truck. The inside information story was obviously a total surprise.

"Yes. Yes, it is. Is there anything else I need to know?"

"I'm afraid so," Heyward said, "but I can't tell you everything yet. I will as soon as I can. Events are still unfolding. Will you be available here for my call? Or is there somewhere else I can reach you tomorrow and Saturday?"

"Oh, I'll be in this office Friday, Saturday, and Sunday. I haven't had any life outside the office since I moved to New York. My office's direct line and my cell phone number are both on my card," Hunt said, handing one to Heyward.

Heyward nodded. "I'll be in touch. Meanwhile, there are a few other unpleasant matters I should tell you about, if you really plan to clean house," Heyward said. He looked at Hunt, a question in his eyes. Was Hunt serious about this? Did he want to know about the office affairs? About Oscar Danbury's revolting behavior? Heyward felt conflicted about how much to tell the fellow. DDD&W's dirty laundry was not Heyward's business, but through a series of unusual circumstances, he was privy to information about DDD&W that its managing director didn't have. Was it Heyward's duty to tell Hunt Frederick everything? Hunt must decide.

Hunt sighed. "Fire away," he said.

❦

Dinah was cooking roast pork with one eye on the clock, waiting for the appropriate time to call Ellie, when an e-mail arrived from Eleanor Athos, as Dinah had to remember to call her.

Dear Dinah,

Aunt Barbara just scolded me transatlantic for not writing. I apologize. It's been so wonderful being at home and away from DDD&W, I lost track of time.

I'm sure you have a thousand questions. Aunt Barbara told you why I was at DDD&W. We were heartbroken when Margaret committed suicide. She left a note saying not getting the job was the final blow. I was furious, and when they turned Elizabeth down, too, I knew there was something really wrong. I decided to get a job at DDD&W and investigate. I was hired as a temp, mostly to type, and managed to get assigned to Patti Sue, which was easy, since everyone hated working with that poor woman. After I got there, I sneaked into human resources and destroyed my file, including my application. The Victor sisters knew me, but I don't think anyone else did. And there was no record I was ever there.

I snooped to my heart's content, hating the people, but what wonderful experience for an actress! That's what I was doing on the thirty-third floor that fatal Friday—snooping. I hadn't reached Hunt Frederick's office, I saw no one, and the first I knew of the dead woman was when you told me about her. But I'd been expecting something awful to happen. I had no idea that the death was murder, but I wanted the police involved, so when I called it in, I said it was murder.

I didn't trust anyone at that cesspool, but when you arrived, I knew you were innocent of any of their vile activities, and I wanted to warn you. I had to be cryptic. I never knew who might find my notes. I entered and left the building disguised as an ugly old woman—the stereotypical invisible person. That's why no one ever noticed me. I wanted to make sure "Ellie" never appeared on the security tapes. But I knew if the police investigated thoroughly, everyone would eventually find out who I was. I called Aunt Barbara and told her about the bookcases, and the death, and asked her what I should do. She told me to get out immediately. So I flew to California before anyone could identify me, but before I left, I arranged to have one of the mail boys leave you one last note. I wanted you on the track of the Stubbs before they were sold. I watched the papers, but the word "murder" never appeared, and I didn't know you were in trouble. I wish I could help you, but I know nothing about the murder.

I know there are plenty of bad people involved: that terrible Parker, the Victor women (although I am sorry they were killed), Moose, Leichter, Danbury. Probably a lot more. Don't trust anyone at DDD&W. It's a nest of vipers. If you want to talk, call me! Good Luck!

As ever, your friend, Ellie.

P.S. I don't know if you'll recognize me when we meet. I've enclosed a jpeg.

Dinah stared at the picture. Ellie the mouse as Eleanor Athos was exceptionally pretty, a typical girl-next-door beauty. Ellie deserved an Academy Award. Not to mention a medal for bravery. She had been annoyed at Ellie for not coming forward, but as it turned out, Ellie had seen nothing, and she'd risked exposure, perhaps worse, by trying to help Dinah.

Dinah didn't think she'd ever had a drink alone. But she wanted to toast Ellie. She poured a glass of white wine from an open bottle in the refrigerator, took a sip, and lifted her glass toward the West. "Go, girlfriend," she said. "Thanks for everything."

～

Coleman was still at her desk at nearly eight Thursday evening when Heyward called.

"We've spoken several times today, but it's always been to exchange information, and I keep meaning to have a longer chat with you. I've got to go to London Saturday night, and I thought we could have dinner at my place Friday night. Are you free?"

"Yes, that would be great," Coleman said.

"I'm going to ask Dinah and Jonathan and a few other people. We've disposed of Parker, as you know, but have you heard that Jonathan and I are going to help Elizabeth Davidson? I called her in London and told her about Parker, and also about the mess at DDD&W. When I described Hunt, and how he's trying to clean house, she said she wants to work with him—to help, if she can. She said her father would want her to. He always wanted her to work at DDD&W, and now the company needs her."

"Good grief! Talk about turning the other cheek. She must be quite a girl," Coleman said.

"I think she is. She's going to let the Americana collection go to the Prince Charles Stuart Museum. She said again she thought that's what her father would want. I'd say that dinner Friday night was a celebration, except that there's still a murderer at large, and I can't figure out how we're going to identify him, or her."

"I know," Coleman said. "I looked at my list of questions about the case, and we've answered them all, and the answers don't help. Poor Dinah is still worried sick."

Fifty-Eight

Bethany and Loretta arrived at DDD&W on Friday morning nearly an hour earlier than usual, but a lot of people were there before them. They followed the crowd to the thirty-third floor, where the masses formed a line near the managing director's office. One of Moose's Merry Men waved at them.

"The Stubbs are back," he called. "We're waiting to see them. Better get in line."

Bethany and Loretta thanked him and fell in at the end of the line. Naomi Skinner walked by, checking names on a list. She stopped and glared at them. "Sorry, no outsiders," she said in her screechy voice.

Bethany, big-eyed in mock surprise, asked, "Why is that?"

Skinner looked at Bethany as if she were a roach in her soup. "Do you see the length of the line? It will take hours for all the *employees* to see the paintings. There's no room for people like you."

"But this is our last day here," Bethany protested. "Can't you make an exception?"

"No exceptions. You're wasting your time." Skinner stalked off, still checking her list.

"What do we do now? Coleman wanted me to take pictures," Loretta said.

"I'll call Coleman. She may have a suggestion," Bethany said.

But Coleman told them to forget about photographing the paintings—they had more than enough information about them, what with Rachel's reports from London, Parker's confession, and Crawdaddy's admission that he'd made the copies, not to mention Heyward's "buying" them. "Just finish up, pick up the check, and leave," she said.

Bethany, who needed no urging, assured Coleman they'd leave by noon. After Bethany and Loretta finished hanging the last of the prints, they sent the hangers home, and Bethany collected the Greene Gallery's check from Theodore Douglas's office. When Bethany handed the check to the messenger who would deliver it to Dinah, she heaved a great sigh of relief. "I can't wait to leave this place," she said. She reached under her sweater, removed the wire, and stretched. "My last official act is to hand everything over to you," she said, passing the wire to Loretta.

Bethany was struggling to hide her excitement. She and Zeke were catching the three o'clock plane to North Carolina to see her family and go through the various rituals that would allow them to become officially engaged.

Bethany hadn't told Loretta her plans, but Loretta knew she was eager to leave early and had offered to stay and close up. Since that involved little more than packing the listening devices, and wouldn't take more than a few minutes, Bethany had accepted her offer. Bethany could use those minutes. She had to change clothes and take care of last-minute packing. She'd be ready when Zeke picked her up to go to the airport. Oh, yes, she'd be ready.

She'd told Dinah that she was going home for the weekend, but not that Zeke was going with her, and not the reason for the trip. Bethany wanted to surprise everyone when they came back. She could hardly wait to get to North Carolina, to enjoy the weekend, and to appear on Monday wearing her magnificent ring, and with a wedding date set. She planned to ask both Dinah and Coleman to be in her wedding. She wanted to ask Loretta, too, but she had too many cousins; she couldn't single one out.

∽

Loretta watched Bethany rush off. What was that girl up to? Bethany never let anyone do a job she was supposed to do. They'd been warned over and over never to be alone at DDD&W, and Bethany had never left her there by herself. But it suited Loretta to have Bethany out of the way. She had plans for the rest of the day and the night, too. She didn't want a bossy boots staring over her shoulder, or telling her to go home. Coleman had asked her to take pictures of the fake Stubbs for *ArtSmart*, and come hell or high water, that's what she was going to do. She'd already taken a shot of the people waiting in line, and when everyone had left, she'd use the card she'd found in Ellie's desk to get in that office. She'd get good photos of the paintings.

But she had a lot of time to fill before she could get into that room, and the first thing she'd do was drop by Moose's office. She wanted another look at the framed photographs on his desk. She was pretty sure he'd be out—he and his cronies took long lunch hours and came back in the middle of the afternoon laughing, talking loud, and smelling of whisky and beer.

Right. His office was empty. She walked in, head high, acting as if she owned the place, just in case anyone passed the door, and picked up a silver-framed photograph she'd glimpsed but never examined closely. It was just as she remembered: an exquisite platinum blonde, even more beautiful than Moose's wife, stood next to a man Loretta had scarcely noticed when she first saw the picture. The photo was signed by both its subjects. She grabbed the picture and stuck it under her jacket. She'd copy it, and one day next week, she'd sneak in and return the original. She rearranged the pictures on the desk so there wasn't an empty space. She was sure Moose wouldn't notice its absence. He wasn't due back for a while, but she better get out of his office. Moose might be a killer. She'd heard rumors that he was a bad guy, but nothing concrete. Anyway, she planned to stay out of his way.

Back in the office, she used her cell phone to call Coleman but reached voice mail. So much the better. She'd leave a message and avoid questions, like where was she, and when did she leave DDD&W, and stuff like that.

"Coleman? Something strange. I ran into Theodore Douglas in the Village over the weekend. He was with two little children with red hair—claimed they were his, said they looked like his wife Kathy. I took a picture of him and the kids 'cause they were so cute, and they all looked so happy. I didn't know who he was at the time, but I saw him in the office yesterday. I didn't remember where I'd seen him, but today it came to me. I compared my picture to one of him and his wife Glenda, and it's definitely Mr. Douglas. His wife is not named Kathy, and she doesn't have red hair. I'm sending you the pictures I took in the Village. I thought you'd want to know."

Now for her major mission. She couldn't go in the office where the Stubbs hung until tonight when everybody had left. That was fine. She still had plenty to do.

Her first stop was the art storage room, where she put aside an unassembled cardboard box to take back to the office. She rearranged the empty crates and boxes in which prints had been delivered to make a lean-to against the wall. She'd hide behind it until everyone left for the night. She'd already stashed her books, a blanket, a bottle of water, a flashlight and extra batteries, two peanut-butter sandwiches, a banana, and her invisibility cloak—an oversized black sweater, black leggings, and black flats. A big change from the hot pink suit she wore to work today. She stood out in the pink; she would disappear in the black. She grabbed the empty box and returned to home base.

She removed the black-and-white flower prints from the walls, wrapped them in newspapers, and put them in the box. Next came Bethany's wire and the bugs from the art storage room, the telephone, the wall behind the pictures, and the restroom. The bugs had been a waste of time and money; they'd picked up nothing but people talking trash. But they'd been worth a try: they might have snared a killer. Too bad they hadn't. Now to call Rob's guy to come get the box. She'd leave it for him with the receptionist.

❧

The technician, who received the box when it arrived at the suite on the fifty-fourth floor, telephoned Rob. "Rob, this is Billy. A box just came up from downstairs. We got all the devices back except the one Loretta Byrd was wearing. They're coded—that's how we know the missing one is hers."

"She probably left it down there, or forgot and wore it home. Keep the recorder on until you get her device back or you hear from her. Let me know when that happens, okay? If she left it at DDD&W, we'll have to figure out how to retrieve it."

"Yeah. What about the pictures? Pictures of flowers in black frames?"

"They must me be Dinah's. Have them dropped off at the Greene Gallery."

When Coleman played Loretta's message, she couldn't believe her ears. Ted, a two-wife guy? A harem must be more fashionable than she'd realized. At one time bigamy seemed to be a Texas phenomenon. H.L. Hunt set the pattern in Dallas—three families—and got away with it bigtime. There wasn't even a social stigma attached. The illegitimate progeny fared as well as the legitimate. Then along came financier Fayez Sarofim, at that time described as the richest man in Houston, who lived with his wife Louisa, heiress to the Brown & Root construction fortune, and their two children, but who established girlfriend Linda Hicks in a love nest nearby, had two children with her, and refused to give her up.

More recently, an article in *Fortune* described a famous Wall Street banker, who had a child with "wife" two. The little boy was four before that Master of the Universe told his legal wife about his "other" family. For years he ran two households, a few blocks apart on Manhattan's East Side.

And there was the Wall Street bigwig, who had a wife and teenaged kids in Greenwich, and another family a few miles away in Westport. Loretta seemed to have turned up still another bigamist. But Ted—my God, the gorgeous Glenda and her mighty family would destroy him if they discovered his other life. She wouldn't have dreamed Ted would take a risk like that. He'd always seemed to be the most conventional of men. DDD&W was full of surprising people, and none of the surprises was pleasant.

Fifty-Nine

J eb sauntered into Heyward's office looking sleepy and satisfied, like a contented cat. He was all but licking his chops.

"You must have talked to Roger Black at Colossus," Heyward said.

"I did. I ruined his weekend. I explained real slow and careful about your new company, and what it was doin', and how Miss Coleman fit in. He was sputterin' and fussin' and not bein' a good listener, so I told him how we stumbled on Colossus's inside-information scheme. I thought for a minute he'd pass out. 'Course, his name is on the letters to Miss Coleman. How could he be so stupid?" Jeb said.

Heyward shrugged. "Arrogance. He underestimated Coleman and Coleman's friends. Probably thought she was a fragile little blonde who'd give them anything they wanted if they frightened her enough."

"He hung the Moose out to dry, just like we expected. Blamed everything on him. Well, that's that on Colossus. I think we're done with them. What's next?"

"Are you set for tonight's dinner?" Heyward asked.

"No problem about tonight. After tonight?"

"I have to go to London for a couple of weeks, and I'll take Hicks with me. You're in charge here. Keep an eye on the business—I think it's pretty much on track. That Swedish team we hired is doing a great job, and I'm sure Coleman is doing fine. You can reach me in London if you need me."

"Okay. See you at seven." Jeb lounged out, whistling "Carolina in the Morning."

After Jeb left, Heyward cleared his desk and packed his briefcase, thinking about the evening ahead and what had to be done before he left for London Saturday night. The penthouse suite in what was now officially the CH Holdings building was large enough to accommodate everyone and everything he'd had in mind. The Fishleys, from whom he'd bought the building, had retained the penthouse during their tenure for their own use but had rarely entered it. It was in good shape but had been plain vanilla. He'd asked Coleman's chic friend, Debbi Diamondstein, who handled both his and Coleman's press relations, to jazz it up. She'd brought in a crowd of people who'd made it glamorous and exciting. He had a date with Coleman Saturday morning. He planned to surprise her with the suite and her new office. He was sure she'd love both, and they'd have some time to discuss the future.

∽

Loretta yawned. Seemed like she'd been shut up in the dark for hours. She looked at her watch: only four thirty. She couldn't go about her business for another six hours. The cleaning people left about ten, and she'd wait an extra half hour or so to be sure they were gone. She'd slip out to the ladies' room for a few minutes after the receptionist left at six and then sneak back to her cave. Thank goodness she'd brought three mystery books with her. At least one had to be exciting. She needed to stay awake.

She hadn't remembered to do everything she should have. She'd forgotten to charge her cell phone, and the battery was dead. She hadn't told her new roommates she'd be out to dinner. She wouldn't be on the lease until April 1, ten days from now, but she was at the apartment all the time, and they expected her to obey the rules—call if you were running late or not coming home, or planned to be out for a meal. They thought she was crazy, giving up her own place to sleep on a bunk bed in a room with three others. But they were fun and good company, and she wouldn't be lonely or homesick living with them. They'd have conniption fits about her not staying in touch, though. And she'd forgotten to turn in that stupid wire. She'd take it off, but she might forget again and leave it in here. She'd been told they were expensive. It was probably safest where it was.

Sixty

Coleman had never seen Heyward's house dressed up for a party. The rooms were beautiful, if too formal for her taste. The word *cozy* did not apply. The black-and-white color scheme seemed cold, despite the touches of deep red in the cushions, the cranberry glass ornaments, and a striking Motherwell over the fireplace.

For tonight's festivities the austere rooms had been decorated with great silver bowls of red camellias and larger arrangements of dark pink crabapple blossoms. Candles in silver and crystal holders glittered everywhere, and the delicate scent of the flowers reminded Coleman of childhood walks in an apple orchard in bloom. The atmosphere was festive, and certainly there was much to celebrate, although not enough. A murderer was still at large, and a cloud still hovered over Dinah. Coleman pushed those worries out of her mind and concentrated on her surroundings.

Heyward had collected many beautiful and valuable objects; it would take hours to see everything. She was admiring a group of exquisite miniatures clustered on the wall in the hall when Heyward came down the stairs.

"Hi, Coleman, welcome!"

The doorbell rang, Horace answered it, and Dinah and Jonathan joined Coleman and Heyward. After exchanging greetings, Dinah turned to look at the miniatures that Coleman was admiring.

"These are lovely," she said.

Heyward smiled. "Thank you. They're my most treasured possessions. I inherited them from my paternal grandmother. I can't make up my mind whether to keep them here or in London. For the time being, I plan to be mostly in New York, so they'll stay here."

"Shouldn't they be in a safe?" Coleman asked.

"No, I like to look at them, and to share them with others. Anyway, I have a terrific security system. I had all the New York services checked out, and hired an outfit called Prestige. They installed the alarm system, and they test it periodically. This place is as safe as a bank vault."

Jonathan smiled. "We use Prestige, too. I researched all the companies as well. They're far and away the best."

Heyward turned to look at him, an odd expression on his face. "You use Prestige?"

"Why not? Just as you said, they're the best," Jonathan said.

"Right. Dinah? When you're at home, do you set the alarm? Or just when you're both out?"

"Oh, it's always on, whether we're there or not. I turn it off when I unlock the door to go in, turn it back on when I'm safely inside. Jonathan worries that someone will break in while we're at home, or worse, when I'm home alone," Dinah said.

Heyward nodded. "Yes, that's what I do, too, and Prestige keeps a record of when the alarm is on or off. Do you realize that means you're alibied for those times Jonathan was away?"

Coleman stared at Heyward. Could this be true? Could Dinah have been cleared since the beginning of all this horror?

Dinah, looking stunned, turned to Jonathan, who took his cell phone out of his pocket, and made a call. He walked into the living room, away from the group, and spoke briefly on the phone. Coleman held her breath, waiting to hear what he learned.

When Jonathan rejoined the group in the hall he said, "You're absolutely right. Their records prove that Dinah never left the house the nights those women were killed."

Dinah's face lit up. "Oh," she breathed. "I can't believe it. All this time, and we always had the answer."

Yes, Coleman thought, so simple. Meanwhile, Dinah was suffering, nearly had a complete breakdown. Why didn't Rob think to check with Dinah and Jonathan's alarm company? For that matter, why hadn't any of them thought of it? But Rob was the pro; he was supposed to know about security. Rob certainly hadn't covered himself with glory during this investigation.

The doorbell rang again, and Rob came in, followed by Debbi Diamondstein, Jeb, and Hicks, Heyward's assistant. The noise level rose as everyone tried to tell the newcomers about Dinah's alibi. Rob looked shattered. Debbi whispered in Coleman's ear that she'd turn the story into a column item, pointing out that the police should have checked with the alarm company but were so anxious to pin the DDD&W crimes on anyone no matter how innocent, they hadn't done any real detecting. And Jonathan thanked Heyward again and again.

At the dinner table, Coleman was seated next to Jeb. She could think of nothing but his nearness. She wanted to reach out and brush that wheat-colored cowlick away from his forehead. She wanted to touch the tanned hand that lay in his lap. She nearly jumped when his knee brushed hers. He was an intelligent and amusing conversationalist, but she couldn't concentrate on what he was saying. It had been a long time since she'd been so attracted to anyone. Her feelings must be obvious. Rob was staring at her, his brown spaniel eyes hurt, and Dinah looked disapproving. Coleman didn't care.

Her feelings were so intense, she was almost relieved when dessert and coffee were served, and even more relieved when everyone stood up and went into the living room.

Jeb followed her. "May I take you home?"

She must have said yes, and she hoped she said good night to everyone and thanked Heyward properly. She rode the few blocks to her apartment beside him in a little red car that Jeb drove with skill and grace. But when they reached the door of the building and he said, "May I come up?" she kept her head and said, "Not tonight." He kissed her and she nearly changed her mind but came to her senses at the last minute and hurried inside.

Her phone was ringing when she opened the door to her apartment. She looked at her watch. 11:20. Who would call so late? She grabbed the phone a ring ahead of the answering machine.

"Ms. Greene? I hate to bother you, but this is Marilyn, one of Loretta Byrd's roommates, and she never came home tonight. I spoke to her around two this afternoon—she was at DDD&W. She didn't say anything about being out for supper, or not staying here tonight. We have a rule you have to call if you're not coming home for supper, and you have to call if you don't plan to sleep here. She hasn't called, and her cell phone is turned off, and we're afraid something's happened to her—"

Coleman frowned and picked up Dolly, who was leaning against her legs. Why was Loretta still at DDD&W at two o'clock this afternoon? She should have left long before two. Dinah had received the check about twelve thirty. "Have you tried Bethany?"

"Yes, I got the answering machine at her apartment, same thing at Zeke's. Do you think they all went somewhere together?"

"No, I forgot—Bethany's out of town. Look, wait near the phone in case Loretta tries to reach you. Call me on my cell phone if you hear anything. I'll start a search for her, try to find out when she left DDD&W. I'll let you know when we find her. What's your name again?"

While she was talking, Coleman had stripped off her green silk pantsuit and pulled on jeans, a sweater, and boots. She gave Marilyn her cell phone number, said goodbye to Dolly, and ran for the door. Something—or someone—had prevented Loretta from leaving DDD&W when she should have. A murderer was on the loose, and no one had heard from Loretta for nine hours. She prayed that she was safe.

She hailed a taxi and gave him the DDD&W address. She called Heyward first. Would he meet her at DDD&W? And call Jonathan? They might need Greg Fry's assistance with the building people, and she was sure Dinah would want to help look for Loretta. Maybe he should call Rob, too, in case they had to deal with the police.

⤙

Rob, alerted by Heyward, reached Billy, the technician who'd unpacked the listening devices, at home. He hadn't heard from Loretta. When he left at ten, he'd left the recorder on. "She must have removed the wire, and left it somewhere. I can't believe she was at DDD&W all that time and never said a word," Billy said. "Last we heard from her was when she sent the box up—"

"Meet me at our suite. Maybe the recorder has picked up something since you left," Rob said.

They converged in the lobby of the Fry building. The guards had been alerted, and one of them escorted Dinah, Jonathan, and Heyward to the thirty-second floor, while Coleman and Rob headed up to fifty-four. Another guard was checking the security tapes to see if they could spot Loretta leaving the building.

The technician had arrived and was listening to the voice-activated tape that they hoped Loretta was wearing. Nothing was heard until 10:47, when Loretta, sounding cheery as a chickadee, said, "Hi! What brings you here this time of night?" A soft voice mumbled a response, and Loretta replied, "Oh, I cleaned out Ellie's desk yesterday. Go ahead and look, but it's empty. Dinah had loaned her some books, and Dinah asked me to look for them. Did you know Ellie? Nobody else around here seems to have ever heard of her."

"Mumble, mumble."

"Damn it, Billy, can't you turn up the volume?" Rob said.

"It's as loud as it'll go," the technician said. "The guy's whispering."

"Shh," Coleman said. "I want to hear what Loretta is saying."

"What did I do with Dinah's books? Packed 'em up and sent 'em to Dinah," Loretta said.

"What books?" Rob said.

"Shh," Coleman said again. "Tell you later."

"—that's why I'm still here—had a lot of cleaning up to do," Loretta said. "Actually, I'm glad I ran into you—I'm longing to see the Stubbs paintings. Will you show them to me?"

"Mumble, mumble."

"Okay. Let's go upstairs. Let's walk since it's just the one flight—quicker than the elevator. I can hardly wait—"

Silence.

"What happened?" Coleman said.

"Nothing good," the technician said. "The tape is working but they're not talking. They were on thirty-two, but I can't be sure where they are now."

"I don't like it," Rob said. "Coleman, let's go downstairs and help look for her. Billy, call me if you hear anything else on the tape."

To Coleman, he said, "Okay, explain. She didn't send any books to Dinah, did she?"

She shook her head. "No, she brought all of Ellie's stuff to me. She was making an excuse to the person she was talking to for having gone through the files. Whoever she's talking to knew Ellie, and was interested in the contents of her desk. That's the first person who's admitted knowing her."

❧

The thirty-second floor was brightly lit and buzzing with activity. The security people had locked the building's exterior doors, and leaving one guard on duty downstairs, half a dozen men had come up to help with the search. The lobby tape didn't show Loretta leaving the building. She had to be in the building. They were certain she was on thirty-two, when they checked the art storage room and found Loretta's hideout. They searched the office allocated to the Greene Gallery and found nothing. They were spreading out over the floor to look for traces of the girl when Dinah spotted the metal knitting needle, one of the pair Loretta often wore in her hair. She leaned over to pick it up, but Rob stopped her. "Don't touch it," he said.

"I have some of Dolly's cleanup plastic bags with me," Coleman said, pulling one out of her carryall and handing it to Rob. "What's that on the point?"

"I'm afraid it's blood," Rob said, his tone grim. He picked up the needle with his handkerchief and dropped it in the bag. "We better call the police, and emergency medical services." His cell phone rang.

"Rob? The tape just came to life. She's definitely on thirty-two. I can hear her groaning. I think she's hurt," Billy said.

Rob looked at his watch. "She can't have been here long. It's not yet midnight. Hurry, everyone. We have to find her fast."

"Why do you say she can't have been here long?" one of the guards asked.

"The tapes tell us the time and the location," Rob explained. "She was talking to someone on this floor around eleven. We can hear her groaning—she's still on this floor. The person who was with her must be here somewhere, too. I don't think anyone could have gotten past us. Unlock every office door, check every room," he told the senior guard. "Make sure all exit doors remain locked so no one can get out of the building."

Jonathan used his cell phone to call New York Episcopal, the nearest hospital, requesting an ambulance, while Heyward called the police.

❧

Dinah nudged Coleman. "There's a big supply closet near the stairs to thirty-three. They'd have to pass it if they walked up. Let's look in there."

Loretta lay on the floor of the closet. She looked young and small. Her face was pale and her black hair had partly tumbled down; the other knitting needle remained in what was left of her bun. Coleman couldn't see any blood. Maybe the blood belonged to her attacker? If so, good for Loretta! Coleman hoped she'd stabbed the devil in a tender spot. Dinah ran back and called to the others, who swarmed around the door of the closet.

Loretta was at least partly conscious and struggling to talk. "Teddy...teddy...teddy," she said.

"Poor little girl. She's asking for her teddy bear," the guard with the Groucho Marx moustache said.

"I don't think so." Coleman said. "I think she's telling us who hurt her." And damn the monster to hell, she added silently.

After they found Loretta, everything moved at high speed. The ambulance arrived and took the girl away. Jonathan and Dinah and Coleman followed in Jonathan's limousine, with Tom at the wheel. Heyward remained with Rob to help conduct the search for Loretta's attacker, and to deal with the police.

Sixty-One

Coleman and Dinah huddled together on the hard orange plastic chairs in the hospital waiting room, while Jonathan paced. After what seemed an interminable wait, Dr. Shah, whom they'd met when they arrived, reappeared. He was smiling. "She has a mild concussion," he said. "She'll be fine. She was a little confused, but she's better now. She's resting, and I'd prefer no one try to talk to her tonight. She needs quiet and rest."

"Thank God," Dinah whispered.

"Can you tell us what happened to her?" Jonathan asked.

"She received a blow on the back of her head. The impact was deflected by that big bundle of hair. Her hair saved her from a much more serious injury," the doctor said.

"When can she go home?"

"Tomorrow, if she feels okay. Someone should be here to pick her up about ten. Unless there's a change in her condition for the worse—and I'm pretty sure there won't be—she'll be better off at home, but she'll have to take it easy," he said.

"Thanks, Dr. Shah," Jonathan said, "We'll be here. Come on, Dinah, Coleman." In the lobby, they met Heyward and Rob coming in and told them the good news. They had news, too.

"It's over," Rob said. "They found Theodore Douglas hiding in the dining room on thirty-three. Loretta had managed to stab him in the hand with that needle, and he left a trail of blood. He denied touching Loretta until he learned she was alive and had identified him. Then he began to talk. I advised him to be quiet and call a lawyer, but he seemed determined to spill everything. He implicated Parker all the way, except that Parker had nothing to do with the attack on Loretta. This was about Loretta discovering Douglas's second family. He recognized her in the elevator this morning and decided to kill her before she told anyone. He planned to follow her home, to the building where he saw her in the Village, and kill her there. He waited downstairs in the coffee shop to see her leave, eventually came back to see if she was still in the office, and ran into her.

"When he confessed to hitting her, he even produced the weapon—would you believe he struck her with a three-hole punch he grabbed off a desk? He used it like a tennis racket to slam her from behind. He was sure she was dead, but if we hadn't turned up when we did, I think she'd have followed Patti Sue down the elevator shaft. He also planned to go after Ellie, if he could find her. He said he became suspicious of her when she disappeared. He thought Ellie might have seen him arranging Frances Johnson's death, and he'd planned to look through her desk for clues to her whereabouts. As for why he killed the Victor sisters: they knew too much and got too demanding."

"Why didn't he divorce Glenda instead of trying to kill poor Loretta to cover up his secret life?" Dinah asked.

"I've thought a lot about his other 'wife' and children," Coleman said. "Loretta said he seemed so happy with his Village family. Living with the Ice Queen must have been horrible, when he might have been with a wife and children he loved. But he needed a lot of money to support his second family—money that had to be kept secret from Glenda."

"Glenda's family would have annihilated him if he'd tried to divorce her," Heyward said. "The Goulds are notorious for holding on to what's theirs. I'm sure he was tied to her with an airtight prenuptial agreement. His job probably depended on their goodwill, too."

"Douglas deserves punishment, but I feel sorry for Hunt. He didn't harm anyone, but his firm is disgraced and falling apart," Dinah said.

"He made *your* life pretty miserable," Jonathan said.

"I think he's suffered enough," Dinah said.

"I'm convinced that Hunt will rise above all this," Heyward said.

Coleman looked at him. "You know what? I am, too. I'd planned to write a big story about Hunt and the missing art and the disastrous merger, but I think that story is over. The real story is what happens next."

Sixty-Two

April

The Greene Gallery was closed Mondays, but Dinah always went in. She was usually alone and enjoyed the time to herself. There was often a lot to do, and this Monday was no exception. She had a great deal to think about.

She sat down at her desk and reflected on recent events. She had so much to be grateful for. No one close to her, including Loretta, had been severely hurt. She and Jonathan had picked Loretta up at the hospital that Saturday morning, planning to bring her back to Cornelia Street with them, but instead, to their surprise, she wanted to go the apartment near Columbia where her friends—now her room-mates—were taking turns making a fuss over her. She seemed subdued but physically fine. She'd asked Coleman for a few weeks' leave to go home to see her family, and Coleman had readily agreed. The girl had certainly earned some time off.

The check from DDD&W would see Dinah through lean times until the Greene Gallery was stronger, and earning more. Debbi Diamondstein thought the print installation at DDD&W was great and would bring in lots of business. She had arranged to have every wall photographed and would see that the photographs reached the right magazines. She told Dinah she might even win an award for the project.

But Dinah's confidence and her faith in people had been shaken by the events of the last month. She would never have dreamed that anyone could think she was a murderer. She was no longer sure she wanted the responsibility—the burden—of trying to make a success of the gallery. If she hadn't taken on the DDD&W job, she'd never have been accused of murder, and Loretta wouldn't have been hurt. Maybe Patti Sue and her sister wouldn't have been killed. She was beginning to think Jonathan was right: she wasn't suited to managing a big commercial art gallery. She certainly wasn't capable of dealing with the corporate world.

Should she turn the management of the gallery over to Bethany? Bethany would run it well. If Dinah didn't have to worry about making the gallery profitable, she could do as much or as little research as she liked. She could write articles and catalog essays. She could find the perfect Midtown apartment, and make Jonathan happy. She could get pregnant, and make Jonathan ecstatic. A quiet domestic life sounded blissful. She wanted babies eventually. Why not now?

The sound of the mail hitting the floor interrupted her reverie. She collected the handful of envelopes and returned to her desk. Openings at other galleries. Bills. Advertisements. A letter from the Art Museum of Great Britain. What could that be?

Good heavens, they were offering her a Samuel Palmer Fellowship, assisting with the research and cataloguing of a major addition to their American Print collection—an American patron had donated his huge collection to the museum. An exhibition was planned, and her knowledge about American prints would be invaluable.

The Palmer Fellowships were famous, but she had never considered applying. They were a tremendous honor, given to the greatest scholars in the print world. Dinah didn't even have a PhD. She'd never heard of a Palmer Fellow who hadn't earned a doctorate. Who had nominated her? Oh, darling Rachel, her good friend.

Four months in London: June, July, August, September. She'd been to London once and loved it. She'd dreamed of doing something like this someday, although she'd never really believed it could happen. Coming now, when she was feeling so low, it was a heaven-sent opportunity. But what would Jonathan say?

Sixty-Three

Soon after his arrival in London, Heyward had telephoned Rachel to ask if he could come to see her, explaining that he needed only half an hour of her time. She'd invited him to join her for lunch and suggested several possible dates. She'd made it clear she wanted to see him. Maybe, as he'd hoped, she'd begun to think of him as a friend. He'd know soon. The chosen day had arrived.

"Welcome back," Rachel said. "Come into the sitting room. Would you like a glass of sherry?"

He declined, and when they'd settled by the fire, he said, "I wanted to talk to you about Simon. He'll be released from the clinic in a few months, and I don't want him to turn up in New York or to return to London. I think you feel the same way. Am I right?"

"I certainly would prefer that he settle somewhere other than here, but how can he be prevented from returning?"

"I think he'll find a new life in Australia. I propose to buy him a contemporary art gallery in Melbourne. It's successful and, unless he ruins it with his plots and schemes, should continue to do well. I'll buy him a house and a car, and provide him with a liberal allowance. I'll guarantee the allowance for ten years, on condition that he doesn't enter the UK or the US."

Rachel nodded. "Simon is a born remittance man—I thought so when he lived in New York. But he is expensive. That is a very generous offer. How can you be sure he will not come back secretly?"

"I'll make sure he's watched," Heyward said. "Is the arrangement I described acceptable to you?"

"Certainly. May I help financially?"

"No, thanks. I created the monster; I should pay the price. I have a happier topic to discuss. Has Dinah told you about the company Coleman and I have set up?"

"She said it involves magazine publishing. Do I have that right?"

"Yes, but I also want to expand into book publishing. I'm interested in the publication of art books, including bringing back out-of-print books. When we established the bookstore in the Print Museum, we couldn't obtain most of the books we'd planned to sell. Even secondhand copies were difficult to find. What do you think?"

"That is a wonderful idea. How may I help?" Rachel said.

"I'd like you to join the board of the art book subsidiary. Be on the lookout for new books we should publish, suggest out-of-print books we should rescue."

"I should enjoy that," Rachel said. She stood up. "Shall we have lunch? We can talk more about this delightful project, and perhaps you will bring me up to date on all the excitement in New York?"

He was right: she *was* willing to be his friend. He smiled to himself. He also had a sister and friends who'd be glad to see him when he returned to New York. And interesting work to do. To think that so recently he'd been bored and lonely. How quickly life could change.

Sixty-Four

Hunt was exhausted. He'd scarcely slept since Heyward Bain's revelations, and the days that followed the attempted murder of Loretta Byrd had been the worst in his life. They made the unpleasant period of his divorce seem like a holiday in Paris.

The confrontation with Moose had been devastating. When Moose had seen the letters from Colossus's Roger Black to Coleman, he'd appeared stricken, but he hadn't been contrite or apologetic, just furious that Black had supplied the link that would send Moose to jail. When Hunt told him that the SEC and the attorney general knew about his activities, and could arrive at DDD&W at any time, Moose admitted everything and, in an attempt to get a reduced sentence, identified two of his young associates as a part of the inside-information scheme.

Hunt had called security to escort the three of them out of the building and arranged to have their offices padlocked. Ever since their departure, every floor at DDD&W had been flooded with investigators. He'd kept his own door closed, and behind it, he'd terminated the three inside-information sellers and twenty tax-dodgers. Counting Harrison, whom he'd ordered Danbury to dismiss, that was twenty-four departures, and he hadn't finished cleaning house.

He'd instructed Leichter to get rid of his paramour, Naomi Skinner, who had briefly been head of human resources. He'd warned Leichter that any more office romances would mean the end of his career at DDD&W. Funds for paying off Skinner, beyond the normal severance package determined by length of service, had to come out of Leichter's pocket.

He'd dismissed Trixie and her helpers and sent out a memo announcing the closing of the dining room and the cafeteria: employees would hereafter pay for their own lunches, and company-financed snacks were no longer available.

The Cobra had written a ferocious letter to Oscar Danbury threatening him with arrest if he exposed himself and/or displayed his disgusting desktop trick again. Hunt had followed up the Cobra's letter by ordering Danbury to bring in an exterminator and professional cleaners to scrub thirty and thirty-one—at his expense. Danbury was now responsible for keeping those floors immaculate and vermin-free.

Hunt had taken some time off from firing the criminal and the incompetent to tell Amy Rothman she had been elected DDD&W's first female partner.

After explaining what had happened to Moose and why, he'd asked her to take over Moose's department. He'd warned her that she'd have to reduce both the number of Moose's Merry Men, and the huge number of accountants he'd hired, while simultaneously reassuring clients. Her eagerness and enthusiasm had been gratifying.

At the end of each grueling day, he went home to his empty apartment and ate Chinese or Indian take-out for his lonely supper. He fell into bed, where he lay awake tossing and turning, thinking of Moose's villainy and the shock of learning that Theodore Douglas was a murderer, thief, polygamist, and criminal coconspirator with the Boston lawyer who'd cheated and abused the Davidson twins. Douglas: the lying vicious partner he'd considered a friend. His only friends at DDD&W had turned out to be treacherous, even wicked. How could he have been so mistaken about them?

He'd been overjoyed to learn that after all she'd been through, Elizabeth Davidson was willing to forgive and forget, and wanted to join DDD&W. Although she was now the firm's largest stockholder, she wasn't demanding an executive role, but humbly asking for a chance to learn. She was willing to let the Prince Charles Stuart Museum have the Davidson Americana collection. There would be no multimillion-dollar suit from the museum, that crazy Scot was off his back, and the Cobra had disappeared. With any luck he'd never be heard from again.

He wasn't sure he could trust anyone at DDD&W except Elizabeth Davidson and Amy. He'd have to get to know everyone who worked there. Find good people to replace the bad ones. Rebuild the firm. Get a life. In that connection, he was determined to make a telephone call. He'd struggled to put Coleman Greene out of his mind ever since he met her and had failed miserably. He hadn't been free to ask her out—she was press, and then she became a client, and he couldn't talk to her about anything he was doing. He'd been terrified she'd expose the dreadful situation at DDD&W before he could improve it. He was committed to saving DDD&W, and he'd had so many problems to deal with he hadn't had time to do anything else. Maybe too much work had clouded his judgement.

But as far as he knew, all of the dirty laundry had been scrubbed and exposed to sun and fresh air. He still thought about Coleman, still wanted to see her socially. He'd start with an apology and an invitation to dinner. Maybe in time she'd forgive him for how he'd treated her.

Sixty-Five

Rob had never felt worse. This case had been a nightmare, and he and his agency had done a miserable job. Ace, to whom he'd assigned tracing the Davidson daughters and their mother, had been unrepentant about his dereliction: he'd been busy at school, and just "hadn't got around to it." Rob had not realized Ace was so irresponsible. Ace was paid by the hour, so firing him had little impact on him, but Rob couldn't use Ace again, and he was already short of staff.

The men who'd failed to get the information about the Victor sisters' lovers from the old woman across the hall from their apartment weren't defensive; when criticized, they'd retorted that they hadn't been given photographs of the various men involved in the case. That was Rob's job, not theirs. All too true, and as for Dinah and Jonathan's alarm system, it simply hadn't occurred to him. He'd been overworked, understaffed, and preoccupied with persuading Coleman to marry him.

But all of that was no excuse for his oversights and his bad performance. He'd try to pick up the pieces somehow, starting with a letter of apology to Jonathan and Dinah. He didn't think anything would improve his relationship with Coleman. He'd seen how she looked at Jeb Middleton.

Sixty-Six

Bethany and Zeke had come back from North Carolina starry-eyed, full of plans, and floating on air. Bethany had wanted to tell Dinah the news first, so she'd made Zeke promise to keep their secret till she'd spoken to Dinah. But as soon as she saw Dinah's face, Bethany knew something was wrong. "What is it?" she asked. "What's the matter?"

Dinah burst into tears. When she'd managed to stop crying and explained that her tears were partly relief because Loretta was all right, Bethany couldn't understand at first. When she finally grasped Dinah's incoherent story, she was horrified. "You're tellin' me I let this happen 'cause I left early?" Bethany said.

Dinah shook her head. "No, no, don't think that. Loretta told Coleman that she had a plan B. If you hadn't left her there alone, she was going to leave with you, and go back later, tell the guards she forgot something, do everything just the way she did. She was obsessed with showing us what a good detective she was. I guess everything that happened before she got here went to her head—" Dinah broke off, staring at Bethany's left hand. "What a gorgeous ring. Are you and Zeke engaged?"

Bethany smiled. "Yes, we're gettin' married in three weeks. I want you to be my matron of honor, and Coleman maid of honor. But I need to know for sure: are you certain I'm not responsible for Loretta bein' hurt?"

"Good Lord, no. You can't stop girls like Loretta from doing rash things. Loretta has to learn everything the hard way. Forget all that. It's over. And I'd love to be your matron of honor. That's an easy decision. Here's one that's not so easy." She handed Bethany a letter.

Bethany, saucer-eyed, read it and said, "What an honor! Wow! You're goin' to do it, aren't you? You can't turn this down, Dinah. It's a fabulous opportunity. And you deserve it."

Dinah didn't hesitate. "Yes. Yes, I am going to accept it. Can you run the gallery and be a newly married lady at the same time?"

Bethany laughed. "You bet I can!" Her face sobered. "But what will Jonathan say?"

"I don't know what he'll say. A husband ought to be thrilled if his wife won an honor like this one, but Jonathan might not see it that way. Whatever he says, I'm going to do it. It's the chance of a lifetime, and if I don't take it, I'll always regret it."

When Bethany told Zeke about the conversation, she said, "You know how sweet she always looks? So agreeable and easy goin'? For a few seconds, she looked just like Coleman does when Coleman says she's goin' to do somethin', and you know nothin' in this world will stop her. That's how Dinah looked. I see trouble ahead. That Jonathan is bossy, and he likes to keep Dinah on a short leash."

"If he tries to stop her, I hope she'll tell him to go to hell," Zeke said. "It's time Dinah got recognition. And it's time Jonathan supported her, instead of putting obstacles in her way. I'd never do that to you."

She smiled. "I know," she said.

∽

Since everything had turned out all right, Dinah and Coleman hadn't called Loretta's parents to tell them about her injury. They'd left it up to her to tell. Or not. Loretta appreciated their discretion, and she'd decided to keep the story to herself. But she felt odd. The doctors said she was fine, and she might look the same on the outside, but inside, where it counted, something had changed. She didn't yet know how it would all play out, but maybe—just maybe—New York wasn't the place she wanted to be—or should be. Maybe she wasn't ready for the major leagues. She'd made a lot of mistakes, had been overconfident, had been determined to show off. Her people judgment wasn't too good either—she'd thought the man who tried to kill her was a nice guy. She'd been naïve, and it nearly got her killed. She was going home to North Carolina, and maybe she wouldn't come back.

Sixty-Seven

Coleman sat behind the big desk in the enormous office Debbi had designed for her. The room was forty feet long, too big for comfort. The view was magnificent, but she'd always disliked heights, and the fifty-fifth floor was way too high; she didn't like looking down on New York. All the walls that weren't glass were bare, waiting for her to decorate them. If she moved the framed *ArtSmart* covers up here from her little office on the fifth floor, they'd be lost. Even if she framed every cover she'd published, not just her favorites. She sighed and looked at Dolly. Dolly's basket was so far away they could hardly see each other. Coleman moved the basket close to her desk every morning, but every night the cleaning people always put it back where the decorators had placed it.

She scuttled crablike across the room, staying close to the back wall and as far from the windows as possible, grabbed the basket in one hand, and cuddled Dolly in her other arm. She put the basket beside her desk and held Dolly in her lap. Dolly wagged her tail and settled down. Just the feel of her warm furry little body snuggled against her helped, but she still felt strange.

A closed door to her left led to Heyward's office. He said he'd leave it open when he was in. But he *wasn't* here. Heyward was in London and wouldn't be back for another week. She missed him. She'd call Dinah, but what was she to say? That she was lonely? She was never lonely. Call Rob? They hadn't spoken since the dinner at Heyward's the night that Loretta was nearly killed. He was hurt by her flirting with Jeb, but he had finally accepted her refusal to marry him. She'd like to be friends, but he wasn't interested. So be it. There was always work to do, and she should get on with it.

The phone rang. She picked up the receiver. "Coleman Greene speaking," she said.

"Hi, Coleman, Amy here. We have a lot to talk about. Are you free for lunch?"

Coleman brightened. "Absolutely. Anywhere but at your place."

Amy laughed. "No chance. Hunt closed down the dining room and the cafeteria, and let Trixie and her trashy troops go."

Coleman sat up straight. "No! What else?"

"Lots and lots of news. Tell you later. How about Michael's? Twelve thirty?"

"Great. I'll see you there." She felt better. She had a friend. Someone to talk to. The phone rang.

Good. She needed distraction. From missing Heyward. From this huge office. From the view.

"Coleman Greene," she said.

"Hey, it's Jeb Middleton. I've been tryin' to reach you for days—were you hidin' from me?"

"Don't be silly. I've been working really hard. I was so far behind, I didn't answer the phone." All of that was true, but not quite the whole story. She'd wanted a breathing spell before she saw Jeb again. She'd been out with him three times. He was almost too attractive, and like everything else in her life, her relationship with Jeb was moving at high speed.

"Would you like to have dinner tonight? Before you say no, I warn you: I'll ask you out every night for months till you say yes."

Coleman smiled. She'd played hard to get long enough. "I'm not about to say no. I was hoping you'd call."

"Wonderful. I made a reservation at La Grenouille, just in case. It's one of my favorites because the food is so good and it's quiet. If that's all right, I'll pick you up at seven."

"Lovely," she said. "I'll look forward to seeing you."

She leaned back in her chair, thinking about Jeb. She felt the thrill of anticipation. She liked being pursued. She also liked a man who chose the restaurant, and told her which it was so she'd know what to wear, but gave her a chance to say she'd rather go somewhere else. What *should* she wear? Something sexy but not too obvious. She had just finished a dark green lace jacket to wear over a green silk slip dress...

The phone rang. Good heavens! This was Telephone City. "Coleman Greene."

"Coleman, this is Hunt Frederick. I'm so sorry about everything that's happened. I called to ask you if you'd let me take you out to dinner tomorrow night, so I can apologize properly."

Coleman was dumbfounded. "Well—uh—what a surprise. I had the impression you didn't like me."

"On the contrary. I've wanted to ask you out ever since we met. But circumstances—oh, Lord, I can't do this on the phone. *Will* you have dinner with me tomorrow night?"

Coleman smiled. "Well, sure. I'd like to hear what you have to say about our early meetings. You certainly managed to disguise your interest in me."

"I can explain. That's what men always say, isn't it? But it's true. Is Le Bernardin okay? Shall I call for you at seven thirty?"

"Perfect. Do you have my address?"

"I certainly do."

When she'd hung up, Coleman stroked Dolly's soft white fur. Dolly looked up at her, dark brown eyes adoring. "That was a surprise, wasn't it? I thought Hunt Frederick hated me, and I sure didn't like him. Looks like I might be wrong about him. Funny, we were all wrong about Ted. I remember what Jonathan said about him—nice, not very smart. We all thought he was a lightweight. No one thought he was dangerous. I certainly didn't. I was wrong about him. Maybe I was wrong about Hunt, and I thought Moose was just a buffoon. And I thought

Rob was a good detective. And I thought I had good people judgment. That's a laugh.

"I don't know, Dolly. So much has happened. I feel as if I've been on a roller coaster. I think we're back on the ground again, but it's a lot higher than when we started. Do you think we can learn to like the fifty-fifth floor?"